SMALL ISLAND

Paradise Crime Cozy Mystery #2

TOBY NEAL

PARADISE CRIME COZY MYSTERY #2

SMALL ISLAND
A Paradise Crime Cozy Mystery
By Toby Neal

"The essential dilemma of my life is between my deep desire to belong and my suspicion of belonging."
— Jhumpa Lahiri

❧ I ❧

I was nursing a goose egg on my head and a couple of black eyes from catching my last murderer when it was time to hunt another one. Just another day in paradise in the tiny town of Ohia, Maui.

"You should be resting," said Keone Kaihale, fondly known by me alone as Mr. K. My superhot (maybe, someday, in my dreams) boyfriend was wearing his white pilot's uniform, which should be a guarantee that I'd be thinking about things other than death.

Which reminded me of death.

There'd been a lot of it in Ohia lately.

"I'll rest when I'm dead," I said, continuing the theme. "Tell me what you know about Jimmy Ching's murder." I swung my legs to the side of the bed he'd carried me to after deciding I needed to rest my head injury. Tiki, my semi-feral cat, hissed and lashed her tail in disapproval at my movement.

For once, she and Mr. K were on the same page as he declared, "I'll tell you, but only if you stay in bed."

"And I'll stay in bed if you fix that pot of coffee I asked for."

"Deal." He got up and went to the counter of the little galley kitchen to wrestle with my ancient, hand-me-down coffee maker. I admired his well-developed lats, delts, and glutes clad in clingy white polyester trimmed in gold braid.

"The airline shouldn't dress their pilots like that if they don't want women objectifying them," I observed.

Keone winked over his shoulder. "You can objectify me all you want, babe. It's the aunties in town I worry about."

I snorted a laugh. "I take it you're talking about our local Red Hat Society."

He gave a theatrical shudder. "One of them actually pinched my butt the last time I ran their gauntlet."

"They're a force to be reckoned with, all right." Pearl, Mattie, Josie, Clara, and Edith basically ran the part of town known as Old Ohia and decided it was their mission to halt the recent development of New Ohia. "I'll defend you next time."

I clutched my aching head and lay carefully back down, not daring to take up more than an inch or two of pillow while Tiki occupied it. She'd extracted payment in blood on more than one occasion. "Talk while you caffeinate me, please. Tell me everything."

"Not much to tell. I showed up at the Hana Airport early, per usual, to take my plane back to Kahului and begin the day's runs. The Hana Police were already there and closed the airport to travel for the day."

"Did you see the body?"

"Nope. It was covered with a tarp, and crime scene tape blocked off most of the lot." Keone poured water into the coffee maker, which belched in appreciation. "But I know a guy."

"Of course you do. You're related to a guy." Keone was the cousin of Pono Kaihale, a detective with Maui Police Department and the partner of Lei Texeira, a sergeant I'd come to know through the murders we'd solved.

"Not Pono this time." Keone pushed the button and came back to sit on the chair in front of the bed. "Pono and Lei barely got home from dealing with your situation last night."

"I remember." I yawned to illustrate my point.

"They're coming out to investigate the latest body, but they hadn't arrived yet when I was there. The medical examiners were also on their way. No, the guy I know is Mama's uncle. He works after-hours security at the airport. He's the one who found the body."

"Ah. And your great-uncle told you about it."

"He knows I have a newfound interest in these things." Mr. K's eyes gleamed. "Ever since I met a certain Secret Service agent turned postmaster who's informally known as the Postmaster Sleuth."

"Uh-huh. Go on." I hid a grin behind Tiki's bulk as she glared doom daggers at Keone.

"Uncle Wiki says it looks like Jimmy came early to catch my flight to Kahului, and someone whacked him. Literally."

"Wait a minute." I sat up too fast, and it felt like my brain swished in my skull. "Ow!" I yelped, falling back into my pillow.

Startled, Tiki yowled and jumped off the bed to hide under the table, taking a swipe at Keone's leg as she passed.

"Ow!" Keone yelled, grabbing his calf. "What was that for?"

"Tiki was disrupted. Someone must pay when that happens." I groaned, but happily reclaimed the pillow the cat had occupied. "Can you shake this outside? I'm worried about fleas."

"I smelled your hair, Kat. You don't have to worry about fleas," Keone said, but he obligingly opened the door of the shack and took my pillow outside to shake it. Apparently, he'd noticed I'd been washing my hair with flea shampoo as a preemptive measure. Darn.

I sat up on my elbows and enjoyed the sliver of view I could see through the open door—past Mr. K's lovely rear and beyond the post office building's muddy parking lot, a coconut palm swayed over the beach and the sun shone over sparkling Ohia Bay. An *'iwa*, or frigate bird, circled over the water and a rainbow dropped from a cloud to touch the old pier. All that was visible from my bed, through the open door of my shack.

However, the whole situation requires a bit of explanation.

My name is Kat Smith, and I'm a Secret Service agent who ran into a spot of trouble with a handsy Congressman I was assigned to protect. I was (temporarily, I hoped? . . . or not?) posted in the teeny, tiny hamlet of Ohia as the postmaster, until the witch hunt for my badge died down.

In the short time I'd been here, I found the body of Ohia's former postmaster who'd been dead six months, solved her murder, and solved the murder of Kermit Hubbard, a shady character from Old Ohia. Despite it all, I fell in love with this place, its quirky people, and—let's be honest—its over-the-top, ridiculous tropical beauty.

And I'm not just talking about my view of the beach.

Keone came back inside, holding my freshly fluffed pillow. "Here. Let me." Mr. K lifted my shoulders and tucked the pillow behind my sore head, patting it into place as he did so. "You're so pretty."

"Don't lie," I said with dignity. I happened to have seen my face in the mirror, and my hair was snarled as if I'd combed it with a tree branch. "Try another compliment."

"Honestly, you're gorgeous," he said, "because you're brave. And smart. And resourceful. And kind. Plus, your legs go on into next week." He patted one of my limbs for emphasis.

"Oh." My eyes prickled. "Can I trouble you for a cup of that coffee? Cuz I'm not going to let you make me cry."

"Crying is good for the soul. Gets rid of cortisol, the stress hormone." Keone went to the coffee maker, which had finished trickling out a pot of coffee. He poured me a cup in my favorite mug, the one that boldly declared, DO NOT SPEAK TO ME UNTIL THIS MUG IS EMPTY.

I loved that mug. It had belonged to Fran Borland, the former postmaster who'd lived in this shack before me. I thought of her as a friendly ghost that would rest easier now that her killer was behind bars.

"Tell me more about the dead body," I said.

"You sure I can't distract you with compliments?" Mr. K deployed his dimple.

"Nope. We have another murder to solve," I said.

Keone rolled his eyes. He wriggled into his seat with his mug balanced on his stomach, and the air of a man settling in to tell a story. "Well, Mama's uncle is named Kawikikaialoha Kaihale, but we call him Uncle Wiki for short. *Wiki* means 'fast' in Hawaiian, my *malihini* warrior woman."

"I like '*malihini* warrior woman' better than 'Trouble,'" I told him.

"You've earned both nicknames."

I snorted and sipped my coffee. "Please go slower with the Hawaiian words full of vowels, please. You know how I struggle with those."

Mr. K gave a wink and continued. "Uncle Wiki was on duty from midnight to eight a.m. at the airport. At five thirty, he did his last round of the parking lot before the waiting area opened to passengers. On that round, he noticed Jimmy's SUV in the lot. The engine was on, and Jimmy was inside, very much alive. Uncle Wiki said he could see Jimmy's face in the glow from his phone. Uncle did another lap, then opened the doors to the airport's waiting area and unlocked the restrooms. It was five fifty-five a.m. by then." He took a sip of his coffee. "Following so far?"

"Yep."

"After he'd opened the building for the day, Uncle Wiki went to let Jimmy know he could come inside. Something seemed strange right away. The truck was turned off and the door was still open— then he noticed there was a body lying face down next to the vehicle. He ran over, thinking Jimmy had a heart attack or something. As soon as he got closer, he saw blood on the back of Jimmy's head. He checked for a pulse. The man was dead."

"Did he find the murder weapon? Whatever Jimmy was whacked with?"

"Nope."

"Was there anyone else around?" My mind was whirling. "Any other cars in the lot?"

"The only other car in the lot belonged to Uncle Wiki himself.

All the staff who run the airport get there around six, after the doors are open. So, at five fifty-five, when Uncle Wiki found Jimmy, no one else was there."

"Huh. That gives a pretty narrow window for time of death," I said.

"Yeah. The cops were all over that."

"The modus operandi matches that of the killer we already apprehended," I mused. "But my perp couldn't have done it because he was in jail by then."

"So, I guess the mystery you solved isn't solved." Mr. K took a sip of his coffee.

"Or it's a completely new mystery." I held out my mug and tapped it against his. "The Postmaster Sleuth is back in business."

❧ 2 ❧

Keone and I had barely finished the eggs he cooked for us on the little stove in the shack when a knock came at the door. Tiki hissed and ran under the table as Mr. K opened the door. "Hello, aunties." His voice was carefully polite, but Tiki was not. She zoomed out from under the table with a yowl, in full attack mode. The Red Hat Society ladies on my doorstep scattered like a flock of chickens. After a comical moment, they regrouped.

"*Aloha*, Keone," the women said in unison. Mattie, Josie, and Edith stood on my porch, each wearing a red hat and holding an offering.

"Heard you took a bullet, Kat," Edith said, holding up her casserole dish. She was a plump garden elf in her peaked, witch-style red hat. "I hope it isn't true."

"Don't worry, Edith. Not a bullet, just a conk on the head," I said, waving from my bed. "Come on in, ladies."

"I'll be right back," Keone said. "Give you a chance to entertain your visitors." He sidled past the three ladies, carefully keeping his tush out of range, and beat feet across the parking lot. All three blatantly ogled him, then turned back to me with smiles.

Wiry, trim Mattie held up her bowl. "I'm vegan, so I brought you

7

a nice tofu and *limu* salad." Mattie was the most physically fit of the group—I'd recently seen her speed walking a hike that would have defeated lesser folks.

Although her salad was a mush of green goo, I'd give it a go for the sake of nutrition. "Thanks, Mattie. Remind me—what's *limu*?"

"Seaweed. I picked it on the rocks myself," she said proudly.

In my many hours standing in the shadow of politicians, I had mastered the art of the blank-yet-pleasant expression, for which I was now grateful.

"And I brought you *haupia*," said Josie, a statuesque Hawaiian woman, holding up a wood calabash filled with coconut pudding. "A little mynah bird told me you love it."

"I do, oh, I do," I said fervently. "Thanks so much, Josie. I'm not much of a cook on a good day, and today's not a particularly good day. Body wise, at least."

"Yeah, you look like heck," Edith said, squinting at me. "How did you get two black eyes from a conk on the head?"

"Not entirely sure. Migrated bruising, I guess." I gestured to the two chairs and patted the bed beside me. "Please, make yourselves comfortable in my luxurious abode. I'm guessing you ladies are here to get the scoop on what went down last night."

"Yep. The coconut wireless has been rattling up a storm. A few wires must have gotten crossed though, because we heard you were shot, for starters," Edith said, taking a seat on my bed, while Mattie and Josie took the chairs. "Give us the scoop. We have a civic duty to pass on the correct information to the community." They were the Gossip Mafia—and they took their job seriously.

"Before I get into all that, I'd like to make a deal with you. I want to know a little more about your lawsuit against New Ohia and Jimmy Ching," I said. Edith was a practicing attorney and represented the residents of Old Ohia in a class action lawsuit against New Ohia. The nearby development had cut major corners in the areas of community support, environmental impact, economic infrastructure—well, everything, really. Jimmy Ching had been its manager and was universally disliked by the Red Hats.

Edith rubbed her hands together, ready to do business. "Looking for a little quid pro quo? We dish, you dish?"

"Something like that." I confirmed and pointed to Josie's calabash. "Speaking of dish . . . can you serve me up some of that *haupia* pudding while I talk?"

"Ooh, she picked my ono grinds to eat first," Josie said with satisfaction, getting up to rifle my spare cupboards for a bowl and spoon.

"It's kind of cheating, bringing *haupia* pudding," Mattie complained. "Of course she'd pick the dessert first."

"We like Kat because she's the type to start a meal with dessert," Edith said. "As are we! And in light of that and our other similarities . . . we brought you a present, Kat."

"Aw, hey. Food is more than enough," I said warily.

"Nope, we want you!" Mattie opened the backpack she'd been wearing and pulled out a bright red billed cap. She waved it around like the flag in a bullfight, perhaps hoping I would find it just as irresistible. "We thought this sleek and sassy model would suit you. Would you like to join the Red Hat Society? You don't have to be over fifty anymore."

"Wow," I said, gazing at the item. It was certainly sassy—made of shiny red satin, the cap was trimmed around the brim in rhinestones. My head would now be visible in a sniper's crosshairs from a mile away. "It's really one of a kind. So . . . sparkly."

"Our hats are a celebration of uniqueness." Mattie laid the cap reverently on my lap. "You just hold onto that and think about it." She smiled proudly.

"And here's your *haupia* pudding," Josie said, handing me an enormous bowl of jiggly white deliciousness.

"So, how shall we do this?" Edith was all business. "Shall we answer questions first, or you tell us what went down last night?"

I dug my spoon into the pudding and took a fortifying bite. If my

9

tongue could have sung an aria, it would have. I groaned in bliss. "I need a moment."

Edith glanced at the big plastic Minnie Mouse watch strapped to her wrist. "Forty-five more seconds."

"Give the girl a break." Josie took a seat and smoothed her bright hibiscus muumuu over her knees. "Slow down, this ain't the mainland. Kat's got a head injury. You always come on so strong, Edith. I've been telling you for thirty years now, you're not in New York City anymore."

I took another bite of mouth-watering *haupia* pudding and considered the hat on my lap. Choosing to join the Red Hat Society should have been a no-brainer. I believed in their feminist, color-outside-the-lines philosophy. But once I put on that hat, I would be identified as The Enemy by whomever and whatever was behind the scenes at the New Ohia development—and that wasn't going to help me find Jimmy Ching's killer.

But how could I say no? All three pairs of eyes were fixed on me, waiting for an answer.

Opal, owner of the neighboring Ohia General Store, knocked on the doorjamb just as the silence between me and the Red Hat ladies was getting uncomfortable. "Yo."

We all turned to her.

Opal's signature look always included a silk or velour shoulder wrap, secured with an elaborate pin positioned over her heart. Today's scarf was lime green, with a trident pin the size of a spatula. "Having a party without me?"

"Just a little catch-up with the local Red Hat Society." I held up Exhibit A: the hideous satin cap trimmed in rhinestones. "They've asked me to join."

Opal put her hands on her hips and glanced around the room. She was a former redhead with pale freckled skin and blue eyes that didn't miss a thing. "I know you ladies think that's an honor, but Kat hasn't been here long enough to know what it really means."

Mattie harrumphed. "It *is* an honor. We basically run this town."

"But not New Ohia," Opal warned.

"It's just a matter of time until we get them shut down . . ." Edith said.

Opal held up a hand. "Kat's the postmaster. She has to appear neutral and get along with everyone. Pua's shoes are going to be hard enough to fill without her appearing to take sides."

The three Red Hatters exchanged a glance. Edith gestured to the cap, resting on my lap like a lurid, scarlet bomb. "You can keep that. When you're ready to take a stand and join us, wear it proudly."

I held up the hat. "Ladies, Opal's right. I am a federal employee in a position of influence. I work on behalf of everyone in the community and cannot appear partisan or biased toward any person or entity served by the post office. I am truly honored by your invitation, but I cannot accept at this time."

Mattie scowled. "All that time I spent gluing on rhinestones. For nothing."

"Well," Edith huffed. "Good to know whose side you're on."

"I'm sorry. I have my personal feelings and opinions, of course, but I can't flaunt them around town. I hope you understand."

Josie leaned over to pat my knee. "It's okay, hon. Eat your *haupia* and tell us what went down at Pua's last night."

Opal came inside and joined Edith and me on the bed. "Make room, Edith. I want to hear this too."

I regaled the four women with a blow-by-blow account of the previous night's events: two murders were solved, and the post office was exposed as a front for money laundering and drug distribution for the Chang crime family. By the time I wrapped up my narrative, I was feeling headachy and tired. "Your turn," I told Edith. "Tell me about the lawsuit and the role Jimmy Ching plays in New Ohia. And could someone get me a refill on my coffee and a couple of Tylenol, please?"

Opal took my mug and the Red Hat ladies dug in their purses for headache remedies, exclaiming amongst themselves about the revelations I'd shared.

When Opal returned with my coffee, I caught her eye and gave a tiny headshake, hoping she would understand. I didn't want the Red Hat ladies to know about Jimmy Ching's murder just yet, though I wasn't sure Opal knew either. In any case, she seemed to get the message and let Edith take the lead once I'd downed my painkillers with a swig of fresh coffee.

"We're gaining some traction on the lawsuit," Edith said. "I'm filing a cease and desist motion with the Supreme Court of the State of Hawaii. That would halt further development of New Ohia until an environmental impact study, community needs survey, and a local infrastructure impact study are completed, all of which were neglected prior to beginning construction. Hopefully, those studies will uncover a way we can get the project permanently sidelined."

"Wow," I said. "How did it get so far? I mean, the whole place is laid out and ready to build on. That clubhouse and pool are down-right fancy."

"Someone's been greasing the wheels. Basically, New Ohia is the result of backdoor deals made with corrupt state officials. They looked the other way while an investment group with deep pockets barreled forward with the project. The whole thing is entirely illegal, and I'm excited to file the papers on Oahu," Edith said.

I took a fortifying slug of coffee. "What's Jimmy Ching's role in all of this?"

"He's the front man—the dude running around greasing palms and making deals," Mattie said with a curl of her lip. "He claimed he was not an investor himself, but none of us believe that. He's the face of New Ohia Vision, Inc., the group that bought the land from the state."

"And the weird thing is, I haven't been able to find out who that really is," Edith said. "My motion includes a demand that the share-holders and board of directors be listed on the public record."

"Huh. So, when Jimmy disappeared last week . . ." I let that sentence trail off.

"We all thought someone offed him," Mattie said. "And good

riddance to that slimeball." She banged her cane on the floor for emphasis.

I was suddenly too exhausted to deal with anything more. "All of this is very interesting, but my head is really thumping. Would you ladies be offended if I took a nap?"

The group got up with much fluttering and sympathy, cleared my dishes into the sink, and headed out the door into the gorgeous Hawaiian sunshine. Opal poked her head back in. "I'll check in on you later," she said. "And we can talk about the situation," she added with a whisper.

I held a finger to my lips and nodded, and she closed the door. I settled my sore noggin gently on the pillow, pulled my covers up, and shut my eyes. My brain, tired and sore as it was, wouldn't stop churning. A lot of people had motive to kill Jimmy Ching, and several of them had been in the room with me today.

I woke up from a dead sleep to the feeling of someone or something touching my face. Reflexes kicked in and I swung up my fist in a left hook and connected. *BAM!* Nobody sneaks up on Kat Smith while sleeping!

"Oof!"

I followed that with the heel of my other hand to their face. *WHAM!*

"Ow!"

I opened my eyes to assess my assailant.

Mr. K was sitting on the floor beside my bed, cradling a bleeding nose, his right ear bright red. He groaned. "That'll teach me to try to wake you up with a kiss."

"Oh, bung nuggets!" I eased into sitting up carefully, cradling my cranium. "I wouldn't have done that if I'd known it was you!"

"Can I get a paper towel or something?" (Only it was more like, "Cad I ged a paber towel ur subting?")

I slung my legs out of bed and wobbled over to the sink, ripping off a pile of paper towels and bringing them back. "I'm sorry, Mr. K. I told you about the PTSD, though, didn't I?"

Keone stuffed the towels against his nose. "Helb me up?" He had changed clothes, which was fortunate—the blood covering the front of his T-shirt would have been hard to get out of that white uniform. "How about some ice? I think my ear is . . ." He made a gesture to the rapidly swelling appendage on the side of his head.

I felt worse by the minute as I cracked some ice cubes out of the old-fashioned tray in my tiny freezer and wrapped them in a dish-towel. "Here—put these on your ear." I guided him to my bed to sit. "Lean forward and pinch the top of your nostrils until the bleeding stops." Drops of blood dotted the floor between his feet. "What was it you were trying to do, again?"

"Wake you up with a kiss." Mr. K rolled his eyes. "Dumb idea."

"Yep."

We glanced at each other and chuckled.

Chuckles turned to full-blown laughter, even though it hurt. We sat on my bed, Keone bleeding and me bruised and concussed, and laughed until we hiccupped to a stop.

"Well," I said, wiping my streaming eyes with paper towel, "I may have been okay with you carrying me across the parking lot, but clearly waking me up is hazardous. Just ask Tiki. I almost shot her head off when she snuck onto the bed our first night together." I pointed to the bullet hole in the wall near my pillow.

"I'll have to take precautions when we go to bed." His eyes gleamed with naughty thoughts.

Or tears. I wasn't sure which.

"Dude, you're talking about a sleepover when I might have broken your nose?" I shook my head. "You're a glutton for punishment."

"I guess so." He smiled. "I set up a beach tent next to the pier. Thought we could go hang out over by the ocean since we both have an unexpected day off."

"That will take my mind off a sore head, for sure."

I shared my Tylenol with Keone, and we got ready for the beach. We changed into bathing suits, grabbed a couple of towels, filled a water bottle, and headed across the road. I didn't even feel guilty walking past the post office, which was doing brisk business as the denizens of Ohia showed up in force to get news on what happened over the weekend.

Mr. K had not only gone home to change while I was visiting with Opal and the Red Hat ladies, but he'd also built a little hut out of driftwood and palm fronds next to the pier. "Thought you could rest in here just as easily as in the shack," he said.

"This is the cutest little hut ever!" I exclaimed, spreading my towel inside the shelter, and easing down on top of it.

"I try to wake you with a kiss and get beat up. I demonstrate my manly building skills, and it's 'cute,'" Keone complained, only half-joking. "You're hard on a man's ego, you know that, right?"

"Yes, I know," I sighed. I wanted to make a joke, but the subject was a bit tender. "I'm a Secret Service agent, six foot one, and wear a size eleven shoe. I am bigger than most men and protect them for a living. But hey, if anyone tries to assault you—besides myself, of course—I'm your gal." I tried to grin. "I warned you I wasn't easy."

He sat down on his towel beside me. "I wouldn't be here if I wanted easy. Can I try that kiss again?"

"I'd love a do-over of that disaster." My eyes fluttered shut and I leaned in, my mouth reaching for his in anticipation.

And Keone Kaihale gave me a peck on the forehead. "We'll have to work up to anything more. I have PTSD."

I elbowed him in the ribs. He chuckled. I settled into a prone position on the towel and sighed. "Thanks for this."

Next thing I knew, something touched me on the leg. "Time to turn over."

I lifted my head off my arms, waking up abruptly. "What?"

"The backs of your legs are the color of a tomato."

That got me flipping over in a hurry. Apparently, the sound of the sea and the warmth of the sun had put me right to sleep with my bottom half sticking out of the beach hut.

Keone held up a piece of driftwood. "I gave you a little poke from way over here."

I glanced over at him. "Fair." Mr. K's nose was swollen, and his ear was still bright red. "I really am sorry for what happened before."

"I was warned. And now I'm on my guard." He waggled the driftwood. "Let's hop in and cool off in the ocean."

Admiring each other in our bathing suits while keeping our injured heads out of the water made swimming in Ohia Bay a little challenging, but refreshing nonetheless. We were back up on the beach and tanning our fronts when Keone's phone chirped.

Down here on the beach, close to the water, was one of the few places we were able to get a cell phone signal in Ohia. The other that I knew of was in New Ohia, through some deal with the devil the developers had made.

"Shoot. The Air Traffic Controller is calling me in. I've got to get over to the airport ASAP—they're resuming flights today." He leaned over and gave me a quick kiss. "I'll see you tomorrow night for that steak dinner we talked about, if not before."

"Sounds like a plan."

Mr. K had barely driven off when a familiar purple truck pulled up to the small unpaved parking area near the pier. Detective Pono Kaihale, Keone's cousin, was an older, thicker version of the handsome Hawaiian I was dating. He and Sergeant Lei Texeira, an athletic woman with a wind-ruffled head of brown curls, walked across the sand to join me at the beach hut.

"Got room for two more?" Lei asked with a smile.

I scooted over as far over as my towel would allow. "I thought you guys would be busy at the crime scene at Hana Airport."

"The medical examiners, Dr. Gregory and Dr. Tanaka, are handling the mop-up. It was a pretty straightforward scene," Lei said.

"The airport was eager to get back to business," Pono added. "We passed Keone on the way here."

"Yeah, he was the one who built this shelter. He'd been hoping to have the day off with me, but duty called."

The detectives settled themselves beside me. The three of us sat in companionable silence as we gazed out at the sparkling waves, waving palm trees, and soft sand. A couple of kids, who must have been playing hooky, were running and jumping off the pier. Seabirds circled the horizon.

Lei sighed, clearly exhausted. "We barely got home last night after the situation with you when our phones were waking us up for the murder at Hana Airport."

"We thought you might've had something to do with it," Pono said, only half-joking. The action had been nonstop since I arrived in Ohia, and not in a good way.

"Not this time. One of your officers dropped me off at home last night with an ice pack for my head, and that was the last thing I knew until this morning," I said. "Did everything go okay, booking the perps?" I was still struggling with the fact that my coworker almost had a hand in killing me. Almost. She'd demonstrated restraint at the last minute. Not her nephew, though. "You got Sonny nailed down for those murders?"

"He's denying everything, but Pua has agreed to testify against him. We also have you as a witness. For now, he's locked up and unable to make bail."

"Huh. Interesting." I sipped more water, rubbing my aching temples. "I thought the cases were all sewn up and the killings would stop. Can't say I'm terribly surprised by Jimmy Ching's demise, though. He's got a lot of haters in this town."

"Why don't you tell us who some of those are." Pono took a small, spiral pad out of the back pocket of his jeans. "Kat the Postmaster Sleuth has ears everywhere."

"What can you tell me about Jimmy Ching's murder? I'll do my part if you do yours," I countered.

"I'm sure Keone gave you enough to get started," Pono said with a wink.

"He did tell me what he knew, but this time, I'm without a suspect," I said. "I haven't had time to work up a threat assessment on anyone."

Pono cleared his throat. "Lei and I talked it over. We'd like you to be the eyes and ears of the Maui Police Department out here. That's what we came to ask."

"Sure." My heart thudded with excitement at the idea of catching the killer. "I'll be your boots on the ground." I wiggled my toes in the sand. "So to speak."

"I wish we could jump in the ocean today, but we've got to go search Jimmy's place. Apparently, he lived in one of the model homes in New Ohia. Maybe afterward we'll have enough time to take a dip and cool off," Pono said.

"What happens in Ohia, stays in Ohia," I said.

"You got it," Pono chuckled.

Lei smiled. "Thanks, Kat. You've got a knack for this." The two cops headed out to do their search. I watched them go, wishing I could be a gecko on the wall to see what they found.

🌺 4 🌺

My nap-filled morning left me well-rested and antsy, especially after my conversation with Lei and Pono. I rinsed off in the ocean, packed up my towel, and headed back to the shack. It would be hard to be the eyes and ears of the Maui Police Department from inside my little beach hut.

I'd somehow managed to burn off all the treats, goodies, and breakfast that I'd eaten that morning. Opal had promised me a catch-up chat, so I took a detour to the general store, my stomach rumbling.

Artie Pahinui was sitting in his chair on the porch, his ukulele in his hands, strumming a mournful ballad. His blind eyes seemed to gaze at the ocean view across the road. A large man, Artie suffered the wear and tear of diabetes in his discolored feet and loss of eyesight. On a side table at his elbow rested a plate of vegetables: carrots, celery slices, and broccoli.

He paused his playing, laying a large hand over the strings of his ukulele to quiet them. "Spare me from some of these veggies, Kat," he said. "Opal has decided I need to cut down on my carbs."

I sat in the chair beside him. "Don't mind if I do. I'm starving." I picked up a chunk of crisp broccoli and crunched loudly. "How did you know it was me?"

"I recognized your walk."

"Huh. Have you guys heard any good gossip about what happened to Jimmy Ching?"

"I'll catch you up as soon as the last customers are done in here," Opal hollered from inside the store. "It's time to read the runes."

"Oh, good." I rubbed my hands together in anticipation. "I'm so fascinated with how she reads the runes, Artie. Between the two of you, you've got the psychic bases covered."

"Lot of good it does us," Artie grumbled. "We sure didn't see what happened with Pua and Sonny coming. Opal is crushed. She considered Pua one of her best friends."

"It sucks," I said, summing up the situation the only way I knew how. "For me too." I touched the goose egg on my head gingerly. "Frankly, I don't know how I'm going to run the post office without her."

Just then, a large white van with "Maui Police Department" emblazoned on the side pulled up to the store. The van doors opened, revealing Dr. Gregory and Dr. Tanaka, Maui's medical examiners.

Dr. Tanaka hopped out of the van and waved at us. "Hey you two! We decided to drive back to Kahului this way because it's straighter with fewer curves. We need some drinks and snacks, big-time."

Dr. Gregory came to the steps, rubbing his paunch. "Extra big-time."

"Anything to help keep our island's MEs fueled up," Opal said, stepping out to join us on the porch. She handed me a wrapped packet, then held the door wide. "I still have some premade sand-wiches and coffee cake left over from Sunday."

"I can vouch for that coffee cake," I told them, unwrapping my lunch. "I had some on Sunday and it was delicious."

The two medical examiners followed Opal into the store.

I had an idea. My pulse sped up as I placed my sandwich on the veggie plate and rose from the chair from beside Artie.

"Where are you off to, Kitty Kat?" Artie asked.

"Just going to have a little peek at Jimmy Ching's body in the van," I whispered.

I scooted over to the van and tested the handle. The door popped open, and I squelched a pang of guilt. This was my chance to get a look at the body and check out what their findings might be. I trotted around to the back of the vehicle and tried one of the double doors. Just like the front door, it opened easily.

Lying on the gurney inside was a zipped up, strapped down black body bag. I frowned. Getting into that quickly was going to be next to impossible. Luckily, a clipboard with a closed metal cover swung from a hook at the foot of the gurney.

"Good enough," I muttered. I glanced back at the store and could see the two doctors were busy shopping and chatting with Opal. I pulled my phone out of my pocket, thumbed to the camera app, flipped open the metal cover on the clipboard, and quickly snapped pictures of the notes written in tiny, precise block lettering. These included an outline of a body with a series of hand-drawn illustrations, arrows, and jottings scribbled all over it.

"Nice." From what I had observed during my previous case, Dr. Gregory talked out loud and performed an examination, while Dr. Tanaka confirmed details, discussing findings, recorded the audio, and took their case notes. The tiny printing likely belonged to her.

I resisted rampant Curiosity, my personal demon. That little devil on my shoulder begged me to unbuckle and unzip the bag and check out the corpse. I at least wanted to see if there were defensive wounds on the hands or arms.

"No. You do not need to personally view Jimmy dead. He was unattractive enough alive," I told myself sternly. "Besides, any exterior damage to the body will be in the notes."

I rehung the clipboard and shut the van's door as quietly as I could, then hurried back toward Artie. I parked my behind in the old wooden chair just as the two doctors exited the store onto the worn front porch.

"Been a lot of nasty activities in your area," Dr. Gregory commented, unwrapping one of Opal's sandwiches. He perused me thoughtfully as he chewed. "I heard you were involved."

I gestured to my bruised head and black eyes. "Don't I know it. I'm ready for things to calm down. At least I get a couple days off from the post office to recover."

"We're sure glad you're here. You have been such a big help to the Maui Police Department," Dr. Tanaka said. "Anything we can do, just let us know."

"I'd love a tour of your morgue sometime," I said, giving in to Curiosity's seductive whisper.

"No problem. Just text me," Dr. Gregory said. I exchanged contact info with the two docs, hiding my glee. These were some useful phone numbers to have.

The couple got back into the van, toting bags of taro chips, bottles of coconut water, and the last of the homemade sandwiches the Pahinuis put together in the kitchen each morning. They waved goodbye as they pulled out onto the road.

Opal put her hands on her hips and addressed me with a frown. "Why are you still wearing your bathing suit? Go home, take a shower, and eat your sandwich. Come back for dinner tonight, and we'll catch up. I'll read the runes then, too."

"She's in her swimsuit? What am I missing?" Artie rumbled with a grin, strumming his ukulele for emphasis.

"A six-foot bikini model with nice biceps," Opal said. "I should have you sit on my porch every afternoon in that outfit, Kat. Even with your black eyes, you'd be good for business."

"Ha. What's for dinner?" I asked, grabbing my sandwich and making my way down the porch steps.

"Got a nice teriyaki chicken in the Crock-Pot," Artie said. "Low sodium. Brown rice and a salad. Should be ready around five thirty."

"Perfect. I'll be back." I set off across the parking lot in my flip-flops.

Once inside, I made a beeline for the bed and opened my phone's photo app. I was too eager to study the photos of the crime scene records to wait until after a shower. Nothing like a few autopsy and crime scene notes to whet the appetite of the Postmaster Sleuth.

I started with the photo of the body outline with the notations on it, using my thumb and forefinger to zoom in on the handwritten notes from Dr. Tanaka. I scanned the illustration—a description of "blunt force trauma to the head" was marked "tentative COD." Apparently, there had been a rounded edge to whatever caved in the back of the victim's cranium, but the weapon left no obvious trace in the wound. Dr. Gregory had taken a swab to send to the lab to confirm. In addition, the victim's hands and arms had been closely inspected and "no defensive wounds" was marked on the chart.

That was the piece of information that I had been most interested to find out, and the answer was clear: Jimmy Ching had not seen the fatal blow coming. He'd been ambushed.

I flipped back to the photo of the first page and skimmed over the details about the body in situ. A little inventory had been made of the clothing he was wearing and the items in his pockets, which included a wallet with cash, keys, and a small folding manicure pocketknife.

This wasn't a robbery. No attempt had been made to make it appear like one.

Frustrated, I flopped back against my pillows. I was glad Opal was going to read the runes after dinner.

I checked the time on my phone and saw that I still had a couple of hours before dinner. That shower could wait a little longer while I took a leisurely stroll around New Ohia. Maybe I could find Jimmy Ching's house and see if Lei and Pono were still there.

While I was keen to search New Ohia for clues, I also wasn't stupid. I threw on a tee and shorts, stashing my miniature Mace keychain in one of my pockets. I strapped on my nylon webbing shoulder holster and loaded it with my Glock 19, concealing the whole accoutrement with my windbreaker.

Armed and alert, I was probably a lot more dangerous than anyone on Maui, murderer or not. I had training, but more importantly, I knew what it was like to pull the trigger. Using a weapon on someone, even someone who needs killing, is a lot harder than people realize. Maybe that's a good thing.

I stepped out onto my stoop rock and locked the door behind me. Time to have a look at Jimmy Ching's model home and see what I could find out.

5

The last time I'd gone into New Ohia, it had been to get a look at a body and to talk to the same cops I was hoping to waylay at the home of the latest victim. Maybe Ohia wasn't such a safe place, after all. I resolved to help make it one.

The artificial waterfall with golden letters that marked the entrance to New Ohia glittered in the afternoon sun. Walking quickly made my head pound, so I slowed as I entered the development. I had to look casual, like a woman just out for a leisurely stroll before dinner. I was highly cognizant of the hidden surveillance cameras connected to the artificial intelligence security system that Jimmy had bragged to me about just a few days ago.

A wide blacktop drive curved upward in an artistic fashion from the entrance. Its shoulders were wide, even, and perfectly mowed, with hibiscus and full-sized coconut palms planted at intervals. At night, strategically placed spotlights dramatically illuminated the landscape. The whole place seemed to have been designed with serene, suburban walking in mind.

Walking here was certainly more pleasant than the rugged, narrow shoulder of Hana Highway, with its hidden mud puddles and zero room for speeding cars to pass safely. Even so, I felt disloyal even comparing the two. They were truly mangoes and coconuts, with nothing in common but the tropics.

I passed the clubhouse with its sparkling pool, sauna, gym, and barbecue patio. Not a soul was in sight. I'd jogged through the development once before and remembered seeing several model homes at the ends of cul-de-sacs. These sat situated on the elevated portion of the property. "Of course Jimmy's house has to be on a hill when I'm nursing a goose egg," I complained aloud as I walked up the sloping sidewalk. But this was still nothing like that time in Beirut—I'd been clobbered by a rifle butt on that assignment. Seeing double, I still had to run for a couple of miles through the city. Life in Ohia turned out to be more dangerous than I'd expected, but it was still mellow compared to the physical challenges of the Secret Service.

Navigating entirely by memory, I made my best guess and headed down one of the cul-de-sacs. I reached the end and was pleased to find I'd been correct. Amid the empty lots marked with fluttering flags sat a completed, Mediterranean-style home. This was the dwelling where I'd spotted Jimmy Ching's big white SUV the last time I jogged through. The vehicle was gone, probably at the police impound.

Also missing was Pono's jacked-up purple truck, Stanley. Lei and Pono must have completed their search of the premises already. A big X of crime scene tape crisscrossed the front door, with a bright red seal stuck across the crack between the door and the frame.

"Well, heckfire," I said, slowing my pace. I'd have to go around to the back, since I obviously could not enter the front door undetected. I also had the security cameras to contend with—I'd need to identify and locate them in order to figure out how to evade them. As much as I was yearning to get into the model home to conduct my own search, I continued at a slow steady pace around the circular pad and back up to the main road.

As I walked, I racked my brain for where the hidden cameras might be located. Part of the aesthetic of the place included no overhead lights or power lines, but the cameras needed a power source.

The light fixtures nestled into the decorative landscaping made the most sense as a place to hide the surveillance nodes, since they too required power.

Nearing the entrance to the development, I veered toward a particularly flamboyant hibiscus bloom, taking my phone out as I approached. The shrub was positioned beneath a coconut palm with its own spotlight. I feigned snapping a perfect picture of the flower, instead focusing the camera on the light fixture. Once home, I'd examine it closely. I turned my meander toward the exit and suppressed the urge to speed walk back to the shack.

Tiki sat on my stoop rock, glaring from across the parking lot as I approached. She always seemed to appear there at five o'clock on the dot, with clear expectations of an evening meal. She lashed her tail and miaowed. I gave her a wide berth as I approached the porch, guarding my bare legs.

"Hey, pretty girl. Thanks for keeping intruders out."

Tiki was not, technically, a pretty girl, but I had hopes that flattery would assist with my campaign to win her over. She was a large, patchy calico with the orangey head of a tabby, minus one ear. When I first met her, she had a rough coat and a weepy eye that was swollen shut. Her fur was improving since she'd been getting regular, nutritious meals, and her bad eye was open again. Not much could be done, though, about the kink in her tail that suggested a long-ago encounter with an automobile.

Catching her for a vet visit, let alone a flea bath, was currently out of the question. The fact that I didn't yet have a car also didn't help. I needed to rectify that situation, and soon.

Tiki narrowed her eyes and complained in her loud, rusty voice that it was five-oh-seven, and I was late procuring dinner.

"I hear you." I opened the door of the shack, noting that the post office, which closed at four p.m., was already locked up tight. Phil Hanoi's vehicle was gone. Hopefully, he'd return tomorrow. Despite lots of rest today, I was still in no shape to meet the public.

Once inside, I filled Tiki's dish with kibble and refreshed her water, then hopped in the shower. Thankfully, though the shack was "rustic," it had been equipped with an on-demand propane water heater that delivered plenty of piping hot H_2O.

Lathering up and luxuriating in the hot water, I was not pleased to spot one of the giant cane spiders Lei told me were "fairly harmless to humans." High in the corner of the stall, it observed me with its multiple eyes—its long, hairy legs cocked to leap.

"Consider cane spiders your friends," Lei had said. "Along with house geckos, they help keep other bugs down."

"Ugh," I told the spider. "Could you please NOT stare at me when I'm naked? Also, no jumping on wet humans. I might squash you out of sheer terror." The arachnid, the size of my hand, seemed to understand and scuttled out of sight into a crack.

The thing wasn't gone.

Nope.

I'd see that big brown monster again next time I showered, guaranteed.

"I think I'll call you Miss Prissy," I told the crack where the spider disappeared. "So you seem less scary."

Out and dressed, my hair wrapped in a towel, I settled on the bed to examine the photos I'd taken, zooming in on them with a thumb and forefinger. The surveillance nodes appeared to be small, shiny, round lenses set within the matte black light fixture.

"Smart," I muttered. "Hiding in plain sight." They were hard enough to see when you knew what to look for; the average person would never notice they were being watched by these tiny, beady eyes. They were probably transmitting info wirelessly, too.

I sat back in the chair, tapping my lips and gazing up at the ceiling, deep in thought. Unfortunately, Miss Prissy the giant cane spider had emerged from her shower crack and crouched on the ceiling in the corner of the room. "Yikes. You stay up there, you hear? Don't come any closer, or I'll have to whack you with my flip-flop."

The spider made no reply. The bare, dangling bulb that lit the shack had attracted several fluttering moths. Nearby, a couple of pale, speckled geckos were lurking in wait for those tasty, winged treats.

"Ew. I was better off not looking up." I went to the sink and poured myself a big cup of water and drank it down, thinking through my options. Now that I'd located the surveillance nodes, I could probably stay out of their view by climbing behind the bushes to move past them. The cameras were aimed at the streets, which made sense.

Also, during Kermit Hubbard's murder outside the New Ohia clubhouse, the killer had worn a hat and loose clothing, which rendered him anonymous. I could have done the same, but not after the surveillance program registered my height and build not once, but twice.

I'd taken my walk through the development today and gone for a jog just a few days ago. That in itself was nothing noteworthy—in fact, if I wanted to, I could begin a new habit of walking or jogging through New Ohia, just to give myself a "reason" to be there. Someone, or at least the AI program Jimmy had alluded to, would be paying attention and learning my patterns.

But I didn't have the time to establish a pattern. I wanted to break into Ching's house now. The longer the place was empty, the more likely that anyone else involved in New Ohia would return to remove evidence that linked them to the development. And I was finally ready to admit that I wanted to know who was behind the shady development of New Ohia—not just who killed Jimmy Ching.

I turned to face the menagerie populating my one-room dwelling. The beady eyes of a cat, two geckos, and one very large arachnid watched me attentively. "Yep. I want to help the Red Hat ladies with their case without actually putting on a red hat," I told Tiki, Miss Prissy, and the lizard duo, whom I'd decided to name Tweedledee and Tweedledum. "That's what I'm really interested in. Lei and Pono would have focused on anything in his house pertaining to his murder. They might have passed over documents related to his job."

Tiki nodded, and then leaned over to lick her genitals.

"Save that for private time, girlfriend."

She ignored me, per usual.

I checked the time and immediately mobilized so I wouldn't keep Opal and Artie waiting on me for dinner. I undid the towel around my hair and rubbed the wet mass a bit more, then got off the bed, folded it out of the way, and anchored it with the strap. I hung my wet towel over the door of the bathroom because things had a tough time drying if the sun wasn't out in Ohia—a side effect of the high humidity.

Tiki paused her personal activity to glower in my direction, conveying clearly that she planned to rest upon my pillow like the queen she considered herself to be.

"You don't get to sleep on the bed until you've had that flea bath," I told her. "There's your nice beach towel to lie on." I pointed to it, folded on the floor.

She resumed grooming, grumbling as she tongued her unmentionables.

I locked up the shack behind me, firming up my new security habit—but it broke my heart a little that I had to do that. Ohia seemed like it should be a safe place to live. Maybe someday it would be again.

6

Opal welcomed me into their cozy living space behind the store. The kitchen was redolent with wonderful smells: tangy ginger, garlic, and soy sauce. My stomach rumbled loudly in response.

"You two know how to make me hungry," I said. "Thanks so much for the invite to eat. I didn't have the energy to deal with cooking, and my headache is coming back."

"Oh, no! Let me get you something for that." Opal had taken off her daily scarf, her silver-white hair gleaming under the light and contrasting with her purple caftan. "And you probably didn't drink enough water," she called over her shoulder as she hurried off.

Artie was at the stove, his big hands moving with confidence as he switched off the burner under a pot of steaming broccoli. "Go have a seat at the table, Kitty Kat," he said.

Three places were already laid at the couple's round table. My spirits, a bit dampened by my lack of progress in solving Jimmy Ching's murder, perked back up again. Whatever new mystery was going on in this town, I wasn't alone trying to figure it out. Artie and Opal would be right there supporting me.

Opal returned with Tylenol and a big glass of water. "Thanks so much," I said, then downed the pills and half the glass of water in just a few gulps. Opal was right, I really needed to stay better hydrated.

Artie began dishing up the food to bring to the table, and Opal appeared at his elbow. "I've got it, honey." She kissed his cheek as she picked up the broccoli steamer and headed for the sink. "Go get comfortable with Kat."

Opal served the food; for about fifteen minutes, there was little conversation but lots of happy lip-smacking. The three of us demolished Artie's tasty teriyaki chicken, rice, and perfectly steamed broccoli in record time.

Satiated, I sat back and sighed. "So, I got a look at the notes on Jimmy Ching's body," I said, switching gears to the investigation.

"What? How'd you do that?" Opal's pale eyes flew wide and she dropped her fork.

"Kat snuck into the van while you were waiting on the doctors," Artie informed her.

"Naughty Kat! What'd you do that for?" Opal asked.

"This is probably a good time to tell you that I plan to find out who killed Jimmy Ching," I told them. "You don't have to get involved. In fact, it might be better if you didn't. It's bound to be dangerous."

Opal frowned, gazing at Artie. Some invisible communication seemed to be passing between them.

"Why don't we clear the table and see what the runes tell us," Opal said at last.

I carried the dishes to the sink while Opal put away the leftovers. Artie got up, washed his hands, and fetched his guitar. He sat down and picked out a melody in the distinctive Hawaiian music style called "slack-key."

Opal left to fetch a white velvet cloth and the leather pouch that held the runes, and I quickly washed up the dishes, loading them in the old-fashioned drainer. Opal returned to the kitchen and sat down at the table with Artie.

"Quit splashing and come sit down." Opal said.

I wiped my hands on a nearby towel and joined them at the multipurpose table. Opal spread the white cloth open and shook the runes out of the pouch into her hand.

"What's our question?" She kept her gaze on the shiny, highly polished kukui nut shells cupped in her palm, each one etched on the back with an ancient design.

"We could just ask who killed Jimmy Ching," I said.

Opal shook her head. "It doesn't work that way."

I thought back to the other time I'd seen her read the runes. That experience had not been straightforward then, either. "I guess we could ask where to look for answers regarding Jimmy's murder."

"But we know where to look," Artie pointed a thick finger in the direction of New Ohia.

"I guess you're right about that," I mused, tapping my lips with a finger. "Hmm."

"Let's just ask what influences to be aware of in Kat's quest for answers," Opal said. "Focus your intentions."

She closed her eyes and cupped the runes with both hands. I stared at her closed hands, thinking hard. *I want to know what's going on in New Ohia that led to Jimmy Ching's death.*

Opal opened her hands and dropped the runes.

One landed sideways and bounced off the table. "Interesting. That's an influence that's no longer with us." She reached down to pick up the shell and examine the design. "A strong female influence is no longer a part of the picture."

She glanced up and our eyes met. "Pua Chang," we both said at the same time.

Opal's blue eyes filled. "I miss her so much already."

"I'm sorry," I whispered.

She flapped her hand. "It's okay. No one made her use the post office to run drugs. At least, I don't think anyone did."

"It's still hard to discover someone you cared for isn't who you thought they were. If it's any comfort, she wasn't a murderer."

"But she raised one and covered for him." Opal grabbed a tissue from a nearby box and honked her nose. "Anyway." She tucked the tissue into her pocket and peered down at the jumble of kukui nut shells.

"The upside-down ones are also out. That leaves us . . ." She took out her phone and snapped a picture of the runes. "That leaves us with a pretty fragmented message." She frowned, moving so close to the shells that her nose was almost touching them. "There are larger and smaller forces at work. The tool is an . . . ostrich? No. Um . . . the instrument of death was not alone, but meaningful. Courage and caution are needed."

I rolled my lips inward and bit them—pure mumbo jumbo. Why was I so fascinated with those little black nutshells? They clearly had nothing useful to say. But I was as disappointed now as I had been when I learned Santa Claus wasn't real. In other words, really disappointed. Aunt Fae told me the tantrum I'd thrown (and the sulk that followed) had lasted for days. "You really know how to milk a bummer, Kat," she'd said.

Apparently, I was a big, bad Secret Service agent who really, *really* wanted magic to be real.

Opal disappeared into that trancelike state that occurred when she read the runes. She reached for her pad and paper and began sketching the reading quickly. "I need to dig deeper for this one," she muttered.

"Well, do either of you want to hear what I found out about Jimmy from the notes on his body?" I asked.

Opal broke her concentration and met my eyes. "Not this time," she said. "Its meaning still isn't fully known yet, but I'm getting a clear danger warning off this read. You should stay away from it, too."

"It?"

"The dark thing that happened to Jimmy," she replied, her eyes once again fixed on the kukui shells.

Goosebumps rippled over my shoulders. I glanced over at Artie, strumming his guitar and humming.

My gaze bounced between the two, both clearly checked out from their tiny kitchen into some other realm.

"Okay then," I said, rising slowly from my chair. "Thanks so much for dinner."

"You're always welcome with us, Kitty Kat," Artie said.

I impulsively leaned over to kiss his cheek. "Thank you."

Opal was still bent over the runes, muttering to herself. She scarcely looked up as I slipped out the door.

Outside, indigo night had swallowed the sun, though a blur of paler blue still defined the horizon. A breeze rattled the fronds of the coconut palms as I made my way across the unpaved parking lot to my shack. Despite the short distance, I was glad I'd left the light on inside to spill out around the door. I was unsettled by the rune reading, however little it had told us.

Tiki welcomed me with a rusty mew from her spot on the towel, glancing hopefully at the folded up Murphy bed.

"Still on that mission, girl. I need to plan this break-in if I'm going to get away with it." I paced back and forth in the small space, too agitated to get ready for bed—and then, I had an idea. Maybe I didn't need to avoid the surveillance system—maybe fooling it would be enough, just like Sonny had done.

I changed quickly into baggy hiking pants and a tank top and threw a long-sleeved black men's shirt that Keone had left in my shack on top of the outfit. I slipped the fat bunch of keys Mr. Hanoi had given me into my pocket and headed for the back door of the post office.

Going into the P.O. building after-hours wasn't technically doing anything wrong—it was my job to oversee the premises. But I wasn't on the clock, and I wasn't going for any work reason, so I found myself glancing furtively back and forth as I unlocked the door.

I flipped on the lights and sighed with relief to see that Mr. Hanoi had not repaired the alarm system that Pua Chang had installed. The plastic wall mount still gaped open with its tangle of wires hanging out, making a mockery of the building's security.

I went straight to the hall closet. Back behind the brooms and mops rested a large, striped golf umbrella that I'd spotted on my first exploration of my new workplace. The giant, ugly umbrella would work fine for what I had in mind. I retrieved the thing and backed out of the office, relocking the door.

The dirt parking lot with its single, yellow streetlight was deserted. It was a fairly safe conclusion that there was seldom anyone around in Ohia after the sun went down. Even the Hana Highway, the only artery back to civilization, was quiet.

Tiki glared from the beach towel when I slipped back into the shack.

"Don't judge. I told you, I'm on a mission."

Tiki judged all right, but her disapproval wasn't enough to stop me. She settled herself into a squat on her towel as I tied on my running shoes and took a flashlight out of the kitchen drawer. "Hold down the fort, girl," I told her. "I'll be back before you know it."

I locked the shack behind me, frowning at the shadowy entrance to my dwelling. "I really need to put in a sensor light out here," I muttered. But that would require a trip to Hasegawa's in Hana or getting myself all the way to Kahului, and I still didn't have any wheels. I really needed to do something about that, too. Or maybe first. "Chicken or egg? Egg or chicken? Stop talking to yourself, Kat."

I set off across the parking lot, dimly illuminated by the single streetlight that marked the turnoff to Old Ohia. Getting wheels and a porch light would be tomorrow's task. I'd take another day off from the post office and figure out getting my own transportation.

Tonight, I was breaking into Jimmy Ching's house.

❧ 7 ❧

There was no point in pretending I was on an idle stroll this time. The umbrella would do most of the work hiding my identity, but I needed to disguise my height as well as I could. Once at the entrance to the development, I hunched over and positioned the umbrella square atop my head. I altered my gait and walked with a hitch through the empty streets of New Ohia. I was tempted to snag a golf cart just for the fun of it but decided to save that escapade for another day.

I hobbled boldly up the driveway of Ching's house and hurried around the back to a flagstone patio. Areca palms in large ceramic pots surrounded a kidney-shaped pool and accompanying hot tub, both sensibly hidden under solar warming covers. The ubiquitous spotlights shone up at the palm trees and lit the bottom of the pool with a turquoise glow.

I wasted no time observing and walked straight to the back door, keeping the umbrella positioned over me as I assessed the lock on a pair of glass sliders. I could appreciate the view from the living room later, looking across the pool and up toward the gorgeous green mountains that surrounded Ohia—though little would be visible at night.

I tested the door. The slider was locked, of course. I peeked at the track and didn't see anything blocking it, so it would be a simple matter to get in. I took out my handy lockpicks—something every agent is trained in, but little is written about. Ten seconds of wiggling and jiggling and I was inside the room. I still had the umbrella open, covering my face and head. I was pretty sure if there was an alarm system, the police would have deactivated it. Still, it was worth checking. I trotted to the house's front entrance.

Sure enough, Lei and Pono must have been provided the deactivation code, and they hadn't turned it back on when they left. Red letters spelled out ACCESS GRANTED across a small LED display.

"Whew. Finally done with this thing." I folded up the umbrella and rested it against the wall.

I had to work fast, assuming that someone was monitoring the cameras—a shapeless figure hidden under a golf umbrella going into the house at eleven p.m. was definitely suspicious, and it was probable someone would come to investigate.

I located the den with a massive TV, pool table, and a burlwood desk that likely served as Jimmy Ching's workspace. The desktop was empty, but I could make out a faint outline in the dust where a laptop had rested. *Son of a toadstool.* Of course, the police would've taken Ching's computer to analyze for suspicious documents and records. I had to hope for something they had missed or overlooked.

The drawers had been jimmied; gouge marks revealed the detectives used force to get in. A formerly locked file drawer was stuffed to the brim with green hanging files, each one crammed full of documents. These were left behind, and I didn't blame them for doing so — labels were things like "Pending Contracts" and "Quarterly Statements," which were probably duplicated on his hard drive.

Fortunately, those files were what I was interested in most. I grabbed a handful and spread them on the desk. Pulling out my phone, I began taking pictures of the contents. Something rattled in the back of the drawer as I lifted out another handful of the dangling folders.

Eureka! A sleek black memory drive had been hidden behind the folders—just what I was hoping for. Glancing at my phone and noting that the time was already at the five-minute mark, I quickened my pace. I continued my rapid photographing, throwing the papers willy-nilly into the folders and stuffing them back in the drawer as I went.

Within six more minutes, I had photographed every paper in Jimmy Ching's files, and my self-allotted time was up. I was still curious to explore the rest of the house, but security could be on their way if anyone had noticed my umbrella-disguised break-in.

I shut the drawers and wiped the handles and surfaces with a tissue. I retraced my steps through the darkened house, retrieved the umbrella, and locked the door to the patio from the inside before sliding it shut.

The umbrella once again engulfing me, I broke into a galumphing, hunched-over jog and made my way out of the development. Once past the burbling waterfall and bright spotlights, I straightened up, closed the umbrella, and headed to the beach. I needed time to bring my heart rate down before bed. Today was a lot of excitement for a woman with a mild concussion.

I wrapped the Velcro closure around the umbrella to secure it and stripped off the big shirt, tucking both behind a log. I rolled up my pant legs and shuffled into the gently foaming surf. The water wasn't bathtub temperature, but it was certainly warm enough to swim in.

I glanced around. Of course, there was nobody on the nighttime beach but a few crabs, scuttling up and down before the waves.

I lived in paradise. I was having an adventure. I might as well act like it!

Live your best life, Kat. You just got away with searching a murder victim's house. Now it's time to celebrate with skinny-dipping. You've never done that before, either.

I stripped off everything and waded down into the inky ocean. Lit only by moonlight, the pale foam from the waves—and my boobs—glowed in the dark.

Taking a deep breath, I ducked under the water. A burst of joy electrified my body—skinny-dipping in the tropical sea felt like rolling in satin bedsheets. The euphoria was thrilling, erasing all my aches and pains. I shot to the surface with a shout and stood up in the water with my arms raised. "Whoo-hoo!"

A pair of bright headlights lit me up and blinded me. A rough male voice shattered my zen. "Who goes there?"

Did I really have to answer that?

"Crud on a cracker." I wrapped one arm over my boobs and the other over my lady bits as high beams blasted my nakedness.

"This is security from New Ohia." The tone was not friendly, even though these guys were getting an eyeful.

Fortunately, the umbrella and Mr. K's shirt were nowhere near my clothing pile by the water. If they didn't find the umbrella, it was unlikely they would put together that I was the person who had been trespassing in Jimmy Ching's house.

"If you keep those lights on, I will report you for sexual harassment," I bellowed in my best Secret Service voice. "This is Kat Smith, postmaster of Ohia, out for a peaceful evening skinny-dip. I will come over and answer any questions you have once you turn off the high beams and I get some clothes on." A strong, authoritative voice is always best in this kind of situation. Not that I'd been in this situation before, or, gosh forbid, ever would be again (*please all the deities*).

The lights went off. The darkness was so complete that for a moment all I could see was a whirling blaze of afterimages. I had never been so conscious of being naked and exposed—and, suddenly, chillingly cold.

"Nothing to it, but to do it," I mumbled to myself. I needed a little pep talk to get out of the water and through this humiliating situation. I waded forward and headed to my pile of clothing. Consciously avoiding so much as a glance toward the stashed umbrella and shirt, I donned my clothes with some difficulty, dragging them on over my wet body.

Ahead of me at the parking pullout, I could hear a whispered dialogue but no actual words. I advanced toward the sound in the dark and stood tall, waiting. Two men were silhouetted in the weak illumination emanating from the open doors of a white SUV emblazoned on the side with "NEW OHIA SECURITY."

"How can I help you this evening, gentlemen?" ("Gentlemen" was a stretch.) I kept my voice assertive and stared the two men in the eyes. Both were shorter than me, wearing navy polo shirts and matching pants with logos and name badges. One of them cleared his throat. I leaned in to read his badge, which spelled out RALPH.

"We are wondering if you saw anyone come out of the entrance to New Ohia, carrying a large golf umbrella," Ralph said.

"No. I thought I was all alone here on the beach, which explains my personal choice of going swimming in the nude," I said. "I did see a car drive off from where you are currently parked, however."

Ralph whipped out a pad and pen with an air of relief. "Did you see what kind of car it was? Make and model?"

I shook my head. "Sorry. Too dark for details."

The other security guy, whose name badge said ARTHUR, scanned me up and down. "Surprised you didn't bring a towel to the beach for your midnight dip."

"I was just planning to take a walk on the beach, and then one thing led to another . . . the water was warm, the moon was pretty . . ." My voice trailed off. "I don't owe you an explanation."

"Well, Ms. Smith, you might want to be cautious doing those kinds of activities," Ralph said. "We've had an intruder in New Ohia. We will be notifying the police."

I reared back in feigned astonishment. "Who would do such a thing?"

"That's what we hope to find out. If you hear any gossip, let us know, please." Ralph handed me a business card.

"Will do."

I waited as the men got into the SUV, closed the doors, flashed their lights goodbye, and drove back to New Ohia. I let out my breath in a great whoosh and went to retrieve the golf umbrella and the shirt, wrapping the umbrella in the shirt to conceal it. I needed to find a place to hide the darn thing. The umbrella was now associated with a crime.

I carried the ungainly bundle across the road toward my shack, grateful for the dim, yellow streetlight. The perfect hiding place came to mind—if the police ever found the umbrella, the choice of location would totally throw them off.

I flicked on my phone's flashlight app, squared my shoulders, and headed around the side of my shack and into the jungle. There was no trail to my destination. Thick bushes reached out to grab me with dew wet leaves, and branches raked my bare, chilled arms. Long grass dragged at my feet, and an impenetrable blackness loomed ahead.

My mind shied away from the unpleasant memory of the "gift" Tiki had brought to my doorstep—a severed hand. I'd never wanted to visit the shallow grave where Fran Borland's body had moldered behind my shack for six months, but I was on my way there now.

"Fran, you seem to be a friendly ghost who is grateful to me for finding your killer so you can rest in peace," I said aloud. "You don't need that spot under the log anymore, so I hope you won't mind loaning it to an umbrella." My voice sounded hollow in my own ears, immediately absorbed by the velvety darkness.

I hadn't been on Maui long enough to know the names of the various bushes, ferns, and low-hanging foliage that plucked and scratched at me as I pushed through a belt of thick growth. The crime scene investigators had beaten a barely discernible path that led to the large, rotten log under which Fran's body had been concealed.

The huge log appeared the same. The hollow space in the dirt beneath it was also undisturbed. Nothing at all was left to show that this had been Fran's resting place for six months.

I shut my eyes, held my breath, and leaned down to shove the umbrella under the log. I paused, remembering at the last minute that

I didn't want to leave Mr. K's shirt there. I tugged the shirt off the umbrella and pushed the thing deeper under the log, out of sight. "No one will find it here. Thank you, Fran."

I straightened up, turned around—and screamed.

🌿 8 🌿

My flashlight app lit up the round, glowing, amber eyes of a ferocious jungle beast. Growling and hissing, its wide mouth revealed deadly fangs.

The scream died in my throat.

I recognized Tiki.

She'd been as scared as I was by the light. She sat down in the leaves, staring accusingly, her crooked tail switching in annoyance.

"What? I was just hiding some evidence," I told her. "Thanks a lot for scaring the pants off me." I giggled in the drunken aftermath of adrenaline, remembering the skinny-dipping mishap. "This has been a night for surprises."

Tiki turned and led the way back toward the shack. I read the thoughts she was projecting like a book: *What the heck are you doing out here in this dang jungle when we could be getting ready for bed and preferably eating a nice second supper?*

"I'm picking up what you're throwing down, Tiki. And I agree with you." We made our way back to the shack, and Tiki waited beside me while I unlocked the door. I still hadn't figured out how she let herself in and out of the shack. It remained a mystery that I wasn't that eager to solve. There was an element of sorcery about it that I saw no need to spoil.

I slipped off my shoes and left them on the porch, their soles caked with the red dirt of a former grave. I wished that sense of magic that I'd had at the beach would return. Instead, it was replaced by free-floating dread as I wondered about New Ohia's security team and what they'd thought about discovering me out for a nighttime swim. "They would have asked me different questions if they were onto me," I told myself firmly.

I opened my tiny fridge, looking for something soothing to drink. Sadly, there was no alcohol to be found, so I made do with a cup of chamomile tea. I unfolded the Murphy bed and climbed onto it, exhaustion flooding me.

Sitting on the bed and sipping my tea, I watched Tiki get settled on her towel for the night. Her paws rhythmically kneaded the terry cloth, and I stared off into space as I thought about next steps. I didn't have the capacity to go through the photos I'd taken of Jimmy Ching's records tonight, or the memory drive I'd retrieved. That chore would have to wait for tomorrow and be accompanied by a nice, big cup of coffee.

Also, tomorrow was Wednesday. I had a dinner date at the steakhouse in Hana with Mr. K to look forward to. That thought gave me enough of an energy boost to turn the light out and snuggle down, reaching below the bed to stroke Tiki's rough fur. "Don't forget, you can join me up here once you've had your flea bath," I reminded her.

She purred in reply, and I fell asleep to the soothing motorboat sound.

I stared back at my reflection in horror, my head aching for want of caffeine and Tylenol. My eyes were still ringed with plum-colored bruising, and I had forgotten to take a shower after my late-night swim. The saltwater had dried in my hair and on my skin, leaving a crusty feeling. My bed head didn't bear description.

After a long, hot shower, I wrapped my locks in a towel and put on a pot of coffee. Remembering Opal's warning to hydrate better, I downed my two painkillers with a full glass of water. Analgesics on board and fresh coffee in hand, I was ready to tackle Jimmy Ching's records.

A knock came at the door just as I settled onto the bed. Tiki hissed and ran under the table. I opened it, expecting to see Mr. Hanoi. I still wasn't sure where we stood about me returning to work.

Instead, it was Opal. Today's scarf was purple satin secured with a glittering, violet, rhinestone ankh. "I was wondering if you wanted to come have breakfast with Artie and me on the front porch."

"Yes, please." I eyed her outfit, impressed. "Where do you find those scarves and pins?"

"Oh, eBay! I'm always on the hunt for the next inspiring outfit." She smiled. "Come on over and I'll warm up some leftover cornbread."

"You don't have to ask me twice. I'll bring my own coffee."

I poured coffee into my favorite DO NOT SPEAK TO ME mug, then unwrapped the towel from my wet hair and hung it over the wood railing that defined one side of my rickety porch. I slipped my feet into my flip-flops and followed Opal in her caftan and Crocs across the parking lot, taking care to avoid the puddles.

"How did you sleep last night?" she asked me over her shoulder.

"Not too bad."

"Artie thought he heard someone scream from over here. Pretty late at night."

"Tiki startled me."

Opal and Artie made it clear last night that they didn't want to be involved with my current investigation. While I missed having them to talk to, it was probably better this way. They had plausible deniability if anything went wrong on my end. I'd hate to get the older couple into any trouble.

I reached the porch, where Artie was seated in his favorite chair with his ukulele on his knee.

"Good morning, Kitty Kat." He tipped his cheek up.

I kissed it. "Sorry if I woke you up last night. Tiki scared the crap out of me in the dark."

"Sounded like it came from a different place than your shack," Artie said, his blind eyes blinking in confusion.

"I was out for a stroll, and she just appeared out of the dark." All true.

"I get it. That cat scares me too."

"And you haven't actually seen her. Tiki is quite something when she looms up out of the dark. She's the size of a large raccoon or a porcupine."

"Never seen one of those either," Artie smiled. "I wasn't always blind, but I've never left Hawaii, and we don't have those critters here."

"We have a lot of both in Maine, and they are not to be trifled with."

"I feel kind of bad that you've been saddled with that cat," Opal said.

"We're getting along fairly well now," I said. "She hasn't scratched me in days."

"I'll get that cornbread for us." Opal disappeared into the darkened store, leaving me to sit beside Artie on one of the chairs worn shiny with use, enjoying the view.

I hoped I'd never get used to the beauty of Ohia Bay from across the deserted Hana Highway. The early morning sun brightened puffy cumulus clouds on the horizon. I plucked a fragrant plumeria from the tree beside the porch and sniffed it. "I could get used to waking up this way. You two are spoiling me."

"We like the company," Artie said, plucking out a song on his instrument. "You liven things up around here."

"I do what I can, probably more than I should." I enjoyed the song and the view while we waited for breakfast.

Opal returned with a couple of steaming plates of cornbread, butter liberally slathered on each piece, and a pot of honey on the side with a spoon in it. "Do you need any painkillers this morning? Sorry to say, but you still look terrible."

"No more painkillers, thanks. I already had my recommended dose this morning. I'm also taking another day off from work to rest," I said. "Can I ask you a few more questions about Jimmy Ching and New Ohia, though?"

"I think I told you everything we know about him." Opal sat down beside me. "Let's just watch the sunrise and eat breakfast, okay? I need to fill my mind with peaceful thoughts after yesterday's rune reading."

"Did you have any more insights about it?"

"No." Her voice was sharp.

"Fair enough." I helped myself to a square of cornbread. Artie played a mellow song, and we watched the morning sunshine fill the arc of Ohia Bay.

I hoped Opal felt peaceful, but I sure didn't. I couldn't wait to get back to the shack and see what Jimmy Ching had stored on that memory drive.

I crossed paths with Mr. Hanoi as he arrived to open the post office. One look at my discolored face and he held up a hand in a "stop" motion. "Don't come in until next week," he said. "I've got the staffing covered."

"Thanks so much." It wasn't until I spoke the words that I realized how glad I was that I didn't have to meet the public looking like an assault victim. Which I was. But still.

Back inside the shack and fueled up on coffee and cornbread, I sat down at the table and opened my laptop. "Good thing I don't need the Internet for this," I muttered. Weirdly, I was getting used to having hardly any contact with the outside world—it allowed me to focus my attention in a way I couldn't before. What was currently occupying my mind, other than the occasional fantasy involving Mr. K and his tight white uniform, was why someone had whacked Jimmy Ching.

A lot of people in town hated Jimmy, but enough to bonk him on the head, permanently? Seemed like a stretch. The computer finished booting up and I plugged in the memory drive I'd found hiding in the back of his file drawer.

Should I have turned this cache of possible evidence over to Lei and Pono?

Absolutely.

Did I plan to do that, eventually?

Yes.

But the two detectives had a LOT to sift through already, and they were focused solely on who killed Jimmy Ching. I was interested in the bigger picture. I wanted to know who was behind the shady shortcuts involved in the development of New Ohia as much as I wanted to know who was behind Ching's murder.

❧ 9 ❧

The memory drive was password-protected.

"Rats."

I had a workaround, as long as the security wasn't too involved—a digital lock pick. I opened a pirated codebreaker program I'd used once or twice on the job and sicced it on the plug-in drive. According to my computer, the drive was named "Jimmy's Stash."

"Stash of what, I wonder?"

"Meeerow," Tiki answered, from the whereabouts of my knee.

"Son of a cow nugget! You startled me, girl!"

Tiki lifted a paw and licked her toes with an air of satisfaction. She'd been nowhere in sight when I entered the shack. "As soon as I finish with this, I'm going to hunt down how you're getting in here," I threatened, despite my reluctance to actually figure it out. Tiki called my bluff and sauntered over to her water bowl, lapping delicately and presenting me with her backside.

"Jimmy's Stash" opened to my digital lock pick. I rubbed my hands together and cracked my knuckles. "Let's see what he was hiding, shall we?"

Tiki muttered something that might have been agreement into the remains of her morning kibble.

A series of documents filled the screen, all of them labeled with a meaningless jumble of letters and numbers. "Okay. More coffee might be needed." My headache was making a reappearance, its dull thudding like faraway jungle drums in my temples.

After topping off my mug, I took a moment to export the files to a hidden folder on my laptop, then I ejected the drive and set it aside. "Not sure how I'm going to tell Lei and Pono how I got this, but I'll figure out something . . . right, Tiki?" She padded over to her towel, turned in a circle, and lay down. "I'll take that as a yes. Now, let's see what's going on here." I opened the first document.

A deed filled the screen, replete with flourishes and legalese. I skimmed down the document and came to the summary outlining a "lease in perpetuity" between the State of Hawaii and New Ohia Vision, Inc. The sum listed was only one hundred thousand dollars.

Aha! The original deal. But that price seemed ridiculously low for a parcel of land that size—twice the size of the whole town of Old Ohia. Now to find out who the players were that made it possible to bypass any and all inspections and zoning reviews.

The next document was a sample sales deed for a plot within the proposed development of New Ohia. I did a double take, rereading the document to make sure I was understanding it correctly. I was a novice in real estate sales, but even I knew the difference between a lease and a sale.

"So, the state is leasing the land to New Ohia Vision, then New Ohia Vision is selling the land to investors who think they're buying something outright. How does that work?" I mulled out loud.

I went on to the next document. This was a completed deed of sale with an individual's name and address on it. I opened a new document and copy-pasted the information into it. This was a lead I could follow up on.

But I still didn't know who had represented the State of Hawaii in this suspiciously cheap "lease," and who really made up New Ohia Vision, Inc. And how did this collection of deeds consist of

Jimmy Ching's "stash?" I still hadn't found anything that directly related to the late, not-so-great facilitator of New Ohia.

I was deep into copying and pasting landowners from the deeds of sale into my own document when a knock came at the door. Tiki hissed and darted under the table, assuming her attack position. I got up to see who might be calling on us.

Not for the first time, I wished I had a peephole to check who was at my door. Even though I shouldn't have had anything to fear in a place like Ohia, reality showed that not everyone who showed up on my doorstep had good intentions.

C'mon, Kat. You're a Secret Service agent. I was probably more dangerous than anyone. Still, I palmed my mini-Mace canister as I turned the shiny deadbolt I'd installed last week and flung the door open in a classic overcompensation move. "Yes?"

Mattie from the Red Hat Society stood on the porch, looking startled, a Tupperware container in one hand and her cane in the other. "Hey, Kat. How're you feeling today?"

"Sorry, I was in the middle of something and wasn't expecting visitors." My cheeks heated. Aunt Fae wouldn't have approved of my snippy tone. I held the door open wider and softened my voice. "I'm better today, thanks. Want to come in?"

"No, dear. That's fine." Mattie thrust the container in my direction. I caught it so it wouldn't fall to the floor. "I felt bad about yesterday. The pressure we put on you. I wanted to apologize."

I wrapped my hands around the dish. The contents were still warm and emitted delicious smells. "That's not necessary. Still, I'm a woman with few cooking skills, so I'm delighted to accept. What is this, by the way?"

"My special enchiladas. I promise you'll like them." Mattie's sharp brown eyes glanced beyond me and took in the open laptop, the memory drive, my empty coffee mug, and the hissing cat under the table. Her small, wiry body seemed to vibrate with curiosity. "What're you working on over there?"

I pinched my lips to keep from telling her. The ringleader of the

Red Hats had some strange juju that made me want to confess all. "Nothing much. Studying the digital version of the postal manual since I have the rest of the week off."

She sagged with either relief or disappointment. "Oh. You were so great at flushing out Fran's murderer, I confess I was hoping you might know something about who broke into Jimmy Ching's house last night."

"Oh yeah? Someone did that?" I widened my eyes, blinking and playing dumb. "Don't they have a ton of security over there?"

"Yeah. Cameras too. But a clever someone used a big golf umbrella to get past all that." Mattie studied me closely, twirling her cane with her hand. Instead of a traditional cane, it was one of those spike-tipped hiking poles made of lightweight metal. I distinctly remembered watching her pep-step incredibly fast down a jungle trail using two of them.

"Interesting. How did you hear all that?"

"I have a nephew whose ex-girlfriend dates one of the security guys. They were all in a flap about it, trying to figure out what was stolen. It seemed to them like the burglar didn't take anything when he or she rifled Jimmy's office." She pointed with her chin to the memory device lying beside my laptop. "Unless it was something very small."

"Huh." I did mental times tables to keep my face from giving anything away. "Wonder what they were after?"

"Information is my guess," Mattie said.

Tiki chose that moment to make one of her mad dashes. She zoomed out from under the table and out the door, taking a swipe at Mattie's leg on her way past. Mattie howled, cursed, and dropped her hiking pole, hopping on one leg as she clutched her injured shin.

"Oh no! I'm so sorry!" I rushed to the kitchen, slamming my laptop shut and swiping the drive as I passed the table. I tossed the device behind the dish drainer as I pulled a wad of paper towels off the roll and headed back to assist the bleeding woman.

Mattie leaned against the doorjamb pitifully as I dabbed at the scratch on her leg. "Now I'm going to need a tetanus shot."

"That would probably be a good idea. Tiki is not really domesticated. Why don't you come in? I have a first aid kit for this very thing—"

Mattie snatched the paper towels out of my hand and applied them to her shin. "You've done quite enough, thank you. Enjoy the enchiladas."

I handed her the fallen hiking pole. "I really am sorry. I can't control Tiki. She's a force of nature."

"Then you should think twice before letting her into your home," Mattie said. "In fact, you should think twice about what you poke your nose into around here, too."

She seemed her age at last as she teetered off my flimsy porch and onto the round beach rock that made my front step, leaning heavily on the hiking pole. She headed off into the parking lot, aiming for an older model, tan-colored Toyota Corolla with a raised suspension and mud tires.

I frowned as I watched her go, crabbed up and whimpering.

I hitched up my sweatpants and headed back to my laptop after stashing the enchiladas in my little fridge. Apology, my left tittie; Mattie Ramirez had just warned me off the case.

But why?

Maybe the answer lay in the reams of material I still needed to review.

❧ 10 ❧

Hours later, I was so engrossed in the documents that the dimming light and a loud knock on the shack's door took me by surprise.

"Fudgy fondue sundae in a Crock-Pot!" That must be Keone for our date. I jumped up off my chair and hurried to the door, easing it open just a bit to check. Sure enough, a handsome pilot stood on my porch, looking tasty enough to nibble on in an aloha shirt that hugged his muscles and a pair of black jeans.

"Are you wearing a dress like you promised?" were the first words out of Mr. K's mouth.

"Uh . . . I don't remember any such agreement." I dimly recalled some discussion involving a dress. Perhaps a joke about how I never wore one? I couldn't remember exactly, but clearly, he took it seriously.

Keone put his hands on his hips. "You promised."

I held up a finger. "Give me five minutes."

"Take six. I'm sure they'll hold our reservation." Mr. K moseyed back to his truck as I slammed the door, my heart going haywire.

I only had one dress in my possession—a little black satin sheath I wore to events on the job in Washington, D.C. My favorite thing about it was a custom pocket sewn into it for my service weapon. Otherwise, the thing was annoyingly skimpy, though conservative enough for the parties I'd attended in it.

Did I mention black satin? It was way too dressy for Hawaii. Not to mention I'd ditched the heels that went with it when I left D.C.

But apparently, I'd promised him a dress, and it was kind of fun to imagine how his eyes would bug out when he saw me in it. The dress clung and glimmered, making promises.

Keone Kaihale knew the score, though. I was a touchphobe with trauma issues. He had about as much of a chance of peeling that garment off me as Tiki did of winning a prize for Miss Cat Congeniality. But I would look good in it, even wearing flip-flops.

Mind made up, I hurried into the bathroom, flung my head down, brushed my hair, scooped it up and bobby pinned it into a loose twist. I shimmied into the dress and threw on a bit of makeup.

I checked my phone—five minutes exactly from start to date ready. I prided myself on my time management. I took my clutch wallet out of my backpack and slid the miniature tube of pepper spray into the dress's hidden pocket, just in case I ran into any trouble. I slipped on my flip-flops and filled Tiki's bowl with kibble. Satisfied that I'd thought of everything, I stepped out, locking the door behind me.

Keone whistled as I approached, hopping out of the truck to open the passenger side door for me. "Wow. You clean up nice, Agent Smith."

"So do you, Mr. K."

We ogled each other, grinning. He finally gestured to the passenger seat. "Your chariot, my lady. Nice footwear."

"When in Hawaii . . ." I hopped up onto the chrome step and got in. "Flip-flops are always the right footwear."

"We don't call them flip-flops, my *kama'aina*-in-training. Those there are 'rubbah slippahs.'" He said it with that pidgin flair.

"Rubber slippers," I said, trying for the island flavor of his tone.

He clutched his chest dramatically. "I love the way you butcher our pidgin. Keep it up." I smiled as he walked around to the driver's side and got in beside me, firing up the mega engine of the jacked pickup. "I hope you're hungry, because the steaks at this place are huge."

"I'm hungry," I said. "No problem there."

I was missing a chance to flirt, but Keone didn't as he twinkled his eyes at me. "Is that so."

But all the banter did was remind me that I was on the verge of making promises I couldn't keep just by wearing a little black dress.

The Hana Ranch Restaurant had a large, covered patio overlooking the ocean. Of course, Keone knew everyone in the place, and they came by the table one by one to check me out as his date (including the chef). Smiling at all and sundry and sipping a frothy drink in a tall glass, I was glad I'd worn the dress. Finally, the staff's curiosity was satisfied, and they left us alone with a pupu platter of raw fish while we waited for our steaks.

I picked up a piece of fish with my chopsticks, then held it out to him. "You take the first bite."

"Sure, but let me show you how to prep it first." He skillfully took the sashimi from my chopsticks with his, then swirled it in the soy sauce and dabbed a bit of green wasabi on top. His teeth gleamed in the low light as he ate the tidbit. "Delicious. Now let me fix you one."

"The Red Hat ladies already initiated me into the world of raw fish enjoyment." I ate it off his chopsticks, surprised by the salty heat and pleasant texture. "It doesn't taste funny at all. Yummy."

"Sashimi can be an acquired taste. You're getting used to our ways quick."

I glanced down at my plate, feeling a twist of pain. "I really like it here."

"But . . ." Mr. K picked up another piece of fish, prepped it with sauces, and fed it to me. "You're not going to be here long. I know. Doesn't mean you can't enjoy paradise while you're on Maui."

"I know." I forced a smile and met his gaze. "It's just hard making sure I don't get too attached to . . . Tiki."

"Who wouldn't love Tiki." His dark eyes crinkled at the corners, but I could tell he got my drift. "Don't overthink it, Kat. You're here now, and you've done a lot of good for Ohia already. Now tell me what you've been up to."

"I'm not sure you really want to know. Let's save that for after dinner, shall we?" I had a feeling what I had to tell him might ruin both of our appetites.

The entrees arrived, and sure enough, the steaks were huge and perfectly done. I couldn't help making some animalistic noises as I dug into mine. "I've eaten the best food in my life since I've been here."

"Ono grinds are important for *ola maikaʻi*," Keone said, the banter gone from his expression. "A good life. Living well is an art."

"Is that so? Tell that to my boss in the Secret Service." I shuddered, remembering the many rubber chicken campaign dinners and state events I'd attended as an agent. My meals had been eaten cold and microwaved as leftovers in plastic containers most of the time. "Enjoying life is actually a new concept to me, believe it or not."

"Stay here long enough and we'll change that," he smiled.

I felt that pang again and drowned it with a hefty swig of my drink. "So, how are things at the airport?"

"The *pilikia* with Jimmy Ching's murder has died down, but folks are spooked. My uncle says he hasn't been sleeping well since he found the body." Mr. K addressed his steak, sawing vigorously. "I think he might need *hoʻoponopono*, and it just so happens that Mama's *kumu* friend from Kauaʻi is visiting, so they're meeting tonight for that."

I held up my hands. "I only understood about every third word of that whole paragraph."

Keone sat back, picking up his drink to swirl it. "*Pilikia* is trouble. *Ho'oponopono* is a traditional Hawaiian method for emotional healing. Our version of therapy. And a *kumu* is a teacher, a wise person."

"I have a lot to learn about Hawaii, that's for sure."

"You could spend a lifetime studying Hawaii and Hawaiiana and not know everything. Outsiders don't realize how well-developed our culture is."

"I respect that." I obeyed an impulse and touched his hand where it lay on the table. "I don't come from a rich heritage like you do. My parents died and my Aunt Fae raised me in Maine. She's the last of her line, which makes me the end of it. We're white. *Haole*, as you call it here. I don't know anything about our origins, but I suspect there's nothing very interesting about them."

"There's a lot that's interesting about *you*, though." Keone leaned forward into my space, his eyes on mine. "I suspect you are descended from a line of Amazon goddesses who somehow ended up in Maine."

"Aunt Fae would have told me if that were the case." I pulled back, busying myself with the remainder of my entree.

"And, you dodged my question earlier about what you've been up to," he said when we were both done.

"Yeah, I did." I set my empty plate aside. "I've decided to find out not only who killed Jimmy Ching, but who's behind the New Ohia development. I don't think we'll be done with the weird goings-on around here until we find some answers to that." I gazed into Mr. K's eyes. "The last time I was investigating, I asked if you were in or out, and you chose out. I'll ask that question again, with the warning that some of the things I've been up to are . . . not things I want getting back to your detective cousin Pono and his partner Lei." I took a deep breath. "Are you in or out?"

Keone narrowed his gaze. A muscle ticked in his jaw. At last, he said, "I'm in."

I whooshed a sigh of relief. "Good, because I really need a partner in all this. Someone with wheels, especially. Opal and Artie have recused themselves on account of a bad rune reading, and it's got me a little spooked."

"Let's tackle this one step at a time. I've got your wheels situation solved, at least temporarily," he said, with a glimmer of mischief in his eyes.

"What? How?"

"It's a surprise." His dimple made a brief appearance. "Now, tell me what you've been up to."

I leaned forward and so did he. Our elbows defined the space around us, shutting the rest of the world out. Someone removed our plates, but we hardly noticed. We were bent around the candle flickering in a red glass holder, forming our little conversation bubble.

I told Keone that I'd got hold of Jimmy's secret thumb drive and was combing through the documents on it, already seeing shady dealings in the paperwork. "I bet a forensic accountant could really put together what's been happening in New Ohia. The main file is named 'Jimmy's Stash' but so far, I still haven't seen how he directly benefits from any of it. His role in the development still isn't clear."

"I always heard he was a hired hand. The face of the development, but not an investor."

"That's what I heard too, but why would he work so hard without a vested interest? And why would anyone kill him over it?"

"We don't know why he was killed yet, though."

"You're right." I leaned over to sip the remains of my melted drink through the straw, making a rude noise as I chased the dregs at the bottom. "It's hard to imagine his death doesn't have something to do with New Ohia, though."

"Have you made it through all the information on the drive?"

"Not yet. I was working my way through all the deeds of sale and making a master list of buyers when you interrupted me for dinner."

Someone cleared her throat. We both jumped and separated, startled. Our server, who'd been introduced as a Kaihale cousin once removed, offered us coffee or dessert.

"No thanks," we said at the same time, then glanced at each other, smiling.

"You guys are too cute. I'll get your check, then," the cousin said and spun on her heel.

Mr. K sighed. "Tanya is a huge gossip. It's going to be all over town that I've got a girlfriend now."

I stared down at our hands resting on the table, awfully close to each other. "Hmm," I said.

He must have seen where I was looking because he took my hand. "Would it be so bad if that's what people thought?"

"This is our first official date," I said. "Seems like things are moving fast."

Mr. K squeezed my fingers. "It's hard to put a stop to the coconut wireless, but I will if you want me to."

I couldn't find the words to speak. My feelings felt like a ball of yarn stuck in my throat. I made a sound like Tiki with a hairball.

I was so conflicted. I liked this guy. I mean, *like* liked him . . . more than I could remember liking anyone in my ridiculously celibate, touchphobic life.

But I was probably going to leave soon. And maybe that would ruin things and upset him, and then his mama would make my guts into garters, and her *kumu* friend would put a hex on me, and the world would never be a big enough place for me to hide from the wrath of powerful Hawaiian women.

Mr. K gently set my hand on the tabletop.

Tanya returned with the check and set it down between us. "Thanks for coming in. Hope we see you both again soon."

Mr. K smiled at her. "Probably not. We're just friends."

Tanya's face fell, and my heart flopped as painfully as a just-landed sea bass hitting the deck of a trawler.

"We should go Dutch," I said as she left.

He drew the credit card slip over and signed it. "I invited you. My treat." He stood up. "Shall we?"

I tripped over the flip-flops—pardon me, rubber slippers—as I stood. He patiently waited for me to get situated with no effort to touch me, and I was grateful. I waved and smiled to the friendly staff and wended my way out, Mr. K polite and silent behind me.

Ugh. Why did doing the right thing feel so wrong?

We got into Mr. K's truck, and he turned the big vehicle onto the road back to Ohia. That awful ball of conflicted feelings still strangled me. Finally, I cleared my throat.

"You didn't have to say what you did to Tanya. About us being just friends."

"Oh yeah?" It was too dark in the truck's cab for me to see his face, but he kept his eyes on the road. "You were pretty clear you didn't want people making assumptions we were a couple."

"I guess that's true. But it doesn't . . . feel right. I think we both know we'd like to be . . . more than friends." I rolled my window down and stuck my face out into the wind to cool my cheeks.

"We're on the same page about that, at least."

"I just don't know how. And I don't want anybody getting hurt, but that seems inevitable." I was glad of the dark that hid my embarrassment.

"Don't worry about it, Kat."

"Because I told you before—I'm not good at relationships."

"Obviously." But Mr. K was smiling as he said it, and I could smile back at his teasing. "That's why you'll have to rely on my superior people skills to help us navigate. I suggest a safe word."

"A safe word? Isn't that for people who are into kinky stuff?"

"Yeah, but in our case, it's for when you start feeling stuck and uncomfortable, and you're not sure what you should do. Then I will know I have your permission to assess the situation and figure out a solution to propose that works for both of us. Who knows, I might need the safe word too."

"Oh, I like that." I turned my face back toward the moist night wind. The truck's lights flickered over the dangling vines, ferns, and tropical tree branches interlaced overhead as we navigated the narrow jungle route. A waft of blooming ginger hit my nose and I shut my eyes, inhaling deeply.

"Yeah. Me too. So, what's the safe word? It should be something unusual but easy to remember."

"Banana," I blurted, remembering mortification when my junior high sex ed teacher showed us how to use a condom by putting one on a large, yellow, curving fruit. That was the moment I was sure I would be a virgin forever. I couldn't imagine ever being comfortable enough with another human to have such an intimate experience.

"Banana it is." I heard the smile in his voice. "Here we are."

We pulled up beside the post office and his headlights lit up my shack. Tiki sat on the porch, her yellow eyes baleful slits of resentment in the illumination.

I sighed in relief as he turned off the truck and I didn't have to look at the cat's grumpy face anymore. "Tiki's not pleased I went out. But I left her kibble and everything."

"She's just going to have to get used to it." Mr. K opened the door and the light in the cab came on. He reached behind his seat for a flashlight. "I've got something for you. Come around to the back of the truck."

"Whatever it is, you shouldn't have." I navigated my way down from the cab, hampered by the dress's narrow skirt. I picked my way past puddles to the truck bed.

Keone already had the tailgate lowered. "Told you I solved your wheels problem. At least for the moment."

He held up the flashlight to illuminate a mountain bike with a rear carrier resting in the truck bed. "This is a battery-assist mountain bike. My mom got it for her birthday and has hardly used it. She offered to loan it to you. If you like it, you can buy it from her."

"A battery-assist bike? I think I've heard of those."

"Yeah, they're better than a regular bike for commuting. You can go up to twenty miles per hour on one. You do have to pedal, but you won't get tired doing long distances. I figure this will be enough for you to tool around between Ohia and Hana, at least. You could probably make it all the way to Kahului if you had somewhere to charge it before you came back."

"Wow. This is great! Tell your mom thank you." I reached for the bike, but Keone waved me back.

"I don't want you to mess up your dress. Why don't you go get the shack open and put the lights on? I'll bring it up on the porch and show you how it works."

I hurried to unlock the shack and let Tiki in. I quickly yanked the lightbulb cord and stepped back outside just as Mr. K hefted the bike out of the truck bed and brought it up on the porch. "I charged it yesterday, so it should be good to go for a while. Here's the charger and an extension cord."

With the door of the shack open, we had enough light for him to show me how the "e-bike" worked.

"I can't wait to try it out tomorrow," I enthused.

"And it wouldn't be complete without these." He opened one of the saddlebags mounted over the back tire's mudguard. "A helmet and this safety vest." Both were bright neon yellow with silver reflective trim, and as ugly as anything I'd ever seen.

"Ugh," I said.

"Mama said you don't get the bike unless you wear the gear." Keone's expression was serious. "And she also said to tell you that if you don't wear the gear, she'll know. She has eyes and ears everywhere."

"Like a scary lady Santa Claus, she can see everything." I

accepted the hideous helmet and vest. "Now I know why she hardly ever used the bike."

Keone grinned. "They are a necessary evil on these narrow roads. I'll lock it up for you." He wrapped a plastic-covered cable around the bike and clicked a combination lock shut. "I set the lock to the date of your first day in Ohia."

"That was nice."

We stared at each other. My hands were occupied with the helmet and vest, but our date was over, and he'd oriented me on the bike. I had no idea how to proceed.

"Banana," I said.

Keone's eyes twinkled. "How about you set down the gear, and then we try a hug."

I set the helmet and vest inside the shack's door and closed it so that just an inch or so of light illuminated the porch. When I turned back, Keone was right there in front of me. My heart thumped so hard that I was sure he could hear it.

"Hug?"

I stepped forward and put my arms around him, and he embraced me.

We stood there awkwardly, but the longer we did, the less weird it felt. Finally, I sighed and really leaned into him. "This is nice."

Mr. K's arms tightened. "Want to try a kiss?"

"*Honi* instead?" His mother had shown me the Hawaiian greeting.

Keone nodded, and we moved apart enough to rest our foreheads gently on each other's and breathe into the warm space between our bodies. My eyes closed, and it seemed like our hearts calmed as our breath fell into sync. Finally, the moment felt complete, and I stepped back.

"Thanks for a wonderful dinner. And the bike. And for saying you're 'in' on my investigation into New Ohia, because there's going to be a lot to do."

"You're welcome. Thanks for a whole new meaning for 'banana.'" He turned and headed into the night.

I pushed open the door. Jimmy Ching's records awaited me.

The first thing I noticed upon entering the shack was a fresh, damp, earthy smell—the jungle after a rain. It usually rained in the evenings, that was nothing unusual. But it didn't usually smell this strong.

My gaze flew to the window over the table.

I'd locked up before I left on my date. But now the only window in the shack, one that faced the tropical wilderness behind the building, hung ajar from its hinge.

"Son of a toadstool!" I rushed over and examined the sill. The pane had been forced open with something that left deep gouges in the weathered wood. The simple hasp had been no match for the assault.

I pushed the window open and peered out. The screen lay on the ground below, and trample marks in the vegetation revealed the path a burglar used to enter and exit.

"Dagnabbit." I whirled around. Tiki complained loudly that she had tried to warn me that leaving was a bad idea. "Lot of good you did, keeping an eye on the place," I grumbled. "You're supposed to be my attack cat."

Tiki turned her back, extended a leg, and licked her lady bits to let me know what she thought of being appointed guard.

I scanned the room. Thankfully, the laptop was still sitting where I'd left it on the table. "What kind of thief doesn't grab an expensive laptop sitting in plain sight?"

Then I remembered.

I hurried over to the sink and felt around in the spot behind the dish drainer where I'd stashed Jimmy Ching's memory drive.

It was gone.

Anger and frustration welled in my chest as my hand groped the empty space behind the dish drainer. Albeit a shack, this was still my home, and I was darn tired of it getting broken into.

I checked my private document stash under my mattress on the strapped up Murphy bed—undisturbed. My weapon was still in its hiding place, too. It appeared that nothing else had been taken.

"I guess they got what they came for," I muttered.

But who knew about the drive?

Just the people I trusted: Artie, Opal, Mr. K.

And Mattie Ramirez.

Our last encounter left me feeling distrustful of Mattie. And she'd definitely noticed the memory drive. But why would she break into my place and take it? And, if she had, why not take the laptop? Anyone with any computer knowledge would assume I'd made a copy of the drive (which I had) and that it would be stored on the laptop.

I sat down quickly and opened the device: my password input appeared. I typed it in, opened the hard drive, and verified that the file was still there.

Whoever had stolen the device hadn't searched my laptop.

Maybe they'd assumed I had a copy in the Cloud, which I didn't —there was no Wi-Fi at the shack. Or maybe they didn't care if I had the info on the drive—they just wanted it for themselves.

I whooshed out a sigh. "Time for me to get some help with this and come clean about stealing that memory device. Lei and Pono need to know what's going on with this."

Tiki let out a protesting mew.

"Tiki, you know how the phone reception is here. I have to go down to the beach to get a signal. You can come, if you want."

Tiki resumed her personal grooming, apparently thinking it over.

I changed out of the dress, hung it back up in the tiny closet, and donned my usual yoga pants and tee. This time, I put my Glock into my windbreaker pocket. No sense in tempting fate by walking around at night unarmed. I'd seen more action in this tiny town than I had during my many trips to the hot spots of the world.

Surprisingly, Tiki followed me when I left the shack to make my calls. As I stepped onto the cool sand of the beach, I wished Mr. K and I had taken a walk down here, and that I'd made my discovery while he was still with me. My feline companion was nice, but Tiki wasn't exactly the same comfort.

Tiki sat on her haunches at the high point of the sand, clearly in no mind to get wet. I continued down to the foamy waves and held my phone up, checking for bars. Sure enough, I had three.

I made my first call to Sophie Smithson, CEO of Security Solutions on Oahu. Sophie was a tech whiz and was one of the best investigators I'd ever met. We'd become friends through my assignment to guard her father, now retired Ambassador Frank Smithson. Frank had been my last protectee before the disastrous Congressman posting that led to my current circumstances, and I sure missed that sweet man.

Sophie picked up on my third ring. "Hello, Kat! How is Maui?" Her husky voice with its crisp British accent was always a treat to hear.

"Well, it's been an adventure." I took a few minutes to fill her in on the events of the week since we'd last spoken. I told her about Jimmy Ching's murder and my determination to find out who was behind the development at New Ohia. "The info I was sifting through was on a memory drive I found in Ching's house. I just got home and discovered that someone broke into my place and stole it."

Sophie exclaimed in Thai, one of her many languages. "This is very concerning. How can I help?"

"Fortunately, I'd copied the drive's contents to my laptop, which they didn't take. But I'm having trouble understanding what the documents mean. Do you have anyone on your team who's an accountant or lawyer?"

A pause. "I know someone, yes. But she's not my employee, and she's expensive."

"Rats. I guess I can keep going through the files by myself—"

"Why don't I check with her and see if she'll help you pro bono or on spec if there's a reward? Hermione Leede is a forensic accountant here in Hawaii, and she's good. She's retired Scotland Yard. If anyone can interpret what you've found, it's her."

"Oh good. Let me know what she says."

"Why don't you send me what you have, too? I can run down the Articles of Incorporation on New Ohia Vision and see who's behind it."

"That would be excellent. There's some kind of swindle going on, but until I know how it works, I won't be able to stop it. Knowing what's going on behind the scenes in New Ohia could also help Lei and Pono figure out who benefited from Ching's murder."

"I'll let you know tomorrow on both counts," Sophie said. "Stay safe."

We said goodbye. It felt good to share my concerns with an outside party.

I knew I needed to include Lei in that loop, but I needed a minute to work up the courage to do so. She wasn't going to be happy with my news—or my actions—on the case.

"Nothing to it, but to do it," I said out loud.

Even though it was nine p.m., Lei picked up promptly. "Hey, Postmaster Sleuth! What's up in Ohia?"

"I have a situation."

"You often do. In fact, that whole town is a situation." She chuckled. "Give me a minute to get some privacy." I heard the sound of a door closing on young voices. "Okay. Lay it on me."

"No pun intended, Lei." I tried to be funny.

"Ha." She waited.

"I decided to get to the bottom of who's behind the New Ohia development," I started hesitantly before deciding to just barrel through it. "To that end, I obtained a memory drive with confidential records on it from Jimmy Ching's house."

"We just searched that house, and it was sealed by the Maui Police Department, so I fail to see how that happened." Lei's voice was frosty.

"I know. I broke in and found it after your search. Hidden in the file drawer behind the folders." I rubbed the pain forming between my eyes. I seemed to forget about my head injury until stress brought it back.

"Keep going. When you're finished, I'll start asking questions," Lei finally said.

"Well . . ." I decided to skip the part about how I evaded the cameras and got into Jimmy's house—why aggravate her more? "I took the drive home and began examining the contents on my computer. I've only had it twenty-four hours, I swear. And I was just starting to figure out something hinky going on with the sales, and while I was out this evening, someone broke into my shack and stole it."

"That's definitely a situation."

I hurried on. "The good news is, I made a copy of the memory drive on my laptop, so I still have all the information. I was lucky the robber didn't take the laptop, or it would have been gone too."

"Burglary is what happened to you . . . and what you did at Jimmy Ching's house. A robbery involves stealing from a human directly, usually with the threat of bodily harm." Lei's voice had not warmed.

"Yes. Whoops. I knew that." I kicked foam around as a wave expended itself over my feet. "I'm distracted. I'm walking around at the beach so I can get a signal to call you. Remember, you asked me to be your eyes and ears—this was my way of helping."

"When we stopped by the other day, it was to ask you to keep an ear out, not start your own investigation, Kat. I think you know that." She sighed. "I'm not gonna lecture you about breaking into Ching's house, because you know perfectly well that was illegal and wrong. Let's move ahead with whatever you found on the memory drive. How can you get me those records?"

"I'm not sure. I could probably go into the post office and use the Internet connection tomorrow and send it to you." I blew out a breath. "I'm really sorry, Lei. I always planned to hand the drive over to you, but I really wanted to have a peek at it first. I'm interested in solving the corruption that might be going on behind New Ohia as much, if not more so, than finding Jimmy's killer. And I know you and Pono have to prioritize the murder investigation."

"We always want to look at all leads in an investigation," Lei said. "I need to know that you're a part of our team, not a loose cannon running around stirring up trouble. It definitely seems like six of one, half a dozen of the other with you."

"I can see how you would think that, but I do want to be part of the team. I'll stay in my lane from here on out." I crossed my fingers behind my back. Bending that rule might be necessary in the days to come, but I hoped not. "I'm starting to care about Ohia and its people very much. It's not in my nature to let evil go on under my nose without trying to stop it."

"Now *that* I understand," Lei said. "Anything else?"

"I asked Sophie Smithson for help. I know you two are friends. She's reaching out to a forensic accountant she knows to see if she will help me understand what the documents from the memory drive mean. It could really save time and effort to have the right person interpret what we're looking at. Sophie also said she would find out who is listed as the leaseholder from the state from the Articles of Incorporation for New Ohia Vision."

"I don't love having more cooks in the kitchen on a case, but Sophie and her team are solid. We can also have a lawyer look at the documents if we need more interpretation. In the meantime, I'd like access to the contents of what was on that drive. Figure out a way to get it to my encrypted email at MPD right away."

"You got it."

"Anything else you need to tell me?"

"No . . . isn't that quite enough?"

Lei laughed. "Yes, I guess it is. I'd better hear from you tomorrow." She ended the call.

I watched the moonlight on the restless water and listened to the palm trees rustling in the breeze. The thing I'd dreaded most since getting my hands on that drive was done. Lei knew. And Sophie was going to help, too. Hopefully, we could stay ahead of whoever had taken that memory drive.

I turned back to where Tiki sat waiting for me near the vegetation line on the beach. "I think that went about as well as it could have," I told the cat. "We deserve a good night's sleep after all of this excitement, don't you think?"

Tiki commented in the affirmative and walked beside me back to the shack.

Unfortunately, once we got back, I realized I still had to fix the window. There was no way I could rest with it hanging open like that.

Securing the window took a few trips around the back of the shack and some creative use of my limited tools. By the time I got it back in place with the screen attached, I was wired. Miss Prissy (the cane spider) and Tweedledee and Tweedledum (the geckos) were disturbed by my repair efforts. All three of them stared down from the wall of the living area.

"You guys are creeping me out," I scolded. "Everyone go back to your cracks, okay?"

Of course they didn't, and Miss Prissy's many eyes on me were worrisome. Only Tiki was following directions—she was already on her makeshift bed with her nose tucked into her tail.

"I think I'll go over to the post office and upload the documents to the cloud now, instead of tomorrow," I told them. "By the time I get back, you critters better be gone."

Someone wanted those documents enough to break into my place to steal that drive. I had to make sure they were safe and in Lei's and Sophie's inbox before I could relax.

With the laptop under my arm and the comforting weight of the Glock in my pocket, I locked up the shack and headed into the dark toward the back door of the post office.

The building's hall light bloomed on when I hit the switch just inside the door. The remains of Pua's security system protruded from the wall, untouched by Mr. Hanoi for yet another day. I was grateful that security wasn't his priority, as it would have complicated my late-night access.

The premises felt a little spooky. I found myself turning on every possible bulb as I made my way to the deserted office labeled "POSTMASTER." The desk was undisturbed, and I wondered where Mr. Hanoi worked during the day if not here.

I found the ethernet cord and plugged it into my laptop, settling down with a sense of relief to be connected to the outside world once again. I uploaded the drive's contents to a secure cloud storage I'd used for Secret Service work and sent an access link to Lei's secure email address at MPD and Sophie's at Security Solutions.

Now that the files were safe and shared, I sagged with tiredness —but the documents still called me. There had to be some record in there revealing how Jimmy was profiting from this scheme.

Unlike this morning, I had a strategy. I had been fixated on reading the documents and trying to understand them, but hopefully Sophie's forensic accountant would help me with that. This time, I knew what I was looking for and moved through the files quickly, ignoring anything that wasn't directly linked to Jimmy.

I found my answer in an unmarked folder. The metadata showed that the folder had been accessed as recently as three days ago. Inside was an Excel spreadsheet with dates, initials, and dollar amounts.

Down at the bottom of the sheet was the information for an offshore bank account at Bahamas Savings and Loan.

Aha!

Someone had been paying Jimmy on a regular basis, amounts varying from $2,000-$50,000. I suspected the amounts might coincide with the dates of the sales deeds I examined this morning—probably some kind of kickback.

A sudden pounding on the glass front doors of the post office made me jump like I'd touched an electric fence. My heart went into overdrive, and I had my Glock out and ready before I even realized what I was doing.

Why had I turned on all the lights? I was lit up like a goldfish in a bowl and there was a killer loose in this town.

Moving quickly and taking cover as I went, I switched off lights as I made my way to the front of the office. I ducked behind the front service counter and flipped off the lobby light as well, hoping whoever it was would just leave. But that peremptory knock came again, loud enough to rattle the safety glass.

"Fudgesicles," I hissed into the darkness.

Slowly, my eyes adjusted to the total darkness I'd created. Peeking over the counter, I could make out a petite female figure in the doorway, backlit by a pair of headlights.

I stood and fumbled through my bunch of keys, making my way to the door. Through the glass, I gazed into Pua Chang's porcelain-doll face, perfectly made up as usual. Her teeth gleamed between scarlet lips in an unfriendly smile. I unlocked the door and pushed it open a few inches. I was not pleased to see my former nemesis.

"What's up, Pua? I thought you were in jail," I said.

"I made bail. I was passing by and saw all the lights on. What are you up to in the post office so late at night?"

Twenty years of service or not, I did not answer to this woman, nor did I have anything to prove to her. I was not the one who had been arrested for using the post office as cover for a drug smuggling operation! I decided no defense was the best offense. "How can I help you, Ms. Chang?"

"You look terrible," Pua said, her expression softening. "I'm so sorry for what Sonny did to you. I swear I didn't know what he was up to."

"It's not me you'll have to convince—it's a jury. But thanks for the apology."

Her dark eyes went flinty again, fast. "There's something going on in New Ohia that you should be aware of," she said. "Can I come in?"

I kept my grip firm on the handle. My shack had just been burglarized, and it could have been Pua Chang as easily as anyone else. Though I was armed, she likely was too. "I don't think that's a good idea." I felt like a fool being this cautious, but Pua had taken me by surprise before. She might be tiny, but she could also be deadly.

Pua smiled that humorless, patronizing smile. "Okay. You're afraid of me. And maybe this isn't the right time or place to talk, anyway. Why don't you come out to my farm tomorrow, so we can speak freely?"

"I don't have fond memories of your farm," I said. "No thanks."

"Then how about we meet somewhere neutral? Tomorrow morning, at the church at the top of Hibiscus Road. I really want to make it up to you by sharing this information."

Who was I kidding? I was dying of curiosity. (Hopefully not literally.) "What time?"

"What time is it now, almost ten? Eight thirty ought to give you enough time to catch up on your beauty sleep. You obviously need as much of it as you can get. See you tomorrow." With that confidence-stealing zinger, Pua turned and walked back to her car.

I pulled the glass door shut and discovered my hands trembling as I fumbled for the key to lock up. I didn't move from the dubious shelter of the darkened doorway until I heard her car drive off.

"What a witch," I muttered to her retreating taillights. "The reason I need so much 'beauty sleep' is because your nephew tried to kill me. You've got some nerve telling me I need more rest." I gathered my laptop from the office and glanced out into the parking lot one last time to make sure it was completely empty before heading out the back door and locking it. Note to self: *from here on out, keep the lights off when you come into the building for a late-night Internet fix.*

The chatter of mynahs outside my window pulled me from a deep sleep. Despite Pua's visit putting me on edge, exhaustion won out and I'd fallen asleep hard once my head hit the pillow. I rolled over and peeked through the bullet hole in the wall that I'd accidentally put in the wall the first morning I moved in. Yep, another sunny day in paradise!

I took a minute to stretch out and check in with my body. For the first time since the attack, it was feeling good. My head only ached a little bit, and when I touched my face, it no longer felt tender.

I got up to check in the mirror. Despite feeling better, the black half-circles still lurked vibrantly beneath my eyes. The puffiness was gone though, and the goose egg on my head had shrunk considerably in just a couple of days.

When I emerged from the bathroom, Tiki declared loudly that it was time for breakfast. I obeyed and filled her bowl, and then put coffee on. While it brewed, I showered and dressed in a sensible pair of shorts, a tank top, a billed cap, and my beloved Nikes.

I grabbed a mug of coffee and my phone and headed down to the beach to make some calls. It was still early, but I wanted Lei to know where to find the file detailing the payoffs Jimmy had been collecting.

I plunked down in the sand and made the call to Lei's cell. As expected, she didn't pick up, so I left a message with the details about the memory drive's contents. I called Sophie next. She didn't pick up either, so I left the same info and told her that Lei was on board with working with both her and Hermione Leede if either woman found time to look at Jimmy's files.

Watching the waves sparkle in the morning sun, I readied myself for my next, less pleasant task: meeting Pua Chang.

✣ 14 ✣

I decided to ride my new-to-me bike to my meeting with Pua. Opal and Artie were sitting at their morning posts on the front porch of the general store when I wheeled the battery-assist bike into the parking lot for a test drive. I put the key in, turned it on, and wobbled around the lot a bit. In a matter of minutes, I wiped out when the "boost" from the pedals hit just as I was making a turn.

"Clearly this is going to take a bit of practice," I muttered, picking myself up. I was glad the parking area was only dirt. I hopped back on and continued to lurch around the lot.

"Where's your helmet?" Opal yelled from the porch of the store. "I'm pretty sure you're supposed to be wearing one of those."

"I'll put it on as soon as I get the hang of this," I hollered back.

"That's not the proper order of things," Opal replied, and I had to admit she was right. I went back and put on the World's Ugliest Helmet and Vest, waved goodbye to my friend, and pedaled up Hibiscus Road toward the church at an amazing speed, considering the incline.

I'd been wanting to visit the church since I first saw it a few days ago on a neighborhood walk. Perched at the top of the hill that sheltered the original town of Ohia, the neat white building was inviting and quaint.

I was there before Pua, so I parked the bike and walked around the grounds. Native plants surrounded the church, some of which I recognized, and many I did not. A fenced graveyard, with headstones and markers ranging from the recent past to centuries old, invited exploration with neatly trimmed walkways winding through it.

Curious about the original settlers of Ohia, I wandered down the path, peering at the markers. Many of them were unusual shapes to my Western eye and marked with characters rather than letters. Often, small bowls containing incense or statuettes adorned their pediments. I eventually found a section with crosses and Portuguese names, then another section of Hawaiian markers. Nothing appeared newer than the last fifty years or so.

"Checking out our ancestors?"

I whirled around. Pua Chang had managed to sneak up on me. No telling how she'd done it. "Do you have relatives buried here?" I asked.

She pointed to a corner of the graveyard sectioned off by a low, lava rock wall. "The Changs are over there."

I headed in that direction, and she followed.

Up close, the family's plot was neatly kept. Rather than head-stones, each grave was marked with a round, black, natural lava stone, whose surface had been planed smooth and polished. They were all the same, as if they'd been bought in quantity and saved until needed. The name CHANG was engraved deep in the stone, with Chinese characters beneath and individual names and dates following.

"I hope to be buried here someday," Pua said suddenly. "I've arranged for it with the pastor who keeps things running out here."

I didn't know how to respond, so I said nothing.

"My grandparents are over there." She pointed. "But they were the last to be put in the family plot. My parents passed on the Big Island." She brushed her hands against each other as if whisking dust away. "They call us the 'Big Island Changs,' but this is where our journey in Hawaii began. Ohia is where we made our first home, coming over from China to work the pineapple fields. Now, I'm the last one here."

As she often had, Pua threw me off. I never knew what to expect from her. Last night's vaguely threatening, yet intriguing vibe had given way to this bittersweet disclosure.

I decided to respond in kind. "I'm the first one of my family to even visit Hawaii," I said. "I don't have the history you do, but I have come to care about Ohia very much. That's why I'm here right now and interested in what you have to tell me about New Ohia."

Pua turned to face me. She was dressed casually (for her) in floral capri pants and a cotton cable-knit vest over a thin, pink silk tee. Pearls gleamed in her ears, and petal-pink espadrilles dressed her itty-bitty feet. She could have brunched anywhere in the world in that outfit. "I told you that I thought you were the right person to take over the post office, and I haven't changed my mind."

"We'll see." I didn't want to talk about the post office and her recent role there. "What did you want to tell me?"

She gestured to a nearby stone bench, and we sat. At the very top of the hill, the spot had a wonderful view over the memorials, past the church, and all the way down Hibiscus Road to the beach and the sea beyond.

"Peaceful, isn't it?" Pua's voice was soft.

I nodded.

"Some of my family members are behind the development at New Ohia," Pua said. "They planned for it to be a way we could return and vacation here, where we started in Hawaii. They'd also make a profit leasing other lots, of course, and collecting rents on the buildings they planned to put up. They saw it as a way for the family to return to our roots."

My heart lurched. The Changs were synonymous with organized crime, which explained a lot about the shady development's cut corners.

"I was so excited to bring the family home to Ohia. I thought the location would be perfect. I helped put the original deal together and tracked down the State of Hawaii contacts. Of course, we had a relative on the land commission who weighed in and helped the lease go through." She twisted her hands in her lap. "But something went wrong, and now everything's falling apart. None of my contacts know what happened or what's happening now."

"Is this since Jimmy Ching was killed?"

"No, it all went sideways well before that happened."

"Why are you telling me all this?"

"Because I want your help getting New Ohia back on track—back to the way it was supposed to be."

I swiveled to face Pua as we sat on the stone bench. "Did your relatives have anything to do with Jimmy Ching's murder?"

Pua broke eye contact and sighed. "I don't know. Jimmy was the front man. He wasn't an investor, but he was promoting the development, finding workers, and coordinating the contractors. He really kept the whole thing going. It's come to a complete halt without him and I'm not sure what will happen next."

"I appreciate you telling me this, Pua. I'm concerned about New Ohia too—specifically, the impact it's having on Old Ohia and the fact that a lot of the usual safeguards seem to have been skipped. Was Jimmy involved with that, too?"

Pua shrugged. "Like I said, he was the front man. The coordinator. Nothing went on over there that he didn't know about."

And profit from, as it turned out. But Pua didn't seem to be aware of those details.

We both gazed over at the New Ohia development, clearly visible from our spot on top of the hill. The sun gleamed off of the solar panels atop the clubhouse and model homes, and the meandering lines of the streets wandered over the plain like dark veins.

"It's important the police know all this," I said. "They're looking for Jimmy's killer and what you've told me is relevant."

"I know, but it can't have come from me." Pua stared straight ahead, her jaw tight. "So I thought . . ."

"You thought I could give them a tip and keep you out of it."

"I hoped so, yes." She smiled, but her eyes were sad. "I will be going to jail for a time, I expect, but this is still my home."

"Maybe we can get you a deal if you help unravel what's going on at New Ohia," I said impulsively. "At least let me propose it."

"It can't get back to my family that I informed the police of their involvement, so no thank you," Pua said. She stood abruptly. "You can pass on the tip I gave you, nothing more—or my life will be in danger."

She grabbed my hand suddenly, gazing into my eyes. "Please, Kat. Promise me you won't tell the cops that it came from me."

My skin crawled. I fought the urge to leap away, my touchphobia flaring up. "I promise." I said, yanking my hand away. I wanted to help Pua. I had wanted to before, and now I wanted to again. I didn't understand it, after everything that happened between us. But I couldn't help it.

Pua turned and hurried away down the path toward her car. The hunch of her shoulders told me that she was regretting everything she'd shared.

Was Pua Chang a master manipulator, or someone caught in the machinations of a crime family who couldn't break free?

❧ 15 ❧

I decided to keep the bike turned off as I rode down the hill; I'd noticed that the power boost came on at unpredictable moments as I pedaled, and the last thing I needed was more speed while navigating a steep downhill grade.

Even so, I whizzed uncomfortably fast down the relatively straight Hibiscus Road, and then hooked a right onto Hana Highway, using the button at my thumb to engage the power assist once I was on the level. I flew past the post office lot, deciding to take a ride to Kahului for supplies to shore up my shack's security.

The difference between an e-bike and a regular one was dramatic. I cruised along the highway at a very respectable speed. As I ascended the curve that led around the bluff that defined the end of Ohia Bay, I glanced back at the village cupped in its valley.

"A little piece of paradise," I murmured, and then hit a pothole going fifteen miles per hour. Lightning reflexes saved me from wiping out as a local truck driver zoomed toward me. Thankfully, he spotted the World's Ugliest Helmet and Vest and swerved to give me a wide berth.

"Eyes on the road, Kat," I told myself sternly. Until I was more familiar with the way the bike responded, I needed to give my full attention to piloting it.

I rode along the narrow road that followed the rocky coast, passing stony beaches and waterfall-lined gulches. Biking this scenic byway was the best way to really experience it. I'd never noticed the details that I was able to see from the bike: torch gingers hiding in the lush ferns, mangoes sprinkled liberally over the road, the way the mynah birds scolded me as they fluttered away from pecking the fallen fruits as I passed.

Eventually, I left the wetter side of the island and entered a wide-open pastureland. The wind whipped down from the erosion-sculpted mountains to push me even faster. It had been a while since I'd enjoyed anything as much as this ride, but the road hadn't been repaved in eons on this section. Soon, I had to slow as my teeth rattled together bumping over the ruts. Finally, after a few rough miles, I hit another paved section and was able to relax a bit.

I thought over my conversation with Pua Chang. I'd only intended to visit a big-box store on this trip into town, buying myself hardware to fix the window, a sensor light for the porch, and a home security system to reduce my vulnerability at the shack. I decided I should probably swing by the police station and talk to Lei and Pono about what Pua passed on.

But maybe not.

What she'd said about her family being behind the New Ohia development was too general. I needed specifics, and that meant connecting with Sophie and her forensic accountant. If the Changs were a part of New Ohia, I had to know exactly how—even if I had some idea why, thanks to Pua.

But as Pua said, "something went wrong." Without Jimmy Ching to keep things going, what would happen next? One thing I knew from my Secret Service work: crime hates a void. Some nefarious entity would be coming out of the woodwork to take Jimmy's place. To prevent that, I had to work fast to find out how to shut the enterprise down.

I squinted into the sunlight, peering down the road. It rolled like an unfurling ribbon over eroded grassland dotted with dry, wind-sculpted trees. This whole zone, water-starved in the lee of the towering Haleakala volcano, seemed more like an African savannah than the lush Hawaii promoted in magazines.

I pulled off the road for a quick break and propped my bike against a wiliwili tree. I recalled Lei and Pono introducing me to the strange-looking tree during my first ride in Stanley. Orange in color with a bulbous trunk and very few leaves, it reminded me a bit of a baobab tree.

I drank some water, stretched my hamstrings, and put the Ugly Helmet on. I was only a third of the way, but the roughest section of road was behind me. I hoped the remaining forty miles were smooth and easy. Pulling back out onto the road to Kahului, I sent up a request to the deities: *here's hoping the battery holds out.* The wind sprang up and gave me an extra push of help.

By the time I did my errands in downtown Kahului, the saddlebags on the back of the bike were full, and the battery on the bike was failing. I manually pedaled the now-dead bike the last few yards into the parking lot of the Maui Police Department, amazed at how difficult it was without the battery assist helping. My still-healing head pounded with the effort, and I was immensely grateful for a chance to take a break.

At the entrance, a double glass door opened automatically into a vestibule. I wheeled the bike over to the wall and dropped the kickstand. I took out the charger and stuck it into a handy wall socket, hoping it would charge quickly for the ride home.

Adjusting my backpack straps, I went through the main door and greeted an officer at a desk behind bulletproof glass. "May I speak with Sergeant Lei Texeira or Detective Pono Kaihale? It's important," I said into the speaker.

A few minutes later, an officer appeared at the lobby door to escort me into the main work area. Lei and Pono were tucked in their cubicle. Pono's side was cluttered with papers, family photos, and Hawaiiana, and Lei's side was clear and organized.

Lei was focusing on her computer and did not respond as I knocked on the door, but Pono rose to give me a hug, which I was thankfully able to tolerate.

"You look like you've got a little sun and wind. Really sets off those black eyes," he said. "How did you get out here? Did you hitchhike?"

"Keone loaned me his mother's e-bike, and I rode it into town," I said. "I had some things I needed to pick up from the store and decided to pass on some information in person regarding the Jimmy Ching case."

"We always have time to meet with the Postmaster Sleuth," Pono said, giving Lei a poke. As his partner turned her head, I spotted her earbuds. She'd been scrolling through records that looked familiar.

Lei took the earpieces out, and I pointed to her screen. "I have some information for you from an informant, but first—I sent Sophie the files last night too. Do you want to check in and see if she has any info yet?"

Lei and Pono exchanged a glance, and Lei pulled her desk phone over and gestured for me to help myself. I pulled out my phone to check Sophie's number and punched it into the keypad. Lei hit the speaker button, and the sound of the phone ringing filled the tiny space.

Sophie picked up right away. "Oh, Kat! Hello," she said after I identified myself. "Did you get my message?"

"No, I didn't, sorry. I just made it to the Maui Police Department, and I'm here with Lei and Pono. You're on speaker. What did you want to tell me?"

"Heri—that's Hermione Leede—agreed to take on the case pro bono. I forwarded the link to her and she's reviewing the files as we speak. I gave her your contact info, so she will be reaching out to you when she knows more. As for me, I was able to get a copy of the original Articles of Incorporation for New Ohia Vision. I'm texting it to you." As if on cue, my phone dinged from my pocket.

"Thanks, Sophie. Anything else we should know?"

"Some of those names are pretty interesting. Want me to run background checks on them for you?" I glanced at the detectives, who were both nodding enthusiastically.

"Heck yes. You rock, lady!" I replied.

"I'll send you my bill—my fee being a promise that you show me around your new town sometime soon."

"You got it," I vowed, and ended the call.

"We love Sophie's background checks," Pono said. "She leaves no stone unturned. It will save us so much time."

Lei nodded, visibly relaxing. "And if Leede can comprehend and explain what's going on, we'd appreciate it. I'm having a hard time understanding the documents."

"Me too," I said, forwarding the Articles of Incorporation to Lei's and Pono's phones. "Which is exactly why I asked Sophie for someone who could." Lei pulled the document up on her computer, and Pono and I peered over her shoulder at it. Sure enough, several of the names listed ended with Chang.

I quickly switched gears, committed to sharing Pua's information before I could change my mind again. "Additionally, I thought you might be interested in a conversation I had with a confidential party this morning."

I briefly summarized my conversation with Pua, leaving her name out of it. "This contact told me *why* the Changs were behind the New Ohia development and is upset that things seem to have gone awry from the family's original agenda—namely that it was supposed to be a place where they could return to their roots in Hawaii."

Lei nodded in comprehension. "A certain postal employee who shares a surname with most of those listed on the Articles has made bail and is out of jail. I wonder if this person could be your mystery informant."

"I can neither confirm nor deny," I said.

"I get it. She can't be known to be talking to us," Lei said.

Pono frowned. "Who? Pua Chang? Because she's obviously your informant, Kat."

Lei and I rolled our eyes. "That can't get out anywhere," I told him. "Pua's afraid for her life."

"And she should be," Lei said. "I was kinda surprised she wasn't taken out in jail, but she must have been able to convince the family she wasn't talking to anyone about the drug operation."

"And if you're wondering, Kat, Pua didn't say a word to us about the postal drug smuggling operation," Pono said. "Because of that, we're going to have to prove every step of the supply chain. She might get out of those charges altogether, especially with Bennie Fernandez, the Santa Shark, in her corner."

"Santa Shark?"

"Fernandez is the best defense lawyer in Hawaii. He looks like Santa but . . ."

"He's a shark. I get it." Was it wrong that I felt relieved Pua might get off? I needed to figure out why I cared about this woman's fate, one she had knowingly participated in making. Maybe it was simply because she hadn't killed me when she had a chance to.

"Anything else?" Lei tipped her head like an inquisitive bird.

"That's it."

"And it's a lot. Thanks," Pono said. He glanced out the tinted window and frowned. "Not much daylight left. How long did it take you to get out here?"

"A little over five hours. Not bad for sixty-three miles, but the bike's totally dead. I left it on the charger in the entryway, and I'm not sure if it's ready for the return trip. There's a lot of uphill going back."

Pono stood up. "I'm overdue for a visit to my auntie, Keone's mom. I'll take you back in Stanley. We can throw your bike in the bed of the truck."

"Thanks, Pono. I appreciate it." I really did. Clearly, the distance to Kahului wasn't something the bike was really meant for.

"While you're at it, make a run at those security guards in New Ohia," Lei told her partner. "They might know more than they're telling. Someone broke into Kat's place and took that drive. They were the only ones who might have known she'd have it."

Pono nodded, and I waved goodbye as we left the cubicle.

I was glad for both the ride and that Pono was going to be talking to the New Ohia Security guards again—but they weren't the only ones who'd known about the memory drive.

16

Pono was quiet as we drove, headed for the turn splitting off toward the "backside" route to Hana that passed through Ohia. I was glad for the silence. I leaned my windburned face on the cool window and stared out at newly planted acres of coffee and citrus trees that were replacing what had been sugarcane fields for close to a hundred years.

"I'm glad it's agriculture replacing sugarcane," I said at last. "It would be a shame if houses filled this valley."

"The island can't support that much growth," Pono said, his big hands flexing on the steering wheel. "Water, power, and other infrastructure are already strained with the development we've had in the last twenty years."

"Water isn't a problem out in Ohia," I said. "I'm growing moss inside my shower."

"No . . . but power, waste disposal, and increased traffic sure are."

"Not to mention the way the market hub planned for New Ohia will gut small businesses like Opal and Artie's store."

Pono darted a glance at me. "You're really starting to care about them."

"Yes, I am. About the whole town." I folded my arms around my waist, hugging myself. "In fact, it's going to be hard to leave when I'm eventually reassigned."

"Could that have anything to do with my cousin Keone?"

I shrugged and kept my gaze firmly out the window.

"I heard from a reliable source that you were seen at the steakhouse in Hana on a date, but that you are 'just friends' according to my cuz."

"The coconut wireless again." My cheeks heated up. "We didn't want people jumping to conclusions that we were a couple, especially when I'll be leaving."

"Yeah, I can see how that would be a problem." Pono rubbed the bristly mustache on his upper lip with his fingers, clearly a habitual gesture.

I was desperate to change the subject. "How long have you and Lei been working together?"

"I've been a cop for longer, but I was Lei's first partner on the Big Island when we both started out. We went our separate ways for a while so she could chase career opportunities elsewhere in Hawaii. She moved to other islands, but when she settled on Maui, we reconnected."

"You two seem like brother and sister."

"That's what we are. True *'ohana* isn't always blood."

I enjoyed the vistas rolling by as we turned onto the winding road toward Ohia. I especially enjoyed the fact that I wasn't having to pedal that dead bike all the way back.

I must've fallen asleep, because I jumped and bumped my head on the window when Pono touched my shoulder. "We are in Ohia. I can drop you off at your place, or you could come with me to talk to the head of security in New Ohia. I kind of want to see his face when you show up with me to question him about your burglary."

"Definitely want to come talk to the security guy." I knuckled the sleep out of my eyes. "Thanks!" I spontaneously hugged Pono and then recoiled just as quickly. "Sorry."

"Don't apologize. Hugs are my love language." He grinned. "Blame my wife Tiare that I know that. We studied the book *The Five Love Languages.*"

"Does it have a chapter on weapons? Tactics? Defensive moves?"

"It's all about giving and getting the love you want. Defensive moves are love killers, Kat. You've got a lot to learn about relationships, sistah." He opened his door and jumped out. "I guessed you'd want to come with me to talk to Ralph, so we're parked in front of the clubhouse."

I could see that in what remained of the daylight. I opened my door and stumbled a little on the chrome step before I found my footing on the fresh black pavement of New Ohia's gracefully curving throughway. My legs had stiffened in the long car ride after all the exertion of biking.

"I'm out of shape for pedaling. And for love, it turns out. Maybe I should read that book." I followed Pono as he headed toward an outbuilding behind the clubhouse with several golf carts parked out front.

"Sure. I'll bring it out for you next time I come."

"I never noticed this structure before." I gestured to the hidden building.

"I'm sure that's the idea. They try to keep the security presence low visibility."

I recognized the head of security when the man opened the door of the building. Ralph was one of the two guys who had seen me naked and lit up in high beams on the beach at midnight. That said, he gave no sign of remembering our embarrassing encounter as Pono introduced us and I shook his hand. He'd probably been distracted by staring at my boobs the last time we spoke and thus didn't recognize my face.

"This is Ms. Smith—she is assisting us with our investigation into Jimmy Ching's death," Pono said after introducing himself. "She experienced a burglary recently from her place behind the post office. We thought we'd check if you'd seen any suspicious activity."

Ralph's expression was carefully blank. "Oh, that's a shame. We had a burglary recently too, as you know." Now he stared at me. "Someone broke into Mr. Ching's house and stole . . . something."

"Yes? What exactly was stolen?" Pono tilted his head a little. He must have learned that from Lei—it was her signature move. "We got your report of a break-in, but nothing was reported missing."

The man's cheekbones reddened. Ralph couldn't admit to knowing I had taken something from Ching's house without admitting that he knew the memory drive existed, which meant he likely knew what was on it.

And maybe, most likely, he'd been the one to steal it back.

Call it my Secret Service intuition, but I now knew who'd stolen the drive.

Ralph decided to feign ignorance. "We're not sure what was taken. Someone thoroughly searched Jimmy's office, but because we don't know what was in his desk, we can't determine what's missing. We suspect that it might have been records of sensitive transactions related to the New Ohia development." Once again, he leveled an accusing glower at me.

My gaze sharpened on the man as I did a mental threat assessment. He had seemed like one of several interchangeable, not-too-bright security guys until this moment—five foot ten, one hundred and sixty-five pounds, with a buzz cut and a hand resting on his weapon.

I upgraded Ralph's status to smart, ex-military, and likely dangerous. The guy was probably in on the scam and knew what Jimmy was up to. Maybe he was on the take as well.

I gave Pono a tiny jab with my elbow. He turned to me with a gleam in his eye. "Did you have something to ask, Ms. Smith?"

I opened my mouth, but nothing came out. So much for Kat, the

Postmaster Sleuth. I had no idea how to proceed. Hopefully, Pono did—the Kaihale men were smooth talkers. "You can take it from here, Detective Kaihale."

"Thanks, Kat." Pono turned back to Ralph. "Tell us more about these sensitive transactions involving Jimmy Ching and the New Ohia development."

We were still standing in the doorway of the security building, so Ralph gestured for us to enter. "Come inside and we'll sit in my office."

Pono and I followed him, passing an alcove lined with monitors showing surveillance of the development. Pono paused, staring at the ever-changing views over the shoulder of the young man seated in front of the monitors. "I thought you said there was an AI involved with your security," he said.

"There is." Ralph's chest expanded with pride. "The views the AI shows are of the high-risk areas. We monitor all cameras as best practice."

"So how did someone get into Jimmy Ching's house undetected between the AI and the human watchdog?" Pono asked.

Ralph scowled. "The burglar knew about the cameras and fooled them with a big golf umbrella. The AI alerted us to unusual activity, but we were short-staffed, and it took a little time to respond. By the time we arrived at the house, the intruder had escaped." I squirmed internally, remembering my hurried passage through New Ohia, hidden by the umbrella currently resting in a former grave.

Pono turned to face Ralph. He rubbed his mustache and then spoke deliberately. "This is a lot of security for a mostly empty development with a clubhouse and a few model homes." He gestured at the wall of screens. "It's a little much, don't you think?"

Ralph glowered even more as the young security guy studying the monitors avoided eye contact with all three of us. "The short answer? We do what we're told. Come into my office, Detective. Ms. Smith stays outside."

"Fudgesicles," I muttered, taking a seat on a folding chair behind the monitoring area. Pono and Ralph disappeared into his office. "I wonder what is really going on."

The young security guy's ears grew red at the tops. He was trying hard to pretend I wasn't there, but that wasn't going to fly with me when there was more that I wanted to know.

"You're doing a great job keeping an eye on all of those angles," I told the back of the young man's head. "Can you explain the AI to me? It sounds so cool."

"Sure," he replied hesitantly.

I took that as an invitation and plonked my chair down beside him. "Wow, that's so nice of you!" I crooned in my best admiring female voice. All women have one for use in emergencies, even me.

He pointed to a series of views. "This is the high-traffic area. The AI takes down every car that comes in and logs its plates. It can send a report at lightning speed to the police if something suspicious is going on."

"Wow," I breathed in awe.

"Yeah. And it memorizes the usual traffic and movement patterns of the residents of New Ohia, and it sends an alert if anyone falls or seems in need of help."

That sounded like a Big Brother scenario if I ever heard one. "Could be nice for the elderly," I ventured.

"We expect wealthy older folks will make up most of our demographic," he said. "Once all the units are sold."

"So." I caught his eye, hunching down in my chair in hopes he didn't notice I topped him by close to a foot. "You're a smart man. What do you think is the real reason for all the security in New Ohia?"

He slanted me a glance that wandered over my chest. "I'm just happy to have a job."

I batted my eyelashes like I was having a seizure and giggled. It was a hideous performance, but I gave it my all. "Oh, come on . . . Phil." I read his name badge. "You must have some idea. Surely, it's not just the boss who knows what's going on at a place like this."

"Well, I have wondered about it." Phil's ears were red again. "Seems to me a lot of high-powered people are going to be making New Ohia their second home, and they want to be protected."

I nodded. "What kind of high-powered people?"

"You know." He leaned closer. "Connected people." His breath smelled like the can of Pepsi at his elbow. I forced myself not to pull back.

"Ah. What makes you think so?"

"Just . . . a lot of cash floating around and bulletproof SUVs coming and going," Phil said. "Call it a hunch."

If I had needed anything more, that was pretty solid confirmation of the mob being behind the New Ohia development.

17

The office door opened, and I sprang away from the young man, folding my chair as I did so. "Thanks for showing me how the AI works," I chirped. "You really know your stuff, Phil."

Ralph was scowling as he followed Pono out of the office. "We're expecting a new program manager within the week," he told Pono. "That person will be resuming Jimmy Ching's role."

"I'm sure you're all looking forward to getting back to business as usual," Pono said. He shook Ralph's hand. "Thanks for the info, and rest assured we're doing all we can to find Mr. Ching's killer. As I said, Ms. Smith here is helping with our investigation. Feel free to contact her at the post office with any new leads."

Ralph narrowed his eyes at me and didn't answer. We both knew that wasn't going to happen.

Outside I took several long, deep breaths of fresh air before I clambered up into Stanley's cab. "What did you find out?" I asked, once my door was closed.

"Wouldn't you like to know." Pono winked, turned the key, and the truck's big engine roared into life.

"Let's compare notes, since, according to you, I'm helping with the investigation."

Pono gestured to the light fixture beside the truck. "The walls have ears around here. Let's go get something to eat at the food trucks before I go by my Auntie's house."

"Oh boy," I said, and my empty belly rumbled in agreement with that plan.

A half hour later, we were settled at a picnic table with loaded plates. As we dug into our food, he glanced up at me briefly. "Wait till I tell Keone that you took his mom's bike to Kahului on your first ride on it."

I shrugged. "It's my only pair of wheels. The best way to find the limits of equipment is to test it right out of the gate."

Pono sucked a draft of root beer from his wax cup, then wiped the foam off of his bristly black mustache. "Sounds like something you learned early on."

I smiled. "I have a special spot for aunties, too. After my parents died, Aunt Fae raised me in the woods on the Maine coast. It's not a place for the faint of heart. She had a cabin with no electricity. We had to harvest our own firewood, and for my first ten years with her, we mostly lived off the land. It prepared me for a career in the Secret Service in ways that are hard to describe."

"So try."

Having finished most of my food, I wiped my greasy hands on a napkin. "The Secret Service is all about anticipation, planning, and working independently, as well as part of a team. We research where a protectee will be going, what they will be doing, and we try to anticipate and eliminate threats before they arise. We don't always work with a partner, and I didn't for most of my career because I worked with lower profile diplomats. This required a lot of taking initiative, which is unusual in a government agency. My upbringing with Aunt Fae toughened me up, though. If we didn't take care of ourselves out there in the woods, there wasn't anyone to fall back on."

"Is she still out there now? She must be getting up in age." Pono's brow wrinkled with concern.

I shook my head. "I was able to convince her to move into town after I left. I wasn't gonna be there to dig her out from under six feet of snow and then go fell a tree with my chainsaw to keep us warm."

Pono's deep brown eyes twinkled in much the same way that Keone's did when he was amused. "I see why my cousin likes you."

I addressed my neglected macaroni salad with assiduous attention.

We were finishing up dinner when Pono's phone buzzed. He picked up, greeting someone named Attorney General Hirono.

I was dying to know what they were talking about, but Pono's side mostly consisted of "Yes, sir. No, sir. Okay, sir." He agreed to keep the man informed before ending the call and sliding his phone into his back pocket. He wiped his hands and stood up.

"Time to get you home." Twilight had fallen and the food truck turned on a string of lights that lit our way. A nearby tree came alive with the loud chatter of mynah birds settling in to roost for the night.

I hunkered down on my bench. "If you think you're not gonna tell me what that phone call was about. . ."

"I will, but in the truck on the way back. I'll also fill you in on my discussion with the security guy, Ralph."

In the excitement over food, I'd forgotten all about our interview with the New Ohia Security dudes. That's what being hangry does to this girl.

Back in Stanley and on the road to Ohia, Pono settled into his seat with the air of a man getting ready to impart news. "Ralph told me he's concerned about the future of New Ohia. He thinks the Chang crime family is behind it, and that anyone who goes against their agenda might have a very short punch card. He believes Jimmy might have tried to get in on a piece of pie that wasn't his. He refused to make any kind of official statement or complaint, however."

"That's pretty much what I guessed as well," I agreed. "Are you sure he wasn't in on what Jimmy was doing? He seemed to know plenty about that memory drive that was stolen."

"He says he thought Jimmy was up to something shady, but he wouldn't own up to anything more about the stolen drive."

I mulled that over. "Other than the names on the Articles of Incorporation, proving ties to anything illegal might be difficult."

"That's what the Attorney General called about. Lei reached out to him and told him that we were picking up a possible organized crime presence in the development of New Ohia. We want him to be in on it from the get-go so he can help us with any warrants. He agreed to be on our team and said he wanted us to consult the FBI on this one, too."

My pulse picked up. This was a step in the right direction! "So, are you? Going to consult the FBI?"

"Lei serves as a liaison between MPD and the FBI. She has a good friend, Special Agent Marcella Scott, whom she runs most things by when we have a possible case in need of their resources. She will be reaching out to Marcella. From there, Hirono wants us to put together a multi-agency task force."

I digested that along with my enormous dinner. It would be good to have higher-ups looking into the corruption of New Ohia. "How can I help?"

"Just keep doing what you're doing. Be our boots on the ground —our eyes and ears in Ohia. Your job at the post office puts you in a unique position of being able to monitor a lot of information as it comes and goes."

"Not to mention my relationship with Pua Chang," I said. "Such as it is."

"That too. You might want to reach out and let her know you're working on what she told you. Take her a plate lunch out at her farm."

He grinned as I rolled my eyes. "I don't like her nearly enough for that."

For once, Tiki wasn't waiting for me on the front porch of the shack, and I felt a pang of worry. Where was that grumpy cat? She could always be counted on to meet me when I came home, mad that I'd left and wasn't back when she wanted to be fed.

I took the e-bike out of the truck bed and waved goodbye to Pono as he headed off to visit Keone's mother before he drove back to Kahului. I locked the bike to the post on my front porch, plugged it into the extension cord, and forced my stiff, tired legs to carry me inside.

As I unlocked it, I heard Tiki's familiar growl.

"Hey, girl!" I got the door open and pulled the light string. My scruffy, kink-tailed, one-eared cat sat beside her bowl next to the sink. She let out a rusty yowl to complain about the late hour.

I wasn't sure when the sight of her head morphed from dread to pleasure, but apparently, that shift had happened for her as well. After letting out that initial complaint she came forward to wind around my legs in greeting.

"Hey, Tiki girl. I need to take a shower after my long bike ride. I'll feed you, then after you eat, do you care to join me in the shower for that flea bath we've been talking about?"

Tiki grumbled gently, conveying somehow that she was open to the idea.

I never thought the day would come when I would kneel on the floor in front of my shower, washing down that filthy cat with warm water and flea shampoo and actually hearing her purr—but it happened.

Apparently, miracles do come true on occasion. Maybe we'd pull off another one and put a stop to the organized crime driving New Ohia.

🕸 18 🕸

I woke up early Friday morning with anxiety tightening my chest. I gave up on sleep, got up, and installed the porch light and home security system I'd biked all the way to Kahului to buy.

Once that was done, I knew why I was feeling worried. I wasn't ready for Monday to roll around without Mr. Hanoi. I'd be flying solo in the post office, and, with barely any training, I didn't feel qualified.

I took a quick shower and dressed in my "professional" outfit of a white polo shirt and dark jeans, tied my hair back in a braid, and dabbed on a bit of concealer to soften the discoloration of my face. Then, I waited for my boss to arrive.

"I know it's Friday and you said to take the rest of the week off, but I'm feeling fine." I waylaid the balding, potbellied Chief Postmaster outside the building as soon as he arrived. "I didn't have much time behind the counter training before everything went down with Pua. Would you let me come back to work early to spend the day with you?"

Mr. Hanoi cocked his head, looking me over. I pressed my shoulders back and stood tall in my Nikes, which meant I towered over the man.

He tapped his chin thoughtfully. "I suppose if you feel okay . . ."

"I do. No headache. I want you to check my work procedures—make sure I'm doing everything right before you go back to Kahului and I'm out here by myself."

That sounded downright sensible, and he agreed with a nod. "I brought your name badge with me this morning." He dug in an old-fashioned postal carrier's bag and produced a bronzed oval with letters engraved on the front. "Here you go."

I took the pin. It read: K. SMITH, POSTMASTER.

An unexpected bubble of something a lot like happiness welled up from my stomach and into my chest. I blinked frantically to clear the suspicious moisture in my eyes. "Thanks." I focused on pinning the name tag over my left breast. "Got it on straight?"

Mr. Hanoi smiled. "Looks good on you, Kat. Let's get to it." He turned and unlocked the door.

After the angst of the last few days, throwing myself into what I was actually here in Ohia to do was a relief. The tasks were tangible and the work so hands-on that, for a while, I was able to forget about Jimmy Ching and the issues of New Ohia. Mr. Hanoi set up shop in the office and watched my progress through the one-way glass while working on his computer.

As I sold a page of postcard stamps to a tourist passing through, I was glad I'd decided to come back to work early. There was a scanner for the retail items, but some of the procedures had special codes and there were many forms to become familiar with.

Two young girls bopped in later in the morning, fighting over who got to unlock their postbox. They were equally grubby and similar in size, with messy black hair that looked like it had been cut with garden shears. "You're so bossy," one of them complained.

"Because I'm older," the other said. "I'm in charge. Mom said so."

"Hey girls." I waved from my counter. "Why don't you take turns? Whoever doesn't open it today gets to unlock it on Monday."

Both girls stopped to glare at me. "Where's Auntie Pua?" the older one asked.

"She's enjoying a well-earned vacation."

"I heard she was in jail," the younger one said. She came up to the counter, looking me over with a cold, unfriendly stare and sizing me up. "Because of you."

I cleared my throat. "You shouldn't listen to gossip."

The kid snorted with contempt. "You shouldn't be here, *haole*."

Her older sister reached into the unlocked postbox and took out a fat manila envelope. "Let's go." She grabbed her sister by the arm. "Hope you feel bad about what happened to Auntie Pua, because you should," she said over her shoulder.

I stared after the miniature mean girls, feeling like the wind had been kicked out of me. "Shouldn't you be in school?" I hollered after them at last.

The younger one flipped me the bird.

I went behind the counter and checked the name on the box they'd emptied: NAKASONE. "Where are your parents, girls?" I muttered. "They need to teach you some manners."

The rest of the morning was uneventful, and I remembered that Heri would be emailing me when she had information on the drive's contents. I grew antsy, wondering if the email was sitting in my inbox while I sat reading my massive postal manual.

I poked my head into the postmaster's office, where Hanoi sat. "Mind if I grab my laptop and check my email using the office connection?"

"Not at all, help yourself," he replied.

I jogged to the shack and grabbed my laptop, flipping it open once I was back inside the building. My leg bounced impatiently as I waited for the signal to connect. After what felt like an eternity, I was able to load my inbox. At the top sat an email in bold letters—From: Hermione Leede, Subject: New Ohia Documents.

I skimmed the email and forwarded it to Lei and Pono. It was detailed, with an invitation at the end to call with any questions. I scribbled the number down on a Post-it and ducked into the staff office that Pua once occupied. The ceramic lotus diffuser puffed away in the corner, unaware that the former occupant of this space would not be returning for some time. I pulled the phone to me and dialed the number I'd copied down.

"Hermione Leede, Forensic Accounting." The woman's voice had a British accent with cut-glass consonants. "How can I assist you today?"

"This is Katherine Smith. Sophie from Security Solutions referred me to you for assistance with a cache of documents."

"Ah, yes. Lovely to hear from you, Ms. Smith."

"Call me Kat, please."

"And please call me Heri."

"Thanks, Heri. What can you tell me about 'Jimmy's Stash?'"

"Well, first of all, it is indeed a stash."

"I know, I found his spreadsheet of payments. Were you able to find out who was paying him. Or how the scam worked?"

"You are correct in calling it a scam, Kat. The original land was leased, but New Ohia Vision was selling parcels as if the land was fee simple. In other words, those deeds of sale are fraudulent."

"I suspected as much. It seemed wrong to me that a lease from the state could convert to direct sales."

"Right. And then there are the apartments. From what I can tell, they have been selling units in buildings that have neither been designed nor approved, let alone built."

"Oh, fiddle-faddle." I thought of the previous postmaster who'd been murdered prior to my arrival. She'd bought one of those units to retire in. "Where was the money going?"

"Well, that's a good question. I have no information from these files on where the bulk of the sales money went, nor who was paying Mr. Ching. It is clear he received monetary compensation whenever a unit or lot sold, which isn't unusual for a realtor—they usually receive a percentage of the sale. However, I found a job description document that revealed Mr. Ching wasn't even a realtor. His title was Project Manager, and the job description was essentially to keep the illusion going that the development was on track and underway."

"What about the ongoing operating expenses of the development? They have security guards, model homes, landscaping maintenance . . ."

"New Ohia Vision has a standard business account, which I was able to locate and verify with a little massaging of someone I know at a local bank. That account is funded through homeowner agreement fees . . . HOA fees, in other words."

"So, these owners are buying lots and beginning to pay monthly fees for the upkeep of the development?"

"Yes. And not only that, but none of the sales were financed in any form. They were made in cash."

I felt a chilly little tingle that lifted the hairs on my arms. "What kind of buyers have that much cash?"

"I'm just speculating here, but it seems to me that buying with cash is one of the unwritten prerequisites for being a part of the New Ohia development," Heri said. "There's a lot of cash hiding somewhere, that is for sure."

"Can you help me find where it is?"

"My best advice is to find out the names on the Articles of Incorporation—those shareholders are the people who know where the money is."

"Thanks so much, Heri."

"You're welcome. I hope this helps. This is just the sort of case I like to sink my teeth into," Heri said. "I'll send my bill to the state when they realize how they've been duped, once we've put a stop to it."

"Perfect." I ended the call and stared thoughtfully at the tiny puffs chugging from the diffuser. What kind of buyers had so much cash? If they had been recruited by the Chang crime family, the whole place could be a front for money laundering.

The thought was chilling.

❦ 19 ❧

Thankfully for my ruminations, the delivery van showed up just then with the day's mail. Chad wheeled in the big canvas bag of letters and stacks of boxes, and soon Mr. Hanoi and I were too busy sorting and filling mailboxes for me to think of much else.

"You work the counter whenever a customer comes in," Mr. Hanoi told me, sorting quickly with gloved hands. "You need the practice."

"I know I do," I agreed. Only a few minutes later, another customer came in and I returned to the counter. I broke into a smile when I saw this one was a friendly face: Josie of the Red Hat Society.

"Kat! So good to see you back at work." The statuesque Native Hawaiian woman towed her oxygen tank over to the wall of boxes and retrieved her mail. Her long, flower-print caftan billowed around her. "How're you doing?"

"Oh, fine." I rearranged the rubber stamps in front of my work area for something to do. "What have the Red Hat ladies been up to lately?"

"Well, Edith is getting ready to file a cease and desist order on the New Ohia development," Josie said. "It's taken a while to assemble all the evidence of the shortcuts that were taken, but she has all her documentation ready now. We're giving her a little send-off at the general store tonight if you want to come by. She has to fly to Oahu to file the papers."

Josie dragged her tank over and leaned on the counter with an elbow. She smelled of coconut oil and plumeria flowers. One of the five-petaled blossoms peeked from behind her ear.

I frowned. "Are you sure you ladies should be making a public fuss about what she's doing? There are dangerous people involved with New Ohia." My thoughts drifted back to the conversation I'd just had with Heri.

Mr. Hanoi joined me at the counter. "What's all this?"

Josie had a gorgeous smile set off by her long, rippling, dark hair lightly streaked with silver. "I was about to share my home remedy recipe for bruises with Kat. Have you two heard of noni?"

Mr. Hanoi grimaced. "That nasty fruit might have medicinal properties, but it smells so bad I can't get within ten feet of it."

Josie huffed in offense. "Noni has a thousand therapeutic uses, and Kat has a tree right in her backyard."

I shook my head. "I don't have a yard, Josie. Just jungle behind the shack—it's a wilderness back there."

"Take a break and let me show you the treasure growing right behind your house."

Mr. Hanoi flapped a hand. "Go ahead, Kat. Take a break and let this lady introduce you to what they call 'carrion fruit' on the continent."

"That smell is why Hawaiians call it 'ghost medicine,'" Josie said. "It's good for many things, including chasing off unhappy spirits."

Jimmy Ching's square, hostile face filled my mind. That man was definitely an unhappy ghost, unlike gentle Frances Borland, whom I'd helped lay to rest. "I need to meet this noni plant. Let's go."

I led Josie around the back of my shack. We made our way through long, bunchy grass, Josie choosing her footing carefully in her bright Crocs while I followed behind with her oxygen tank. Fortunately, the slim green tank was equipped with wheels, and I was able to work it over the rough terrain toward the wall of trees and shrubs that marked the beginning of the jungle behind my shack.

I gestured to the thick greenery. "I can't tell one from another. But if we were in Maine, that would be a different story."

"Well, if you are going to be part of our town, you should become familiar with our native plants and their uses." Josie pointed to a nearby tree. "This one is the hala tree."

The hala seemed like something Dr. Seuss had dreamed up: a spindly stem that was more plant than wood, crowned by a bouffant-like tuft of long, spiraling green leaves edged with tiny thorns. Tucked beneath the leafy heads were pineapple-like fruits. I pointed to the yellowish orb marked by hexagonal sections. "Is that edible?"

"No, but sometimes people make leis from the fruit sections. When they're dried, the fibrous pieces make a good natural paint-brush, too. You can find them washed up on the beach, ready to play with."

"I'll have to look for some of those."

"Hala is one of our most useful native trees. It's a variety of pandanus plant. Hawaiians—and Polynesians elsewhere too—use hala leaf fiber for weaving floor matting, sleep covers, even sails for canoes."

"That's amazing." I stared at the long, swordlike, thorny leaves. "But hard to imagine."

"Let me show you. Each leaf requires a good deal of work to prep for use." Josie leaned down and picked up a fallen frond-like leaf about a yard long. Dried, it had gone a nice mellow silvery color. She used a sturdy thumbnail to pierce a slit in the edge, easily peeling away the sharp row of thorns and dropping them. "We hang the leaves to dry them, then cut strips once they're dried." She demonstrated separating a fibrous, silvery strip with her nail. "All weaving is done with various lengths cut from the dried leaf."

I could see what she was talking about—the strip she made was flexible and strong. I rubbed the piece of hala between my fingers. It was soft, and the scent was pleasantly haylike. "It feels and smells good."

Josie took a few more steps into the foliage, her Crocs perfect footwear for the wet terrain. "There's your personal noni tree." She pointed to a large branching shrub. Unlike the hala tree, this plant was a normal-looking bush with woody branches and big, glossy, dark green leaves.

"Where are those famous fruits that smell so bad?" I asked. Just then, I stepped on something unpleasantly squishy. A foul odor, much like the smell of decomposing roadkill, wafted up to hit my nose.

"Gack!" I squealed, leaping back, tripping over the oxygen tank, and landing on my butt in the grass.

Josie grinned. "You just found a ripe noni."

I lifted my Nike to examine the reeking, translucent yellow pulp adhering to the bottom of my shoe.

"Look at that, you crushed it up already. Noni is good for all kinds of infections and wounds. This one is prepped and ready to use on your bruises now, because it's best applied as a poultice," Josie said.

I didn't reply, not sure if she was serious.

Josie threw her head back and laughed at my expression. It sounded like angels throwing a luau in heaven. "My *malihini* friend, your face is priceless."

"I'm sure glad I didn't run into this fruit before you had a chance to tell me about it." I scraped at my shoe with a stick, shuddering. "I would've thought I stepped on a giant dead slug or something."

Josie rummaged around in the leaves on the noni bush and plucked a yellowish-white fruit about the size of a pear. She handed it to me. "Noni's not really ripe until it's transparent, like the one you stepped on. But you can take this one in the house and let it mature for juice or medicine. You can also make tea from the leaves. The pulpy fruit is good for digestion."

I shuddered. "I'll take it under advisement. Now that I have you alone, Josie, please tell the Red Hat ladies to be careful about what they say or do about the New Ohia development. I am helping Lei and Pono with the investigation into Jimmy Ching's death, and we've discovered that there are dangerous people involved."

"The Chang family, you mean?" Josie leaned down to help me up. Her grip was strong, though her breath wheezed around the cannula in her nose. "Everybody knows they're behind how the development has been sped forward."

"Well, that's even more of a reason why you should be careful. Especially Edith. She could become a target," I said, frowning.

"Edith knows what she's doing," Josie said. "All it takes for evil to have its way is for good people to be silent."

"I want everyone to be safe," I said. "I couldn't stand it if any of you were hurt."

"Of course you want us to be safe. You're a Secret Service agent," Josie said.

I tapped my shiny, new, brass name tag. "But now I'm postmaster. I'm watching out for everyone in this town, even the two naughty little girls who came into the post office today and told me off."

"You must be talking about Sandy and Windy Nakasone," Josie said. "Those girls are tough, but they've had to be. Their mom died when Windy was born, and their dad works construction in Kahului. He's gone most of the week. They're pretty much raising themselves out here."

I frowned. "Can't anyone do anything?"

Josie shrugged. "Not unless you have a car and permission to drive them to school. Sandy says there's no one to take them if they miss the bus, and the bus comes at five thirty in the morning."

"Is it legal for them to be alone so much?"

"What's the alternative? A foster home?" Josie shook her head. "At least out here, we all look out for them. Folks wash their clothes and bring over home-cooked meals a couple of times a week. We make sure they get to school most days. Pua took on a big part of helping them."

No wonder those girls resented me. I had nothing to contribute to their welfare. My own set of wheels were still charging from the ill-advised foray into Kahului. "What about the school? Can't they do anything?"

"The girls get two meals a day there through the federal free meals program and after-school supervision with a teacher. They're fine." Josie paused to make eye contact with me. "Kat, I know you mean well, but watch out for making enemies."

"Okay," I said. "I hear you." I followed Josie back to the parking lot, wrestling her oxygen tank through the grass. I'd been warned to mind my own business, and I had plenty of that to worry about.

Out at Josie's van, I helped her get in and settled with her tank. "If you're interested in learning more about Hawaiian medicine, art, and crafts, I host a weekly gathering," Josie said unexpectedly. "You are welcome to come."

"I'd like that," I said, and surprised myself by how true it was though I'd never been interested in such things before. "I can't promise I'll ever want to put that goo on my face, though."

"We'll ease you into it with some tasty tea. It's not bad when you add honey."

"I'll take your word for that."

I was pretty excited to learn more about Hawaiian culture. Yeah, maybe I wasn't ever going to be a fan of how noni smelled. But maybe I could learn to make a basket for Tiki to sleep in out of hala leaves or something like that.

I smiled as I went back into the post office to resume work—but not for long when I saw the man waiting at the counter to meet me.

🦋 20 🦋

"This gentleman specifically asked for you," Mr. Hanoi said, gesturing to a barrel-chested white guy with a bad comb-over and the red nose of someone who liked his five o'clock gin and tonic a little too much. "Roland Thompkins is the replacement project coordinator for New Ohia."

I pasted a smile on my face and advanced to shake Thompkins's hand, glad I took a moment to scrub the foul-smelling noni pulp off my shoes and hands. "Kat Smith, Postmaster."

"Pleased to meet such a lovely lady in a place like this." Thompkins gave me an icky once-over that made me feel like I needed a shower. "Thought I would take a moment to say hello to one of the most important people in Ohia, who's right at the hub of our town's activity." Thompkins had very shiny veneers, but they didn't make his smile real—nor did his damp, doughy handshake.

"I'm just a newbie in this town. The most important folks you need to meet are Opal and Artie Pahinui, next door at the general store. They've been here forever and know everyone," I said. I was eager to get Opal's take on Jimmy Ching's replacement. Maybe the runes would have something to say about this guy.

"I'm moving my things into Jimmy's former model home in New

Ohia. Stop by anytime if you want to know what's going on with our project. Folks won't even miss Jimmy. And . . . I'll be handling all inquiries with law enforcement. I hear they've got some sort of special relationship with you," Thompkins said.

What had he been told about me? And by whom?

"I'm on a friendly basis with the detectives looking into Mr. Ching's demise, but no more than anyone in my position." I accompanied some eyelash-flapping with a deprecating smile.

"Well, speaking of your position—how about you sign me up for a mailbox? I'll take the one Jimmy Ching used."

Mr. Hanoi guided me to the proper forms, and I went through the process of assigning a post office box to a new customer.

"Good thing you're taking Mr. Ching's box," I said. "Because we have a waiting list for the others. The bigwigs at New Ohia sure were lucky to get you to replace him so quickly." More eyelash-flapping. "What made a move to a place like Ohia appealing for a man like you?"

"An opportunity for a quieter life with plenty of time for sunshine, pretty girls, and golf," Thompkins said, and burped out a guffaw as if he's said something funny.

Nope, I definitely didn't like Roland Thompkins any more than I'd liked Jimmy Ching. Eventually, he left, taking a brass post office box key with him. He got into the same big white SUV Jimmy Ching had driven until the day he was killed beside it.

I glanced at Mr. Hanoi. "You know about Jimmy Ching, that guy's predecessor, getting whacked, don't you?"

"Sure do." My boss busied himself restocking certified mail forms. "And if I were you, Kat, I'd keep my head down and stay out of trouble."

I'd been warned twice in one day, but trouble always had a way of finding me.

Mr. Hanoi and I were wrapping up the workday in the post office when the phone rang with a call for me. I took the handset from my boss and answered with a brisk greeting. "Kat Smith, Postmaster."

"You have no idea how sexy that sounds." Mr. K gave a playful growl. "Thought I'd try to reach you on your work landline before you went off the grid for the weekend."

I would have to think about what he said about my sexy voice another time. "Thank you. I understand." I was highly conscious of Mr. Hanoi, hovering in the background, restocking flat rate boxes in the lobby. "What can I do for you?"

Keone's tone sobered. "I was wondering what you're up to tomorrow. There are a lot of things you still haven't seen in our area."

"That sounds interesting," I said perkily. "Thanks for thinking of it."

"How about I swing by tomorrow morning around nine and we take it from there?"

"Perfect. Glad I could help."

He laughed and ended the call.

I hung up too. A warm, fuzzy feeling bloomed under my sternum, and I was smiling.

Mr. Hanoi jingled his keys to lock up. "Got a date for the weekend, eh?"

I hadn't fooled him at all.

"Some sightseeing with a friend," I said. "There's still a lot I haven't seen around here."

We locked up the building, and as he walked to his battered truck, Mr. Hanoi laid a friendly hand on my shoulder. I tried not to shrug it off as my touch anxiety ratcheted up. "Don't hesitate to call if you need me to come out next week. I've really enjoyed this chance to get back in the field."

"Thanks so much for your help, Mr. Hanoi. I'll feel a lot more confident opening on my own on Monday."

"One thing we always say: no matter what else is happening

personally or in the world, the mail must be delivered. All of us in the Postal Service hold that mission close to our hearts."

"As a Secret Service agent, I can attest to dedication to duty," I said. "Meanwhile, it's been great to learn from the best."

Hanoi flapped a hand dismissively, but I could tell he was pleased as he got into his truck and left.

Facing a wide-open afternoon, I decided to head over to the general store. I was missing my friends, Opal and Artie; I'd hardly seen them lately. Plus, I was thirsty and had root beer on my mind. Instead of racing over to the beach to get in a swim, I headed next door for a little catch-up and refreshment.

Opal perked up beside the register as I approached through the dimly lit, musty-smelling shop. "I swear we're telepathically connected. I was just thinking about you and wondering what the heck was going on with the Ching investigation."

"Good to see you, too, Opal," I greeted her. She adjusted her scarf in a little mirror behind the counter. Today's pin was a garish phoenix done in rhinestones. "I thought you wanted to stay out of this murder investigation, and that the runes weren't favorable to your involvement."

"That doesn't mean I'm not still curious. But I dug a little deeper into the reading, and the runes were basically warning us. Signs point to . . ." She paused, staring off into space, still adjusting the purple velour fabric.

"Signs point to what?"

"That's the thing, there were a couple of symbols that were contradicting each other." She jiggled her pocket, and I heard the familiar clacking sound of the kukui nut shells rattling in their pouch. "Maybe what we need is a second reading." Her eyes gleamed with anticipation. "There haven't been any customers in a while. Let's close up early. Kat, would you mind doing the honors?"

"With pleasure." I hurried across the expanse of the cluttered store to flip the OPEN sign to CLOSED. I swiveled the deadbolt on the front door with a satisfying click. "All set."

Opal took her scarf back off and spread out the purple fabric over the countertop. Next, she took the mesh pouch out of her pocket and shook it in both hands.

"Is there a reason you use your scarf to toss the runes onto? Like, it gives extra energy or something?" I asked.

"Nope. I just like to have a fabric surface for the shells to land on, so they don't try to escape." Opal dumped the shiny black nut shells into her palm, breathed on them, shut her eyes for a moment, and then dropped them onto the purple velour. "See that? Even with the material, one of them escaped."

Opal bent down to pick up the errant shell and tapped its surface. "This one represents a strong male energy that is now missing from the reading. I surmise it refers to Jimmy Ching's untimely departure from this life." She set the rune to the side and hunched over the rest for a long moment.

Finally, she said, "I see similar themes to last time. Opposing forces. Darkness. High stakes. But this time, the two contrary messages are gone." Opal glanced up and met my eyes with her clear blue ones. "The runes are warning us, all right, but now the message is clear that we all need to band together to fight a larger negative force."

"I concur with that," I said. "I met Jimmy Ching's replacement today, and he seems every bit as scheming and slippery as the other guy."

Opal walked to the store's fridge and fetched us a couple of cold drinks. She handed me a root beer. I took the chilled bottle from her hand, unscrewed it, savored the spicy smell, and took a long, bubbly, delicious swig.

"Mmm." I waggled the glass bottle at her. "Now I know you're psychic. I had root beer on my mind." I filled Opal in on what I'd found out about Jimmy's murder since I'd last talked to her.

"The Red Hat ladies are gathering here soon to give Edith a send-off for her latest court filing," Opal said when I finished. "But you have enough time for a quick swim before they get here."

I pushed past my phobia to lean over and give Opal a quick hug. "I like the way your mind works. Or is it the way my mind works?"

We both laughed, and I headed out to get that swim before the heavy hitters of Ohia gathered for a send-off party on the store's front porch.

The sun was beginning to slant behind the erosion-carved, lush green headland that marked the boundary of Ohia Bay. I ran across the two-lane Hana Highway in my bikini, tossed my terry cloth robe on a rock, and dove into the water.

The feeling of cool, salty Maui water sluicing over my skin was delicious after the stress of the day. I'd picked up a pair of goggles while at the general store, so now I was able to keep my eyes open and watch for fun things to see underwater.

The bottom of Ohia Bay was mostly sand, but here and there rocks appeared, decorated with coral and waving seaweed. Small, brightly colored fish darted in and out of their habitat, paying me no mind as I swam by like an ocean liner overhead.

Moments like these made it hard to ever imagine going back to my hectic urban lifestyle in Washington, D.C. All those plastic meals and standing against the wall, bodyguarding a politician I didn't like with my own body. All the lonely hours, waiting outside in the hall while important people lived their lives in the next room, never a part of anything but my elite squad. All of the endless, tension-filled anticipation, followed by flurries of terrifying stress when a threat was detected.

How had I done it for so long?

I propelled myself through the water—until my hand hit something hard. Was it a floating piece of wood?

I pulled back abruptly and treaded water, then gasped as a brownish head with yellow-ringed, hazel eyes appeared. Then, the enormous shell of a green sea turtle emerged from the water, bobbing like a floating island beside me.

"Wow," I breathed as the critter looked me over. Apparently, I'd interrupted its swim as it had interrupted mine. But only mild curiosity showed in those wise eyes before it submerged suddenly and disappeared.

I took a deep breath and stuck my face under the surface, watching the turtle swim away. Its large flippers moved like a bird's wings to propel it gracefully through the water.

My smile felt like it would split my face. Apparently, Maui wasn't done revealing its magic and surprises.

I was in a thoughtful mood as I finished my laps, wrapped up in my robe, slid my feet into my rubber slippers, and crossed the street to my shack. Unlocking the door, I was greeted by Tiki seated on her haunches beside her food bowl.

"I met a sea turtle today," I told her.

The cat was unimpressed. She advanced to me, her crooked tail waving from side to side, letting me know that she was happy to see me . . . and it was time for food.

"We've come a long way, baby," I told her. And we had. Of course, I was quick to feed her so we didn't regress.

I dragged a comb through my long, wet hair and threw on a pair of shorts and a tee. It would have to do for now. I picked my way across the puddles to the party developing on the front porch of the Ohia General Store.

All the ladies were there, wearing their red chapeaux. Mattie Ramirez came toward me, raising her cane and waving the red satin, rhinestone ball cap monstrosity she'd made. "I thought you could put it on just for the occasion," she said.

I took the hat and smiled at her. "I am off-duty and there's no one here but Red Hat supporters, so I guess that will be fine." I settled the thing on my head. Clara, Josie, Mattie, Pearl, Edith, and Opal all burst into applause. Artie, seated in his chair, strummed a dramatic chord on his guitar.

Opal advanced to hand me a root beer. "Now I know your libation. Let's toast to Kat in a red hat and Edith's filing!"

The ladies joined with me to clank our various cups, bottles, and cans together.

"I told you it was just for this occasion," I said, sipping my root beer. "Don't get ahead of yourselves, now."

"Well, you're with us in spirit," Pearl said, propelling her wheelchair closer to me. "Help yourself to some *pupus*." She gestured to a side table, heavily laden with appetizers from different cultures represented in Hawaii.

"Don't mind if I do." I grabbed a paper plate and loaded it up with Japanese, Hawaiian, and Hispanic finger foods. Once we were all settled with our selections, I turned to Edith. "Tell me about this filing and why you have to go to Oahu to put it in."

"It's taken a while to gather documentation of the abuses and oversights that have contributed to New Ohia being built so quickly," Edith said around a mouthful of teriyaki shrimp. She wiped her hand on a napkin. "I filed early on Maui, hoping to get a pause in the work, but they denied it right away. They claimed there wasn't enough documentation. So I've taken the time to pull together a good deal of evidence to submit with my paperwork, and I'm going over the Maui judge's head. I'm hoping that the negative influences behind New Ohia don't have a presence in the state court, too."

"I wouldn't count on that," I said. "There's a certain well-known crime family, which shall remain nameless, that seems to have quite a reach. The detectives and I have found good evidence that they are involved with New Ohia."

"I know all that," Edith said. Under the comical red felt hat she wore, the lawyer's eyes were bright and determined. "I'm prepared to take this all the way to the State Supreme Court if I have to."

"Are you sure we should be talking in public about your plan?" I waved a bamboo skewer laden with chunks of meat and vegetables at the empty parking lot.

"We're keeping it under our hats." Pearl rolled toward me in her fancy chair. Her red kanzashi hairpins wobbled and swayed, heavy with decorative sparkling beads. "In a manner of speaking."

"Please be careful," I admonished Edith. "These people are serious about New Ohia."

"Oh, I know," she assured me. "I'll keep an eye out coming and going."

I sure hoped that was going to be enough. "I'd feel better if you had company. Someone to help and protect you."

Edith cocked her head so that she could see out from under the brim of her hat. "Are you volunteering to guard me, Agent Smith?"

A slow smile moved across my face. "I guess I am."

❧ 22 ❧

My impulsive offer to protect Edith on her mission was how I ended up unlocking the post office in the middle of a party and heading straight over to the phone on my desk. I dialed a number I'd memorized.

"Mr. K? I know we were supposed to go do something fun tomorrow, but I have to accompany Edith Pepperwhite to Oahu and protect her while she files papers against New Ohia," I said in lieu of a greeting.

"Well hello, Kat. Can you slow down a bit and fill in the blanks for me?" Keone said.

I gusted out a sigh. "I owe you that much."

I told Keone about Edith's filings in the lawsuit against New Ohia and my concerns for her safety. "The Red Hat ladies are all partying on the porch of the general store as we speak. They say they're keeping a lid on Edith's activities, but I don't believe that for a minute. I'm afraid the bad element we're dealing with could get wind of her plans to file and . . ." I couldn't bring myself to put my worries into words.

Mr. K was silent for a long moment. "Did you know I have my

own airplane?" His voice was tentative, hopeful—like a young boy's. I'd never heard that tone from him before.

"Uh, no," I frowned. "What's that got to do with this?"

"Well, it's a little three-seater. It's been my hobby project for years, and I've started taking it out," he said. "Maybe this weekend would be a good time for a maiden voyage to Oahu."

My chest filled with a feeling—I had no idea what it was, but it made my cheeks hot and my heart pound. I wished I could hug him, maybe more. "Are you thinking what I'm thinking?"

He laughed. "I don't know. What are you thinking?"

"Never mind," I said, embarrassed.

"I might be thinking what you're thinking, if what you're thinking is that I could fly you and Edith over to Oahu undetected by anyone but Air Traffic Control," Mr. K said. "On the negative side, you'd have to be prepared for a pretty bumpy ride and aware this is my project plane that I've never flown that far."

"In other words, it might not be the safest option," I said.

"No. It's safe. I wouldn't try flying that far, especially with passengers, if I didn't have total confidence in my craft and my piloting," Mr. K said. "But if small aircraft aren't your cup of tea, or Edith's, it won't be an attractive idea no matter how good it would be for hiding your plans."

My mind raced. Edith and I would be able to dodge a ton of risk exposure by taking a small private plane instead of one of the major commercial airlines.

"Tiny aircraft don't bother me a bit. I've had para jump training. I can't speak for Edith's stomach, but she seems pretty brassy for an older lady. I have a feeling she'll be excited."

"Then I'm game to take you up. We can meet tomorrow morning at the airstrip."

I restrained myself from clapping my hands. This resolved so many worries. "Is there any way you could take us on Sunday instead? I will still have to stay on Oahu with her until the courthouse opens on Monday, which will mean missing work."

"Unfortunately, I'm flying my normal shifts Sunday and Monday," Keone said regretfully. "Saturday's my only day off."

"Okay. I'll call Mr. Hanoi and see if he can cover for me Monday."

"I assume Edith has made some secure lodging arrangements on Oahu for the weekend?"

"I'll firm up the details with her."

"Good. Then I'll see you both tomorrow morning at six a.m. We'll leave early so we can get a start across the channel before the winds come up. That stretch between the islands can be rough to cross."

"Thanks, Keone. You're a lifesaver."

"High praise from a Secret Service agent," Keone said. "You know how to butter me up."

"Ha." I was missing a chance to flirt with him, but my tongue tied itself in a knot whenever I tried. "See you tomorrow."

After my call to Mr. Hanoi, I headed back to the party with a spring in my oversized Nikes. The butterflies fluttering around in my stomach only increased as I told Edith about our opportunity to dodge the crowds in Kahului.

As I'd hoped would be the case, Edith was excited. "And I have a great place for us to stay for the weekend," she said. "You won't believe how great it is, and I promise it's secure." She refused to say anything further on the subject, other than that she couldn't wait to fly with me and Mr. K at oh-dark-hundred.

Edith picked me up the next morning in a tiny, lime green electric car. She'd dressed like Snoopy in pursuit of the Red Baron in a vintage leather pilot's hat with goggles and ear flaps, and a scarf wound around her neck. She wore an antique brown bomber jacket, and her bottom half was clad in World War II military pants that had been modified for her stature.

"I've been waiting half my life to wear this outfit," she said with a chuckle, flicking the silk scarf at her neck. "Thanks for giving me an excuse to break it out of the mothballs."

Edith must have meant it literally because as I folded my giant self into her subcompact, the chemical odor of naphthalene surrounded us.

She put the car in gear and pulled out, leaving Tiki on the porch glaring after us in the predawn light. "Hope you made arrangements for that cat to get some attention, or I'll fear for your life when you get back," Edith said.

"I sure did. Opal's dropping off kibble on the porch," I said. "I wouldn't dare deprive Tiki now that she's used to food on a regular basis."

"It's starting to look like she's attached to more than just food," Edith observed.

"She's just the post office stray." I couldn't afford to care too much about Tiki or anyone else in Ohia . . . or so I kept telling myself.

As always, the drive to Hana was gorgeous. I never got tired of the way the morning sun lit up the ocean's horizon, gilding fat cumulus clouds with salmon pink and gold. Between the tight curves of the narrow, winding road, the view of the sunrise was framed by dangling tropical vines and coconut palms—the area truly was paradise.

Mr. K had not been kidding about the size of the plane. The aircraft was small enough to pull with a handle on the front, and Mr. K towed it like an oversized child's toy out of a hangar on one side of the minuscule airport. Granted, he was huffing and puffing as he pulled the plane, but he was handling the load fine on his own. As much as I enjoyed watching his shoulders bulging, I trotted over to lend a hand and speed up the process. We soon had the aircraft positioned and pointed down the empty runway.

Keone leaned over and gave me a quick kiss on the cheek. "Thanks for giving me an excuse to take my baby out."

I liked that kiss. In fact, I wanted more. I faced him with a smile. "And thanks for taking us to Oahu in your very own plane. I wouldn't mind a bit more of a snog, if you're in the mood."

Yep, he was in the mood, and we proceeded with no ill effects. In fact, I forgot I'd ever had symptoms of anything other than enthusiasm.

Eventually, I felt a tap on my shoulder.

I broke away to see Edith grinning at us from under her flight cap, her goggles fogged up. "I thought you said something about getting started before the morning winds come up," she said.

"I just need to grab a few more things," Keone said and jogged back toward the hangar.

"Well, I declare. Now I know why our resident, most desirable bachelor is offering us a free ride," Edith said, eyes sparkling.

"We're just friends."

She bounced her brows and cocked her hip. "And I'm a purple elephant."

"Okay, really good friends," I said. "With entry-level benefits."

Mr. K came out of the hangar carrying a folding stepladder, a metal tool kit, and a bundle of parachutes and life jackets. He propped the stepladder against the wing, stowed the toolbox, and handed us each a parachute and a flotation device.

"Put the PFD on your front, and the parachute on your back," he said. "Can't be too careful. Safety first."

Edith fumbled with her gear, suddenly pale. "I'd have no idea how to parachute," she said.

I helped her untangle the straps and handed her parachute back to Keone. "If, for some reason, we need to eject, I'll strap you on my front, okay? We'll go tandem."

Keone nodded once he saw that I knew what I was doing. I demonstrated doing a double jump with Edith, talking her through it and showing her my plan. He stowed the extra parachute and helped Edith up the ladder.

"You need to sit in the back for weight distribution, but you'll fit behind us just fine," he told her. Returning to the tarmac, he grinned. "Sure comes in handy to have a girlfriend with jump training."

"Special friend," I corrected.

"That too. Gimme another kiss."

So I did.

Getting into the aircraft was a bit of an athletic feat, even for me. I climbed the ladder, shimmied over the wing, and folded myself like a jack-in-the-box into the tiny space beside Mr. K. Our fearless pilot handed both Edith and me headsets, and we stayed quiet through the preflight check, letting him focus uninterrupted on the various dials, settings, and gauges.

The plane sounded like my Aunt Fae's sewing machine as it fired up at last. Keone switched his headset to another channel to talk to the control tower. Edith's fragile, age-spotted hand crept between the seats to grab mine.

I could feel the fear in her tight grip and was able to tolerate the contact for that reason. Nothing helped me rise to an occasion like being able to comfort, protect, or care for someone else. That was a lot of what I was about as a person. Maybe that was why I'd stayed with the Secret Service long after the bloom wore off that particular rose.

Edith squeezed my hand harder. I let her, and even tightened my grip in return as we bumped down the narrow asphalt strip and leaped abruptly into the sky. The engine was noisy, but the windows sparkled. The ground dropped away, and Keone grinned reassuringly at us, giving a thumbs up.

The view that I enjoyed flying into Hana upon my arrival was played back in reverse, except without the bumpy air of that particular flight. Maui's coastline was just as lush today, and I enjoyed the nearby waterfalls, valleys, and waving bamboo forests. Turquoise waves beat against beaches of black sand and lava stone, and I watched a pod of whales swim below us and spout. Edith's hand gradually relaxed and she let go. I gave a sigh of relief.

We soon reached visual range of the edge of civilization—Kahului. Keone turned the craft out toward the open sea, lifting the controls to bring us to a higher altitude. Wind out of Oahu caught us, and the turbulence was steady but predictable for the next forty-five minutes. Soon, the green bulk of Oahu appeared. Edith seemed to be handling the stress okay though her goggles magnified her eyes. They were enormous when I glanced back at her.

Oahu's Koʻolau Range was particularly green, dramatic, and well-lit on this beautiful morning. Pearl Harbor was easily the prettiest water I'd seen in years. It was so clear that the shapes of the ships sunk during World War II were clearly visible on the sandy bottom, each their own lasting reminder of that terrible event.

As we circled in and headed for the landing strip, I wished the flight could've been longer. Edith's bony hand emerged from the backseat to pat Mr. K on the shoulder.

"You're one heck of a pilot, young man."

"Thanks," Keone said, and of course, that's when everything went haywire.

✴ 23 ✴

My first indication something was wrong was when Keone frowned at his instrument panel and stabbed a button several times. My second was when he peered out his window and his mouth formed the silent shape of a curse. My third was when he pulled up on the controls just before we were about to hit the tarmac and we lifted back into the sky. I watched him talk unintelligibly on the headset to air traffic control.

Edith's hand grabbed my shoulder with the strength of a zombie rising from the grave. I reached back to pat it.

"Is everything okay?" Her voice was high-pitched and tinny in my headset.

"I'm sure it's fine," I said, without looking back to make eye contact. "Keone's a professional."

He came back on our channel. "Well ladies, we'll be coming in a little hot on our next pass. The flaps are stuck. I've asked for extra runway to coast on our next attempt. We'll be landing at a faster speed than usual and rolling a bit further than you're used to, to discharge the momentum. No big deal, but we need more space for this maneuver than we were initially given."

"No problem. Edith and I know we're in good hands," I said.

Mr. K spared me a grateful look before banking the craft for another attempt. I put my hand into the space between the seats and waggled my fingers. Edith let go of my shoulder and clutched my digits instead. We held each other tight as the little plane circled and came in on the approach once more.

A few minutes before we hit the asphalt, Keone lifted the nose slightly and cut the engine. The noise that had filled our ears for the last hour went silent. "I'm trying to slow us down as much as possible," he explained. I squeezed Edith's hand and gave Mr. K a thumbs up and a grin (perhaps more of a grimace).

We glided in, swift as a gull on the wind and just as quiet. As the little craft touched down on the runway, I could tell that we were going too fast. We bounced back into the air, but Keone's hands were steady on the yoke. We came back down more gently the next time, and thankfully, we stuck that landing.

My not-too-distant memory of aiding in a landing blowout was still fresh in my mind, but after a longer than usual taxi onto a side ramp, we glided to a stop. Keone grinned at us both and turned the engine back on. "Heading to our gate now."

When I removed my hand from Edith's at the private interisland terminal, I noticed my fingers had assumed the shape of a claw. That was a small price to pay for having given the little lawyer some comfort.

Keone got out and hurried off to find a stepladder, and I turned to Edith as we removed our headsets. "Having fun yet?"

Edith removed her fogged up goggles, clutching them by the strap. "These useless things didn't help with that adventure one bit. I missed the whole thing with all the condensation."

"You didn't miss much. We were never in danger."

And if I crossed my fingers behind my back when I said it, I was pretty sure Aunt Fae would forgive me, considering the circumstances.

Our rideshare picked us up outside of the airport, delayed only slightly by Keone and me making sure my PTSD was getting better with repeated exposures to anxiety-provoking kiss stimuli.

The vehicle was a classic—a former blue and white patrol vehicle now equipped with fully-loaded surfboard racks, decorated with tropical stickers, and sporting a hula dancer with swaying hips that wiggled at us from the dash. Our driver, a large man with a bald head and an enormous handlebar mustache, was eager to tell us about the best nightclubs to visit in Honolulu.

"We're here on business," I said, cutting him off. "No time for nightclubs."

"Speak for yourself," Edith said, adjusting her leather flight cap's flaps. "I'm in the mood for a good time after a recent brush with death, young man. Give me the rundown."

"In that case, little lady, I've got a great salsa place in downtown Waikiki I can recommend," the driver said over his shoulder with a wink. "You look like you can still bust a move."

"Oh, you know it, baby." Edith was going to give herself a stroke if she batted her eyelashes any harder.

The two gabbed about nightlife in downtown Honolulu as I stared out the window. Besides the tropical flora, a radiantly blue sky, and a plumeria-scented breeze competing with exhaust fumes, the freeway into the city might have been any urban highway on the main continent of the USA.

I missed the quiet of tiny Ohia already. How was I ever going to go back to my former life? But how could I not? There was no future for my career in Ohia—I had reached the pinnacle of available employment opportunities with the postmaster job. I couldn't afford to buy a house in the area, and I couldn't see the shack being my forever home. Sure, things were going well with Mr. K, but then I'd made it this far with a prospective boyfriend before only to end up back at square one.

Frankly, I was a little scared by how well things were going with Mr. K, especially after this morning's successful kiss fest. I could see the potential for serious heartbreak when he inevitably ditched me because my issues were too much to overcome.

My depressive mulling was interrupted as we pulled up before an impressively large, natural stone building surrounded by a thick fringe of ti plants, with full-grown palm and hala trees dotting its lawn. Lettering at the top of the imposing façade read BERNICE P. BISHOP MUSEUM.

"Here's our digs for the weekend," Edith chortled. "Let's get this party started." She threw the door open and hopped out.

The Bernice Pauahi Bishop Museum was a dignified, massive stone building that held the weighty feeling of history. I stared up at the edifice, adorned with Hawaiian and U.S. flags. Edith grinned beside me, clearly pleased that she surprised me by booking us in the guest-house of the museum.

"You're going to love this place," Edith said. "Now give me a hand up these steps. My energy is zapped after that scary plane ride."

"Your vigor level is just fine, Ms. Pepperwhite, Esquire. We both know you could run laps around me, never mind your age," I teased, but I took Edith's arm anyway.

"Ha!" Edith chuckled, leaning on me. Maybe she really was "zapped" by the morning's events—I wasn't feeling too zippy either. "I'm the Energizer bunny of the two of us, for sure. We'll get settled into our accommodations, and then I'll take you around the museum on a private tour. I used to be a docent here, you know."

"No, I didn't. Staying on the premises is a great surprise," I said.

The guesthouse was around the back of the main building—a rambling, light-filled cottage decorated with flowers and orchids off the museum's primary enclosure. An elderly Hawaiian friend of Edith's, Noelani Oweo, welcomed us.

"I'm the special visitors' concierge for the Bishop, and it's our pleasure to welcome you back, Edith. And to meet you, Kat." She unlocked the building for us and handed me a stack of towels. "It's not glamorous, but it's comfortable. Make yourself at home."

Soon, I was sitting on a bed in my own bedroom, kicking off my shoes and rubbing my feet. A ceiling fan swished overhead, and I picked up a brochure from the nightstand to scan. The Bishop Museum was a large complex that housed several research and education facilities.

I got up and walked to the window. The hardwood floors felt cool against my overheated soles. From my vantage point, I could see the various buildings making up the museum's complex surrounding the gracious, grassy lawn.

"This is incredible," I said, looking out over the century-old palm trees and the open grounds around the main building. Everywhere around us were unique, native plants and striking sculptures in various styles.

"I hoped it would be a treat for you," Edith responded, poking her head into my room. She dabbed at her damp forehead with a handkerchief. "I need to take a load off. Can you find me something to drink?"

"Of course, right away." I headed into the kitchen and opened the fridge. "There's some ginger ale here. Is that okay?"

"Fantastic. I'm going to lie down for a moment," Edith replied, pulling her hot-looking flight pants off.

I returned to her room with a couple of frosty glasses of ginger ale, setting one down on the table beside the bed. Edith already had her head on the pillow, her short white hair a disorderly cloud around her face. "Thanks, hon. And can you close those blinds?"

"Sure." I headed over to rotate the wooden louvers closed and as I did so, I spotted a man standing outside the back door of the museum. Unlike the rest of the museum's visitors wandering in duos and groups, this man stood apart with his arms folded over his chest, scanning the grounds. He stood in the shade of the trees, his short-sleeved white shirt fluttering in the breeze.

I squinted, trying to see his face, but he lifted one arm across his sunglass-covered eyes so I couldn't make out his features. He was of medium height, weight approximately one hundred sixty-five, and there was something familiar about the way he stood. This guy was no idle tourist.

"What's the holdup with the blinds?" Edith said, her eyes shut. She'd finished half the glass of ginger ale and set it aside.

"Edith, I think there's someone looking for us. He's standing outside the main building."

"Maybe he's waiting for someone," Edith murmured. She was clearly falling asleep.

I rotated the blinds shut and the light dimmed. My travel companion was already tuning up a snore when I tiptoed out of the room and closed the door.

I paused outside the door, listening for Edith's steady, snuffling breathing to make sure she was out. I tiptoed barefoot across the creaking wooden floor to the window in my room and targeted where I'd seen the man before.

I scanned the grounds and visitors milling around.

There was no sign of him.

I heard voices faintly through the windows. I tracked an attractive blonde in a grass skirt walking with a group, pointing out an ancient carving to them. A cluster of children sat on the grass around another woman with a pile of books for a presentation.

I peered at the main building of the museum and caught something—a flash of white that moved behind the second story window. I squinted, straining to see more clearly, and suddenly I knew who I was looking at: Ralph, New Ohia's head of security.

✫ 24 ✫

The dude I'd already upgraded to Possible Threat was out of his uniform, but his short black hair and almost military bearing were distinctive.

Ralph being here, at the Bishop Museum of all places, could not be a coincidence.

Edith said that no one knew she was coming to Oahu for the filing, but she'd had to make the arrangements with the Bishop for our lodgings. Who had she talked to? I should have followed up on that. Edith's trip had been planned in advance, which increased the risk of exposure.

I was so lost in thought that when the door to the cottage opened, I nearly jumped out of my Nikes. I raced into the main room, anticipating the worst.

"Hello, Kat," Noelani said, stepping inside.

"Oh, Noelani! I thought you were someone else." I willed my heart to slow down.

"I see Edith is resting. Is everything okay?" Noelani carried a fruit basket full of mangoes, papayas, bananas, and a big fat pineapple.

"She's just a little overtaxed from the flight. I think she'll be on her feet in no time."

"Good," Noelani said. "I'm glad you ladies are here. When do you want to go over to the museum for your visit? I can accompany you and Edith."

I didn't want to go anytime soon and risk running into Ralph patrolling the exhibits. "Later this afternoon. I think I'd like a rest, too." I took the basket from her. "Thanks so much for this, Noelani. Can I get your number? I'll text you when we're ready."

Noelani's warm brown eyes crinkled. "Perfect. I'd like to keep in touch with you. Any friend of Edith's is a friend of mine."

We exchanged contact info and said goodbye. This time, after she left, I locked the door. No one else would be walking into our accommodations unannounced.

I didn't think I'd be able to relax as easily as Edith had, but once the blinds were closed and my eyes shut, I dozed off quickly. But when I woke, I was drenched in sweat and my heart was racing. I'd been dreaming . . . or had I?

I'd been running through a maze of corridors, and at times I could hear the sound of someone crying. I couldn't tell if it was coming from in front of me or behind me. I had to find the source of the sobs and find it fast. But when I turned a corner and was about to see who was so distressed—I woke up.

"*Ugh*. I hate nightmares." I stared up at the ceiling fan, lazily turning above me as I lay on the bed. I was in Honolulu, in a great setting and in no danger, even though a creepy security guy was hanging around outside. "I'm the dangerous one with my combat training," I reminded myself. I decided not to tell Edith I'd recognized the man as Ralph, the New Ohia Security guy. I'd wait until the time seemed right to give her that news.

Edith poked her head into my room. "I heard voices earlier. Were you on the phone? And where'd that basket in the kitchen come from?"

"Noelani came by and brought the fruit basket. Very nice of her."

I glanced at the clock on the nightstand. "Holy Rip Van Winkle, it's nearly three. We should get going if we're going to see the museum before dinner."

I stood and straightened my tank top, looking out the window at the grounds and the Bishop Museum beyond them. "I just had a bad dream. Going to see the exhibits should help clear my mind."

"Perfect," Edith said. "Because we have a lot to see."

It turned out Noelani couldn't join us; the timing didn't work out for her. The Bishop Museum was a gigantic building, and as Edith held forth about each display, I was glad I'd had a rest before we took on the place.

The exhibits, on three different floors, were a study in Hawaiian history: the coming of the first Polynesian settlers, the arrival of Captain Cook, and Hawaii's annexation by the United States. We wandered through a timeline of the early missionaries, the introduction of the sugar industry, and the overthrow of the Hawaiian monarchy in 1893. My eyes stung at the injustice of the events as Edith recounted them before a portrait of the overthrown Queen.

But it was the room of ancient artifacts that held my attention the most. The brilliant red and yellow feathered helmet and cape of Hawaiian royalty and tall ceremonial staffs decorated with rows of bright feathers were breathtaking. A club edged in shark teeth, slings, knives, poi pounders, and calabashes were all tools of a well-developed society that had thrived before the arrival of Captain Cook.

All the while, I kept my eye on the exits and took defensive positions in each room, should Ralph or anyone else with nefarious intentions approach us. But there was no sign of him or anyone else surveilling us.

Edith took photos of everything, and once she'd snapped a shot of the statue of Kamehameha the Great, we left the museum and walked slowly toward the beach. There were a few tourists and locals walking the sidewalks, most of them smiling and exchanging greetings with us as cars whizzed by on the road. Thankfully, I saw no sign of Ralph or anyone else who appeared suspicious along the way.

The beach was beautiful, with the waves lapping gently and the aqua expanse of ocean in the distance. We sat in the sand and watched a few boogie boarders riding the surf. Red, orange, and yellow hibiscus bloomed in a hedge along the beach.

"The guy I saw looking for us was a security agent from New Ohia," I told Edith at last. "Who could have leaked where you were going to someone like him?"

She frowned, adjusting the brim of the crushable straw boater she'd put on for our outing. "I just called Noelani, and she made the arrangements. I didn't tell her why I was coming to Oahu, but I didn't ask her to keep it secret, either."

"Do you trust Noelani?" I felt bad even asking that.

"Of course I do!" She huffed indignantly. "Noelani's been a friend forever."

"Then she won't mind us asking who she might have talked to about your visit here," I said. "We need to find out who knew." I took my phone out. "No time like the present. I'll put her on speaker."

Noelani picked up quickly. "Hi, girls! How did you like the museum?"

"I loved it. Thanks for the great hospitality." I stared out at the people walking along the beach and the wind tickled my hair. "I have you on speaker, and Edith is here too. We have a question for you."

"Hi, Noelani!" Edith said, hollering loudly enough to make a passerby jump.

"Hi Edith! And like I said, any friend of Edith's is a friend of mine. What can I help you with?"

I took Edith's elbow and drew her closer, holding a finger up to signal being a little quieter. The attorney nodded and we both hunched over the phone.

"Was there anyone you might have mentioned Edith's trip to?" I asked.

There was a short pause. "I told a friend of Edith's from New Ohia. She works for the museum—a young lady by the name of Ana. I didn't give her any details, but I did tell her you were coming to Oahu."

"Ana might have tipped off the man we saw," I said to Edith.

Edith frowned. "Could he have followed us?"

"That's impossible because we took an unscheduled, private flight," I reminded my lawyer friend. "The guy had to know we were going to be at the Bishop Museum."

"I never should have told her. I didn't know it was a problem." Noelani sounded upset. "I'm sorry, Edith, I really am. I didn't think it was a big deal."

"It's fine, but please don't mention we're here to anyone else," Edith said. "I'm not just here for fun. I'm doing some confidential lawyer business in Honolulu. It's a sensitive case."

"Of course, Edith, I understand. If there's anything else I can do, please let me know. And I do apologize about Ana."

I ended the call and Edith groaned, covering her face with her hands. "Ana, Ana, Ana," she said.

"Who the heck is Ana?" I asked.

"My granddaughter," Edith said.

❧ 25 ❧

I probably shouldn't have been surprised that Edith had a granddaughter, but there was something about her that was so . . . singular.

Solo.

What the heck, I'll just say it—old-maidish.

She just didn't seem like the kind of woman who'd ever fussed over a kid, let alone the next generation of kids. But clearly, judging by her upset expression, that was exactly what she was doing right now.

"I got Ana a job here at the Bishop," Edith said. "Not an exciting job, she works janitorial." She sighed again. "My granddaughter has . . . problems."

I scooted over to sit closer to my much smaller companion. "What kind of problems?"

"Drug problems to anesthetize the chip on her shoulder," Edith said crisply. "I had a daughter while in college, back in the days when it was better for women to be married while raising a baby. I'd never intended to get pregnant, so I gave my child up for adoption. She looked me up when Ana was born just to read me the riot act about how I'd done her ill, even though her adoptive family was a perfectly lovely couple as far as I knew." Edith stared at the sparkle of sun on the ocean for a moment before continuing.

"When she was grown, Ana sought me out and told me she wanted to get to know me. Of course, I took her in, no questions asked." Edith's jaw tightened. "Ana cozied up to me so she could get my passwords, assume my identity, empty my bank accounts, and rack up my credit cards. She robbed me blind—all the while flouncing around Ohia, doing drugs, and seducing married men in town."

"Oh, Edith." I could think of no words of comfort.

"I had her sign a contract confessing to her crimes before I shipped her off to Oahu. I told her I'd hold onto it as long as she never came back or bothered me again. If she did, I'd turn her in to the police. That was a year ago. We haven't spoken since." She sighed. "But I also couldn't bear to tell anyone about our falling-out. Noelani didn't know. No one did."

"With that kind of bad blood between you, it seems likely Ana would take any opportunity that presented itself to do you wrong— like tell Ralph that you were going to be here."

"Especially since Ralph was one of the men she slept with," Edith said miserably.

"Well, now we know how Ralph knew where to find us," I said, rising to my feet and scanning the beach for any sign of the security operative. "And if Ralph knows we're here, then the rest of his team and that nasty replacement for Jimmy Ching probably know too." I grabbed Edith by the elbow and drew her to her feet. "I hate to say it, but we need to stay in the guesthouse until the filing and keep a low profile. Who knows how far New Ohia Vision will go to prevent you from filing that cease and desist order?"

"Dagnabbit," Edith said, but made no protest as I tugged her rapidly across the sand, working my phone with my other hand to call a rideshare. Poor Edith. All the starch had gone right out of her at the reminder of her granddaughter's betrayal.

I bundled the elderly attorney into a battered purple Prius, and we headed back to the Bishop. I got out first, holding the door for Edith and scanning the area. The museum was closed, and shadows were lengthening. The breeze had mellowed, and mynah birds were gathering for their evening gabfest.

The coast was, temporarily at least, clear.

"I really wanted to take you to get a bite to eat at one of my favorite restaurants in Waikiki," Edith protested at last. "Surely we can do that."

"Nope. It's takeout food for us, and full lockdown until Monday morning," I informed her. "And we need to take steps to stop Ana from getting into our lodgings. She probably has a set of keys."

"Oh no!" This seemed to give Edith a bit of energy to hurry toward our cottage. "I didn't think of that."

As soon as we reached the door and discovered it was unlocked, I knew we were too late.

Ana, or one of the security guards from New Ohia, had tossed our rooms thoroughly. Our suitcases were dumped out, and our clothing and belongings kicked around. Even the bedding had been stripped from the beds and the mattresses moved.

Edith went as white as her hair and swayed on her feet. "Oh no!"

"Sit down." I guided her over to the couch. "I'll make sure the place is clear and see if anything was taken."

I hurried through the small guesthouse. Though everything was thrown around, nothing seemed to be missing or destroyed. I went into the bathroom and recoiled from a message written on the mirror in lipstick: DIE, YOU MEAN OLD BAG! Clearly, the person who ransacked our rooms was Edith's estranged, deranged granddaughter.

"I'll just be a moment, using the facilities," I told Edith, shutting and locking the door behind me. A handy bottle of glass cleaner was stashed under the sink. I soaked the message and scrubbed it off with paper towels. No reason to stress out my traveling companion further.

Once the lipstick was gone, I did my business and then cleaned up our overturned toiletries. When I returned to the main room, I was relieved to find Edith sipping a ginger ale, the color coming back into her cheeks.

"You'll be glad to know I didn't leave the court papers here," she said. "I kept them and all of my valuables right here in my fanny pack." She patted the zipped pouch around her waist.

"Thank goodness!" I unslung the backpack I carried in lieu of a purse and held it up. "All my valuables are secure as well. This is kind of like shutting the barn door after the cow is gone, but can you call Noelani and tell her we need the locks changed today? If that's not possible, we'll need to book a hotel somewhere."

"I'll tell her the truth about Ana," Edith said. "I'm sure they won't want an employee who would do something like this working at the museum." Her statement made me wonder why Edith referred Ana to the Bishop in the first place. She'd have access to priceless items as an employee. Love could be blind when it came to family.

"Can I have a bit of privacy to make this call?" Edith asked. "I feel awkward."

"Of course. I have plenty of cleanup to get started with." I glanced around. "The good news is Ana didn't take anything. She also didn't break anything. It's just a mess. My guess is she was looking for the papers to give to her boyfriend."

"She also didn't want to give the cops any more ammunition than they'll already have when I turn her in," Edith said stoutly and took out her phone. "Because I'm sending the police Ana's signed confession after I call Noelani."

I was relieved Noelani hurried to have the locks changed on the guesthouse, so we didn't have to relocate. She also revoked Ana's access and status as an employee. The police sent officers to take Edith's statement, but Ana herself could not be located, and her phone was disconnected.

All of that took the remaining wind out of Edith's proverbial sails. By the time we'd finished with her police report, cleaned up, remade the beds, and eaten some takeaway pizza delivered to the front steps of the Bishop (I wasn't taking any chances allowing access to our cottage), she seemed to have shrunk in size even more. I helped her to bed and tucked her in.

"Things will be better in the morning," I said, smoothing the blanket over her.

"I doubt that very much, but at least we've only got one more day to go before the filing and then we can go home to Ohia," Edith whispered. She was a little Yoda propped on the pillows, her eyes closed, a nimbus of pale hair around her fragile skull.

I kissed Edith's forehead and didn't even feel a shiver of touch PTSD. I turned off the light and shut the door gently on my new friend, already asleep.

Edith could rest easy. I would be watching over her.

Once a Secret Service agent, always a guardian.

You'd think a whole day stuck inside the guesthouse while beautiful Honolulu carried on without us would be a hardship for Edith and me, but it wasn't. We recharged our depleted emotional and physical batteries by playing Scrabble and watching the Sunday crowds on the museum grounds through the louvers.

Edith slowly shed the despair that seemed to have weighed on her like a lead blanket. Turning in her granddaughter had been tough, but she'd done it—and without any handwringing or second-guessing, either.

"We all make choices," she said after acing me with a seven-letter word. "And we live with the repercussions."

"Wisely said." I shook my head and gathered up the Chinese food cartons that once held our dinner. "I give up. Let's go to bed. We've got a big day tomorrow."

Once again, I slept better than expected. Noelani had the museum's security team on alert and the surveillance cameras tuned in to our abode. One thing I'd learned in the Secret Service was that once you'd done all you could to manage risk in a threat situation, the best thing you could do was to fully rest so you were ready for anything.

Monday morning rolled around, and I prepared as best I could. I walked laps around the grounds of the museum checking for anything suspicious, then showered and dressed. I had coffee ready and my bags packed by the back door long before Edith came out of her room.

The attorney had dressed carefully in a stretchy black pantsuit with a bow tie at her neck. She carried her aviation hat and bomber jacket and towed her little hard-sided case.

"To the courthouse we go," she said, patting her waist pack. "Let's do this."

❧ 26 ❧

"From the car to the courthouse," Edith said, "and then from the courthouse to the airplane." She was pale as a gecko's belly as she touched the fanny pack containing the filing. Our rideshare, a big F-150 with an extended cab and surf racks, dropped us at the steps of the Honolulu courthouse. I got out first, keeping my gun hand clear and scanning for threats.

The steps were deserted but for some mynah birds hopping around. Morning traffic whizzed by in the background. We arrived right when the clerk's office inside opened in order to minimize exposure.

"It'll be over before you know it." I closed the truck's door and waved our driver off. I stepped to the wide cement staircase, looking and listening carefully. I led Edith up the stairs toward a pair of glass doors. Beyond them, a security station with a metal detector screened for weapons. I'd have to surrender the weapon I carried there.

As we reached the top of the stairs, a shot rang out.

Nearby, a mynah squawked, and its tail feathers exploded. Edith squeaked and stumbled on the steps, landing on her tush. She started to rise, but I thrust her back down with a hand and moved to cover her with my body. I guided her forward to tuck behind a pillar.

"Stay low, you're still exposed!" A second shot cracked, and a chip of concrete exploded from the step only a few feet away. "We have to get inside!"

The glass doors were closed, but through them I could see a pair of court bailiffs in dark blue uniforms, each with a service weapon in hand, running toward us. They opened the doors, and the bailiff on the left spotted me. "Get down!" he shouted.

I squatted low and drew Edith's metal suitcase in front of us, peering around its fragile cover to see where the shots were coming from. Across the street from the courthouse, behind one of the large monkeypod trees the area was famous for, I spotted the barrel of a rifle.

But that wasn't where the next shot came from. The sound rang out from a rampart beside the stairs, where the mynahs fled after their comrade's near-death experience.

"We have to move!" I shouted at Edith, who was perched frozen against the pillar. The bailiffs behind us yelled into their radios, calling for a lockdown and backup.

I reached behind me to grab Edith by the elbow, lifting her to a crouch as I backed toward the doors—and safety. "You're in the line of fire," I told Edith. "We have to get inside!"

More shots sounded, and something whizzed past my cheek. I glimpsed a woman behind the rampart, her hair hidden under a ball cap and wraparound sunglasses hiding her eyes—but the boxy black shape of a Glock in her hands was unmistakable.

"Ana! No!" Edith yelled. "Stop!"

The woman fired at us in answer.

The bullet tore into the aluminum suitcase I held but didn't pass through it, thank the deities. I pulled the shield of a suitcase after us as we headed for the door, the wheels clattering on the cement. "Cover us!" I shouted to the bailiffs.

The first man stood by the front door, pistol drawn, guarding it, as the second ran past him to hold the door open for us. I let go of the fragile cover of the suitcase and tugged Edith through the doors. The bailiff let go of the door and it closed behind us. Hopefully, the glass was bulletproof.

A third guard, posted at the security scanner, headed toward us, his eyes wide and a radio clutched to his ear. "Get down!"

I didn't take the time to ask why. I simply squeezed Edith's elbow and tugged her to the floor. The gun felt heavy in my hands as I sat up and held it steady, my arms stretched out and my eyes on the doorway. Edith's body was warm behind me, though her breath sounded ragged, and I could feel her trembling. She was okay—she was alive.

My ears still rang from the shots. My nostrils flared at the stink of gunpowder. My body vibrated with tension. Colors seemed too bright, and the sound of yelling outside was too loud.

Adrenaline was a potent drug.

"Holy cow," Edith said.

"Yep," I told her, not taking my eyes off the door. "I saw two shooters. One was a woman."

"It was Ana," Edith said.

"I'm sorry, Edith."

"Yeah, me too." She sounded miserable.

"Let's get further inside." I had to protect Edith until the situation was resolved. I helped the little lawyer to her feet, still keeping her behind me.

The bailiff came forward from behind the scanner. "The police are on their way. The shooters got into a getaway car and took off. The threat is over."

Edith pointed to my arm. "You're bleeding."

I'd worn a short-sleeved T-shirt that morning. I brushed my arm with my thumb, then clenched my teeth. The cut stung. "It's nothing. I'm okay," I told Edith. "Probably got cut with a flying cement chip from the stairs."

The courthouse foyer was small, with a pair of benches on either side of a low table topped with a potted plant. Edith, shaking from head to toe, needed help through the scanner area after I handed my weapon to the bailiff.

"I never fired a shot with this," I told him.

"Ballistics will verify." He bagged my gun. "Please take a seat on the bench so the police can get your statement."

"This attorney and I came here from Maui to file an important document. The shooters tried to prevent that. We're going to file, then we'll make a statement for the police."

"That's not procedure." The bailiff frowned. "The whole building is in lockdown right now."

I squinted at his badge. "Officer . . . Bowman. With all due respect, we are going to file this cease and desist order at the clerk's office. The threat won't be over until we do." That last statement earned us a security escort all the way to the court clerk, and an over-ride of the lockdown so that Edith could file her motion at last.

Late afternoon sun slanted over the steep, green ridges along the edge of Maui as Edith and I flew toward Hana later that day. Mr. K was not piloting the little commuter plane we were on, and I was almost relieved. The post-adrenaline crash had set in for both of us, and I didn't have the energy to catch him up on our harrowing experience.

Edith had fallen asleep, her mouth hanging open. Snores fogged up the window she leaned against. I adjusted her leather aviation hat to give her a little more privacy and tucked the bomber jacket more securely around her. Truth was I could have used a nap as well, but my job protecting her wouldn't be over until she was out of my custody.

We'd called ahead, and Josie was meeting us at the airport. She'd promised to give me a lift back to Ohia after we saw Edith safely home, together.

I stared out the window at the nearby cliffs, reflecting on the hours since the attempted shooting on the courthouse steps. The Honolulu Police, the FBI, and the Oahu prosecutor's office were all looking for the shooters. Edith and I had been questioned extensively. I'd asked for a phone call and rang Sophie's friend and FBI Agent Marcella Scott to help us get out of there, since she was already working on building the case against New Ohia Vision. Thankfully, the beautiful Italian FBI agent facilitated our departure before poor Edith keeled over from tiredness.

"You two get back to Ohia," Marcella told us sternly down at the Honolulu Police station. She'd met us there with her hunky husband, Detective Marcus Kamuela, whose connections helped speed up our interview. "And stay out of this case from here on out! We've got it handled."

"I sure hope you do, Special Agent Scott," I murmured, watching our rapid approach to land at Hana's tiny airport. Because now we knew how far those gangsters behind New Ohia would go to protect their investment.

The flight landed without any theatrics. I unbuckled my belt and pulled my backpack out from under the seat in front of me.

Edith woke, yawned, and straightened the flaps of her leather pilot hat. "Oh, I feel like a limp noodle!" she said. "I'm not used to so much excitement these days."

She sounded more like her old self. She'd been remarkably steady during the ordeal, especially considering it was likely that her granddaughter had been one of the shooters. "Those bailiffs were amazing," Edith gushed. "I'm so glad they were there. I don't think we'd have made it inside without them."

"They did a good job," I agreed.

"But not as good a job as you did, protecting me." Edith kicked the metal carry-on stowed under the seat in illustration. The police removed the slug from it and saved it as evidence before returning the case to her. "We should be safe now that the motion is filed on

Oahu." Edith blinked up at me through her flight goggles. "Right, Kat?"

"I sure hope so," I said. "No guarantees."

Edith groaned.

I patted her shoulder. "Things will be better in the morning."

"You keep saying that," she grumbled, preceding me up the narrow aisle as I toted our bags. "But to quote you, 'no guarantees.'"

In the parking lot, Josie hurried to meet Edith, tugging her oxygen tank along. "Edie, honey! Are you okay?"

"Absolutely fine," Edith said. "Thanks to Kat, here."

Though we'd called ahead and briefed her, Josie wanted a blow-by-blow account of the whole weekend. I let them drive ahead in Josie's VW van so they could talk, while I followed in Edith's lime green subcompact.

Edith's house was a tidy plantation-style home with a postage-stamp lawn in Hana. Lush potted orchids lined her porch, and a sweet calico cat greeted Edith with a happy mew. The kitty, whose name was Butter, twined around my legs in welcome.

"Couldn't be more different than Tiki, the cat who lives with me," I said. "Tiki will scratch you just for fun."

"Give her a little noni juice in her water," Josie advised. "It's very calming for the nerves."

"Speaking of. I'll have some of that noni tea if you wouldn't mind fixing some," Edith said to Josie before turning to face me. Josie went off to brew the tea while I endured a long hug from Edith. "Thanks so much for everything. You're my heroine, Kat. You never hesitated. You must have been a terrific Secret Service agent."

I swallowed past a lump in my throat and shrugged. "It's the training."

Edith shook her head. "It's not just that and you know it."

Thankfully, Josie reappeared. "I'll take Kat home, and Mattie will come stay with you, Edie, until I get back. She's on her way."

"That's too much fuss," Edith protested.

Josie looked to me for backup. "Could Edie still be in danger?"

I assessed the attorney. From her pale face to her rumpled clothing, she seemed in danger of collapsing. While it was a stretch that
Ralph or Ana would seek her out here, company right now couldn't
hurt. "That's a good idea, Josie."

I took off to check that all the windows and doors were secure
before we left and Mattie arrived to stay with Edith.

❦ 27 ❦

Josie took me home, and I was grateful that she seemed all talked out as we drove the winding, darkened road from Hana to Ohia.

We pulled up at my shack, and I smiled for the first time that day to see Tiki sitting on the beach boulder that made my front step. She was waiting for dinner, her yellow eyes slitted with temper as her tail lashed impatiently. She let out a complaining yowl.

"Nothing like having a sweet pet to welcome you home," I said.

Josie stopped me from getting out of her car with a hand on my arm. "Please take very good care. There could still be danger here in Ohia, for you . . . and not just from your grumpy cat."

"Thanks, Josie. I'm a professional, and I'm armed. I'll be fine." HPD had checked that my weapon hadn't been fired and returned it to me, though without any ammo. Good thing I had extra in my drawer. I stepped out of the van and patted the roof of the VW in goodbye. Josie pulled away with a wave.

I turned back to face Tiki. "I hope you didn't shred the chairs or anything with me gone." She turned on her rumble purr now that we were alone and came to stand by my side as I unlocked the door.

I'll admit it. I stood for a moment after I'd turned the key with my eyes closed, bracing myself. I really didn't want to face a scene like we'd dealt with at the Bishop Museum guesthouse. There's something personally violating about having your stuff torn apart and thrown around like so much confetti. It's demoralizing.

But what would anyone be looking for in my place? They'd already broken in and stolen the memory drive, and I'd taken my laptop with me.

I took a deep breath, blew it out, and pushed the door open. It gave a creak like a coffin opening. Thankfully, my shack was undisturbed. Fatigue hit me like a wheelbarrow of cannonballs after I ate and showered, but that was to be expected after surviving a serious threat situation. I put a Band-Aid on the cut on my arm, took a preventative Tylenol, and drank a liter of water. I'd be fine in the morning.

And then, I woke to the sound of someone knocking on the door of the shack.

Also, Tiki was sleeping on my head again. I spared a second for gratitude that we'd finally had that flea bath as she leaped off my pillow to glare out from under the table.

The knock came again.

It was early, judging by the dove gray light coming through the bullet hole in the wall. Completing my assessment, I concluded I wasn't feeling social or particularly hospitable; in fact, I was downright grumpy and wanted another hour or six of sleep.

"Who is it?" I hollered.

"Keone. I heard what happened on Oahu from my cuz." His voice sounded upset.

But Mr. K was the one person I really wouldn't mind seeing.

I tossed my covers aside and padded to the door, combing my hair with my fingers and tugging down my sleep tee to so it covered a little more than my hoo-ha.

I opened the door, cocking a hip and leaning on the jamb. Early morning air wafting up from below reminded me I wasn't wearing a bra.

"You rang?" I purred.

Keone stared at me, his eyes widening.

I enjoyed watching his expression change from worried frustration to something much warmer. He stepped inside and grabbed me around the waist, hauling me in for a kiss.

Sadly, gentle reader, being grabbed does not work for me even when I've invited it and think I'm ready.

My knee came flying up to hit him where it hurt, and I had him face-planted on the floor with said knee between his shoulder blades before I could tell my reflexes to stand down.

"Ow," Keone said, against the floorboards.

"Oh, son of a thermometer. I'm so sorry!" I jumped up. "Are you okay?"

"I will be. Eventually." He curled up on his side, his hands over the family jewels. His eyes were shut, and he breathed heavily; his tan skin had gone greenish.

"What can I do?" I exclaimed frantically, pushing my hands into my hair and pulling on handfuls of it. "Do you need ice? Can I help you up onto the bed?"

Mr. K opened his eyes slowly, as if even his eyeballs hurt. His gaze started at my feet and traveled a long way up my legs, and then over the rest of me. "Maybe you could take that shirt off. That would make me feel better, I think."

I was eager to make amends. I whipped the sleep tee off over my head and knelt beside him. I folded the warm shirt and lifted his head to set it underneath like a pillow. "How's that feel?"

I was only wearing my sensible bikini underwear, now. They were pink and spelled out TUESDAY all over because I've always weirdly loved day-of-the-week panties.

"Much better, thanks." He was frankly ogling, and I didn't mind a bit. He'd earned it.

I leaned down and kissed him. "I'm so sorry," I whispered against his lips. "I thought I was ready, but you moved too fast."

"I keep forgetting," he whispered back.

"Me too."

We kissed until Tiki made a rude noise and butted her head against my thigh, reminding me she was watching. "All right, all right." I stood up and walked over to the closet with its built-in shelves. I opened the door and reached in to grab some clothes for work.

"Those panties," he said in a strangled voice. "They say 'Tuesday.'"

"Yep." I glanced back over my shoulder. He'd sat up, but his hands were still cupped over his groin. "These panties remind me what day it is. But I'm running out—I only have enough clean ones for two weeks. I have to figure out my laundry situation."

Keone watched me dress with a glazed expression on his face. He was probably still fighting nausea, poor thing. "Men are so vulnerable down there. It's kind of God's cruel joke on them," Aunt Fae used to say.

"It's early on a workday, Keone. Why'd you come by, again?" I tugged a navy polo shirt down over the white lace bra I'd donned and tucked it into my jeans.

His brows drew down in a scowl as he slowly rose to his feet, grasping the table leg for support. He sat gingerly on the bed. "I heard someone shot at you and Edith while in Oahu. After your place was vandalized the day before."

"Yeah. It was a little hairy at the courthouse, but once I got Edith inside, we were safe. And the bailiffs were great." I hurried to fill Tiki's bowl with kibble before she took a bite out of one of us. "Want some coffee?"

Mr. K didn't answer.

I glanced over from where I was rinsing out the carafe.

Keone's expression was what one of my romance novels would've called "thunderous."

"And you didn't think to call me and let me know? At any point, about any of it?" His voice rose. "I heard all this from Pono, who heard it from Lei, who heard it from the FBI!"

"We were fine." I didn't like his tone. "I handled it. Or rather, I handled it with help from a number of professionals, including Agent Marcella Scott, her husband, a detective, and others. Like I said, the bailiffs were right on top of the threat and drove off the shooters."

Keone breathed loudly through his nose as I got the coffee going. Finally, as the pot was coughing up some caffeine juice, I pulled out one of the chairs and sat on it. "This is one of those relationship things, isn't it? Banana."

"Your safe word." His knitted brows gradually smoothed out. His gaze searched my face. Finally he said, "Yes, it's a relationship thing."

"Explain what I did wrong."

"When a guy and girl are . . . hanging out . . . even in a relationship that isn't defined, like ours . . . and when the girl is in danger, even after the fact, the guy wants to know. From her. Not someone else."

"Why? It's not like you could have done anything, and you'd just have worried." I leaned forward earnestly. "Help me understand."

Keone rolled his eyes heavenward. "It's . . . caveman stuff. Hard to explain."

"Okay. I understand. I'll call you next time something happens."

"Even if it's already over and I couldn't have done anything to help," he said, his brown eyes drilling into mine.

"Yeah. Even then."

He smiled at last and patted his knee invitingly. "Good. Are you feeling up for a kiss? Because I'm all better now."

That was quite enjoyable and might have gone somewhere involving taking my shirt off again, only someone knocked on the door. "Kat? Are you in there? It's Opal."

I sighed and got off of Keone's lap, tucking my polo back into my jeans as I opened the door. "Hey, Opal."

My storekeeper friend wore a bright yellow scarf around her shoulders today, with a giant rhinestone heart on it that was so sparkly it made me squint. "What happened on Oahu? Josie called to tell me things got gnarly over there." She peered around me and spotted Keone. "Oh, hi. Why don't you both come over for some coffee cake before Kat has to open the post office? You can tell us all about it, and we've got some news for you, too."

And with that, she marched off. Her yellow Crocs were the exact same shade as her scarf.

"Guess you're going to get the whole story when I tell it to Artie and Opal," I told Keone. "I hope that's okay."

"Next time, tell me first," he grumped.

I patted his jaw. "I would have, but we were too busy making out. Let's go update the coconut wireless."

As always, Opal's strong coffee and Artie's potent, sugary coffee cake got me talking rapidly, and I was able to fill them and Keone in on a blow-by-blow account of our trip to Oahu as we sat in their cozy kitchen.

"So you don't know for sure who shot at you?" Keone asked through a mouthful of coffee cake.

"Not entirely. More than likely it was Ana, Edith's granddaughter, and Ralph from New Ohia Security," I said. "Edith identified the female shooter as Ana, but when pressed couldn't positively swear to it. The woman had a hat and sunglasses on, and her hair was concealed. Anyway, the FBI is taking the lead in the investigation at this point, but Lei and Pono are the boots on the ground here on Maui. I'll give them a call from the post office when I get to the landline. Someone needs to check Ralph's whereabouts."

"Do you think Edith is safe now that the papers are filed?" Opal fiddled with her scarf.

"I wouldn't have left her last night if I didn't think so," I said stoutly, even as I felt a quiver of alarm. "The backers of New Ohia are affiliated with the mob, yes. But they're businessmen. They won't want to attract more attention by going after a lawyer like Edith. I think the attack at the courthouse was probably initiated by

Ana, and now that her name and face are everywhere, Edith should be okay here."

But my alarm antennae wouldn't go back down once raised, and Opal seemed to confirm it as she said, "Let's see what the runes say."

Without further ado, she undid the garish pin and whipped off the cloth. She shook the kukui nut shells into her palm, closed her eyes, breathed on them, and dropped them on the fabric-covered surface.

Artie closed his eyes and settled back in his sturdy chair as Keone and I leaned forward with Opal to study the pattern the shells made.

"This isn't good," she announced, after a long moment of silence. "I see danger. Darkness. And a deadly force that is very nearby."

"Couldn't that refer to New Ohia being nearby?" I asked, playing devil's advocate.

"I see a red hat," Artie said suddenly, his resonant voice authoritative.

"That does it," Opal said. "I'm calling the Red Hatters. Someone should go stay with Edith and guard her until there's some break in this case. The ladies can take turns keeping her covered."

Keone nodded. "It can't hurt."

I hadn't known what to expect from Mr. K as far as the psychic activities of my geriatric friends were concerned, but he seemed to be taking Opal's and Artie's insights as seriously as I was inclined to.

I glanced at the big wall clock over the row of ceramic roosters in various comical poses decorating a shelf in the Pahinuis' kitchen. "I've got to go open the post office now if I'm going to have time to call Lei and Pono before business hours." I leaned over to give Keone a quick kiss. "See you later, Mr. K. Thanks for stopping by this morning."

"Anytime." He gave a slow smile that melted my innards. I lifted a hand in goodbye and hustled off to the shack to get my keys.

Lei wasn't surprised to hear from me when I reached her on the post office phone. "Marcella called yesterday. I'm up to speed. We're on our way out to interview the new guy in charge of New Ohia, Roland Thompkins, and find out where Ralph's been the last few days."

"Oh, good." I blew out a breath. "Sounds like things are moving along. But I'm worried about Edith. Do you think she's safe?"

"Probably, now that the papers are out of her hands and filed at court," Lei said.

"Yes, but . . . what about her granddaughter, Ana?"

"There's a Be On the Look Out for Ana Davies at the airports and with the Coast Guard," Lei said. "We'll pick her up. She's not a professional; she won't last long on the run."

"Okay. I hope you're right about that. On our end, the Red Hat Society ladies are going to take turns keeping Edith company until we know the threat is over."

"That can't hurt. Pono and I will check in with you after we interview Thompkins, and let you know what's going on over there with the security guy."

"Sounds good." I glanced up at a loud pounding on the front panels of the exterior door. It was nine a.m. "Duty calls. The mail must go on." I said goodbye, wishing I felt more reassured.

Ohia was isolated. We were on our own out here.

28

The day flew by as I was the only postal worker on hand in Ohia. I was grateful for the extra time my boss had taken to supervise my work and train me. Though the mail took past noon to sort into all the boxes, and I was flummoxed by a certified mail package going to Tonga, a quick call to Mr. Hanoi got me over the hump.

I didn't have time to think about the case until it was four p.m. and I was locking up. I'd hardly had time to pee let alone eat anything, so those were the first orders of personal business once I'd secured the premises.

I was heading back to my office from locking the front doors when the phone rang on the main desk. I glanced at the clock; better to answer it than have an angry customer show up tomorrow. "Ohia Post Office. Kat Smith, Postmaster."

"Kat?" My Washington boss's familiar voice brought me to full attention with a jolt. "I've been trying to reach you on your cell phone, but it doesn't even go to voicemail."

"Ben. Hey." I sat down on the padded stool behind the counter with a thump. "Isn't it super late in Washington?"

"Before midnight, so not bad. Security never sleeps."

"How's our nation's capital?"

"Blood in the water and sharks circling, as usual," my Special Agent in Charge said. "More importantly, how's life in the back of beyond?"

I glanced around the post office fondly. "Great. I've been unexpectedly busy."

"Well, I hope you aren't getting too comfortable there. I've got a new posting for you. Starts at the end of the month."

"What?" My empty stomach tightened, and my mouth went dry.

"Yeah. The Congressman accepted an apology letter from the agency with assurances that your behavior was being addressed, so he called off his goon squad."

"I signed no such letter, nor did I do anything wrong," I said hotly.

"Be that as it may, we issued one on your behalf. You can't reason with some of these guys. I made a judgement call to throw him a bone. Meanwhile, the Vice President, the first female to occupy that office, wants to make a statement. She's requested an all-female detail. I thought you'd be perfect for it."

My heart thudded in my ears. "This is pretty sudden. I need a little time to think about it."

"I thought you'd be thrilled. This is your dream job," Ben said, surprise coloring his tone.

"Of course it is. But I'm . . . in the middle of something here." I couldn't imagine leaving Ohia before I had answers about what was going on with our latest case.

"You can have a couple of days to think about the VP detail, then I have to offer the slot to someone else," Ben said frostily and ended the call.

Back at the shack, my bladder relieved and Tiki appeased by a food offering made while I wolfed down a quick baloney and cheese sandwich, I mulled over Ben's offer. Was the case really my biggest reservation in accepting? I honestly didn't want to think about it right now. Better to focus on finding answers in the next two days.

I was hot and sweaty; a quick swim would be great to cool off, and down by the water I'd have enough signal to call Lei and find out how their interviews in New Ohia had gone. I did a few laps in the bay, watching for sea turtles and washing the stress of the day out of my hair. After, I sat on my terry cloth robe as close as I could get to the water and called Lei on my cell.

She picked up right away. "Where are you, Kat?"

"The beach."

"We're wrapping things up here. We'll stop by."

Moments later, the purple truck known as Stanley pulled up, but neither of the cops got out. Instead, Lei rolled down her window and gestured for me to join her.

"What's the scoop with Ralph?" I put a sandy foot on the chrome step and peered inside the cab. "Is that a snow cone you've got, Pono?"

He held a white paper cone with a bright blue ball of fine, colored ice that he was eating in big bites. His tongue was already the color of the syrup.

Lei had her hands full with two of the cones and handed me a striped one. "Yours is mango, banana, and coconut. We call this 'shave ice' in Hawaii. Much better than a snow cone on the continent."

I took the frozen treat. "Wow. Where'd you get these?"

"A truck came through New Ohia. The driver said Opal sent him over to bring us refreshments after he went through Old Ohia."

"She's so thoughtful. And so are you, for bringing me one." I chomped into my shave ice. The tropical flavors melted delightfully on my tongue. "This really is different than a snow cone."

"Made differently," Pono said, slurping melted juice from his cone. "It's a big block of ice that's literally shaved, versus a grinder chopping up cubes."

"I'll have to see this sometime." I took another bite. "Now, what's the skinny on Ralph?"

"We've got news for you," Lei said. "But it isn't good. How fast can you shower and throw on some clothes?"

I frowned, slurping my rapidly melting tropical shave ice. "What for?"

"We have a task force meeting back in Kahului and we'd like you to come."

"I have to be back by nine a.m. tomorrow to open the post office," I said. "Not sure how I can do that."

"We'll figure something out," Lei said, with a flap of her hand.

I couldn't miss out on this chance to be a part of the larger team investigating the mess of corruption that was the New Ohia development.

"I'll be ten minutes, max."

Finishing the shave ice, I jogged across the road and met Tiki's accusing stare from my top step. "I know, girl. I'm quite the traveler these days. But I'll be back tomorrow. I need you to keep an eye on the place."

She glared and switched her crooked tail, but refrained from swiping me with her paw as I went inside. "Progress," I told her as she followed me inside.

Precisely ten minutes later, after letting Opal and Artie know where I was going and asking Opal to give Tiki some kibble, I hopped into the back of Stanley's extended cab and we got on the road toward Kahului.

Moving aside a soccer ball and a gear bag, I leaned forward between the front seats to speak to the detectives. "Now can you tell me what you found out talking to Thompkins, the new Big Cheese?"

"You'll just have to hear it all over again in the meeting," Lei said. She looked tired, her tan pale around the edges, her curly hair escaping its ponytail.

"You going to make Kat wait all the way to town to hear anything?" Pono teased. He tapped his big hands on the chrome chain-link steering wheel, and his wedding ring clinked. "Our Post-master Sleuth got shot at yesterday. She's earned a preview of coming attractions."

"You're right." Lei said. "But I'm *pau hana*. I'm just gonna put my head against the door and you can give her the bullet points." Lei grabbed a beach towel from the footwell and rolled it up to make a pillow.

"What's 'pow hah nah'?" I asked.

"Means finished work for the day," Lei said sleepily, her eyes closed.

I learned a lot of new lingo when I hung out with these two.

Pono glanced at me, serious now. "Roland Thompkins was not very cooperative. He's every bit as much of a sleazeball as Jimmy Ching. More, in fact, because he's not from Hawaii."

Being "from here" was pretty important to Hawaii people; it appeared to go a long way to adding credibility and gravitas to someone's status. Being from Maine, and sometimes called a "Maine-iac" because of it, I understood that. Everyone from elsewhere was "from away" to locals.

Pono went on. "Thompkins didn't want to give us any information about Ralph or the security team and what they were up to. We had to threaten an FBI shutdown of operations to even get him to show us Ralph's time sheet. Turns out the man was scheduled off the last two days and hasn't reported in to work today. Thompkins, and the rest of the security team, claim not to know where he is. His cell phone went straight to voicemail."

"Surprise, surprise," Lei murmured against her makeshift pillow.

"In other words, all you got was stonewalling," I said.

Lei grunted an agreement, her eyes still closed.

"Except we did get confirmation about Ana Davies and her relationship with Ralph. According to one of the guys, they were having an affair," Pono said.

"That's what Edith told me. Do you think they shot at Edith and me under orders from Thompkins?"

"It's possible, but that guy will deny it until he's blue in the face." Pono downshifted around yet another sharp turn in the bumpy road. "Give us a blow-by-blow account of what went on over on Oahu."

"Sure." I occupied the rest of the drive to Kahului telling the detectives about our interesting weekend at the Bishop Museum and the events that followed.

"And it seems like that might not be the last of the excitement," Pono said.

"I sure hope it is," I said, but I agreed with his assessment. The trouble at New Ohia was far from over.

❧ 29 ❧

The meeting room at Kahului station was one of those personality-free conference rooms that could have been anywhere. Smelling faintly of Lysol, it contained a long Formica conference table, a couple of flags and a podium at one end, whiteboards all around, and no windows.

Lei introduced me to her commanding officer, Captain Omura, and a couple of detectives, Abe Torufu and Gerry Bunuelos, who has been added to the team. The forensic accountant, Heri Leede, was piped in on video along with Special Agent Marcella Scott. Yes, the room could've been anywhere, anyplace, but the faces around the table were a refreshing blend of ethnicities, and that made it Hawaii.

Captain Omura opened the meeting with a brisk, no-nonsense manner. "What do we currently know about Jimmy Ching's murder?"

"Excuse me, Captain, but can we start with what we've come to know about New Ohia?" Agent Scott asked, her voice a little staticky in the feed. "Once we clarify the players in the bigger scheme, who had motive to do away with Jimmy Ching might be clearer."

"All right, then. What do we currently know about what's going on with New Ohia?" Omura tapped her red nails together with a clicking sound.

Heri Leede cleared her throat. Her white hair gleamed against a bright orange sweater set. "As a forensic accountant, I can tell you that the cash and legal documents trail is pointing squarely to a corporation made up of members of the Chang crime family. Something seems to have gone wrong within the group, however, because Jimmy Ching's death just doesn't make sense from a paperwork point of view. Ching was doing an effective job promoting the development and keeping the place going, so New Ohia Vision could continue laundering money and fraudulently selling lots they didn't own. I haven't found anything in the documents or accounting that points to wrongdoing on his part."

Marcella chimed in. "The cabal behind New Ohia has far-reaching tentacles. We are going to need all of our interagency resources to hunt down the connections and stop this essentially illegal development."

"Where does the attack on Kat Smith and Edith Pepperwhite fit into all of this?" Captain Omura asked.

I opened my mouth, but Lei replied first. "Someone sent a security agent from New Ohia to spy on Edith and Kat before they made their filing. Edith's granddaughter, a minor criminal named Ana Davies, has been identified as a potential instigator for the attack; there was also a male shooter who we believe is the same security agent sent to spy on them, Ralph. Pono and I had interviewed him about Jimmy Ching's death. Neither of them have been captured at this point."

"I have a theory." I spoke up, getting eye contact with each of the people around the table. "By taking out Edith Pepperwhite, New Ohia could cut off the head of legal resistance to the development. The citizens of Old Ohia would be hard-pressed to find another lawyer willing to take their case, so that's motive." I blew out a breath and went on. "Ralph and Ana either took matters into their own hands by attacking us or were under orders from New Ohia Vision to stop the filing from going forward."

Nods all around the room at this.

"We're pulling out the stops to find those two," Agent Scott said. "Hopefully, we bring them in soon."

"And now, back to my original question," Captain Omura said. "What do we know about Jimmy Ching's murder?"

"Not much," Pono said, leaning forward on powerful forearms marked with tribal tattoos. "He was whacked in the parking lot of the airport with no witnesses, by someone who was aware of the security guy's hours and rounds. The cause of death was blunt force trauma, and there were no useful forensics on or near his body. So far, we've discovered no personal motive, so our working assumption is that he pissed off someone in his own organization."

"It's safe to assume, since he was getting kickbacks as a part of his job, that he might have skimmed money or done something else to offend his bosses," Lei said. "But we don't have anything concrete."

"So you have no actual suspects," Omura said flatly.

"Maybe Ralph the security guy did it," Lei ventured. "Acting on orders from higher up. His behavior since has certainly been suspicious."

"Since the man is missing, pursue that angle," Omura said. "See if you can trace his whereabouts the day of the murder. Let's consider him a person of interest in more than just the shooting attempt on Ms. Pepperwhite."

Lei offered to take me home to spend the night at her house, and Mr. K, in an act of heroism, told me he'd pick me up early the next morning before work, as he didn't have a flight that day.

"It's your reward for calling me and telling me what's going on," he said, after I rang him from the police station. "We'll get a couple of hours in the car together."

"I really need my own wheels," I said. "I hate bumming rides off everyone."

"I've told you before that I don't mind driving."

But that wasn't the real issue. Committing to getting my own wheels was tantamount to staying on Maui, and I had a job offer and a ticking clock to address first.

The offer Ben made me for the VP protection detail hung on the tip of my tongue to tell Mr. K, but this didn't seem like the right place or time. Maybe in the car on the way back to Ohia I'd find the words.

Lei and I were quiet as she drove toward her place after the meeting in Kahului. The last of the sunset gleamed on the waves along the coast. Lit by the first stars and a fat, yellow moon, the evening painted the sky with streaks of indigo and deep purple.

"I really appreciate the hospitality and that you and Pono invited me to the task force meeting," I said, as we turned off Hana Highway into the verdantly green jungle area of Haiku where she lived.

"It's the least we could do. You didn't have to accompany Edith to Oahu, but it turns out you probably saved her life," Lei said.

I shrugged. Compliments were hard for me.

Once inside her compound, the family's big Rottweiler, Conan, sniffed my pant legs suspiciously and detected *eau de hellcat*. He gave an inquiring "woof!" in a concerned tone.

I patted his enormous head. "I know. I'm worried about being owned by that cat, too."

The case and my career dilemma were pushed from my mind by the cheerful chaos of the family's bedtime routine—which involved baths, stories, laughter, and lots of hugs between Lei, her husband, their son Kiet, and toddler daughter, Rosie.

Watching them, I could see how different my life might have been had my parents survived and maybe added a little brother or sister to the mix.

Later, tucking myself into the twin bed in Lei's back office, I stared at the ceiling and realized something new about myself: I wanted what Lei had, someday.

A beloved partner.

A home of my own.

Maybe even a couple of kids running around.

A dog. Or a cat.

What the heck, why not both?

But how could I get from where I was right now—alone, single, rootless—to somewhere so different?

I fell asleep with salt on my cheeks.

❧ 30 ❧

Right on schedule, at oh-dark-thirty in the morning, Keone pulled up to the gate at Lei and Stevens's place. Lei was up and the coffee was perking. I was vertical and on my feet, though not much more. I pushed the security button by the front door to let Mr. K into their compound.

Conan the Rottweiler rushed the truck, barking to wake the zombies, but that soon turned to groveling and whimpering for attention when he recognized Mr. K.

"Come in and grab a fresh cup of coffee," Lei invited from beside me on the porch. "I'll fix you both some to go."

"Heck yeah," Keone said, shutting his door with a bang and stretching his arms overhead. "Don't mind if I do."

I watched him walk to the porch, petting Conan and murmuring to the dog in that nonsense way people talk to pets. I tried to ignore the warm tickle in my tummy the sight of Mr. K gave me. Leaving this guy for Washington was going to hurt, dang it. After all my attempts to stay detached . . .

Keone reached me and smiled like he liked what he saw. The guy was delusional. I could only imagine my appearance after crying myself to sleep, getting out of bed without brushing my hair, and pulling on yesterday's clothes.

"Good morning. Hug?" He asked.

"Yes, please."

We walked awkwardly inside with me holding on like a koala. Lei grinned at the sight and held up a pair of travel mugs. "I want these back sometime."

"Wouldn't dream of keeping it," I said, letting go of Keone to take a bright yellow, lidded metal cup emblazoned with the name Haiku Elementary School.

"You two better get moving if you're going to beat the tourists and make it to Ohia by nine a.m.," Lei said.

"Just need a quick bathroom stop," Keone said, and she directed him down the hall.

Once he was gone, Lei turned back to me. "Hope you don't plan on breaking that guy's heart."

"Hey," I scowled. "What about me? Keone's the heartbreaker."

She shrugged and took a sip of her coffee. "Just saying. Dude's a goner, I can tell."

I was still pouting over that when we got into his truck and pulled out.

Keone glanced at me. "What's up? Something new on the case?"

"No." I leaned my chin on my hand and stared out the window, taking a morose sip from the mug as the jungle and sky and a waterfall went by. "Got a call from my old boss in Washington."

I stopped. Did I really want to tell him this? No, I did not.

"Go on," Keone prodded.

I sighed. "He wants me for a special all-female protection detail for the Vice President. My dream job."

Silence.

I glanced over at Keone. His hands gripped the wheel tightly and his jaw was bunched, but he met my gaze squarely. "Good thing we kept this whole thing just friends."

"Yeah." Misery made it hard to speak. "I have a short window to give him my answer. I have a feeling I won't have much of a future in the Secret Service if I decline."

"Of course you have to take it," Mr. K said. "When would you leave?"

"End of the month."

"Ah."

We didn't say anything more all the way to Ohia, and that was a long way.

He pulled up beside the post office at eight forty-five a.m. Tiki was waiting on the porch.

"Just time for a shower and change," I said. "Thanks so much for the ride."

"Kat. Wait a minute."

I paused, hand on the door handle as he turned toward me. "If it would make any difference at all—I wish you'd stay."

I met his eyes. "I appreciate that, but I don't think I can."

He nodded. "Makes sense. This place doesn't have much to offer a woman like you."

I got out and shut the door but paused to address him through the open window. "It's not that. Ohia is wonderful. My new friends are wonderful. You're . . . wonderful." I blinked hard because there was something in my eye, by golly. "I've put a lot into this career, and I want a few things out of life before I'm ready to step out of the fast lane."

"We'll have to discuss what those things are sometime." Keone's expression was neutral as he raised a hand in goodbye and pulled away.

We hadn't made a date to get together. Maybe I'd seen the last of him.

I turned to face the shack and Tiki. For the first time ever, that darn cat advanced to twine around my legs and give a rumbling purr, just like a normal, friendly feline.

"Oh, dang it." I needed to get into the shower so I could bawl my head off before I had to face the public from behind the counter of the post office.

The workday flew by. Ohia was definitely a lot to handle without a second person on staff. It seemed like every time I tried to leave the counter to use the bathroom or, gosh dang it, eat something, an impatient DING! would come from the front counter.

Tough as it was to keep up, all of it kept me from having time to think about the clock ticking on my career dilemma. Or the case.

That is, until Roland Thompkins came in and flashed his veneers at me. "Hey little lady."

"Not exactly little." I stood to my full height and eyeballed his comb-over from above. "I prefer Postmaster Smith."

He didn't miss a beat. "Postmaster Smith, I need to order one of those commercial mailing machines. We're sending out a promo campaign." He held up a large postcard with a photo of the sunset over Ohia Bay on one side and the nine-hole course with model homes overlooking it on the other side. "Sweet, isn't it?"

I opened my mouth to say "you can't sell what you don't own," but I wasn't supposed to have a clue about their scam. "Let me get that information for you," I said.

My stomach felt like I'd swallowed a tackle box of sinkers as I got on the computer and helped Thompkins order the commercial machine. How many more folks would be duped into buying into New Ohia before we could shut it down?

The development coordinator's visit was near closing, and after a small rush of customers coming to check their boxes, I locked up. The evening stretched ahead, empty of activities and full of angst.

I needed something to do, and I was out of clean clothes. Opal had told me there was a laundromat in Hana. I'd load up my stuff and take the bike there, buy something to eat at a food truck, and keep my mind off Ben's proposal—because I was no closer to feeling clear about saying yes to his offer than I had been yesterday.

The chore of riding down the road with a bag stuffed with laundry and tied onto my backpack, eating at one of the food trucks while the clothes washed and dried, and then riding back took me well into the evening and burned off some of my low mood.

Meanwhile, my feline companion's temper had veered dangerously toward the murderous with the onset of night and my absence. She growled and lashed her tail from the top step, visible because of the sensor light I'd installed on the porch.

"Hey girl. Let me plug in the bike and I'll share my leftovers with you."

Tiki hissed, but refrained from attack, temporarily appeased by this bribe.

I hooked up and locked my wheels, feeling a pang as I remembered Mr. K's mother's generous loan of the e-bike. Would she want it back? I'd planned to buy it, though it wasn't a substitute for a real car as I'd learned the hard way.

I fed Tiki her kibble, topped by a generous dollop of barbecue beef left over from my dinner, then hopped in the shower. I'd splashed in a few puddles between Ohia and Hana and my legs were muddy.

Tired as I was, I was wound up by the interaction with Thompkins. That guy oozed entitlement, and the thought of that postcard mailer going out to unsuspecting people made my blood fizz with rage.

I dressed and put away my clean clothes, then turned to face the room. The geckos clung to the screen of the back window, but my resident spider was thankfully out of sight. For the first time since I'd moved to Ohia, I wished I had a TV to drown out my thoughts. Maybe a walk around New Ohia to see what was going on in the development would help me unwind.

I sat on the bed and put on my Nikes. "Want to come out for a nighttime stroll, Tiki?"

To my surprise, she did.

New Ohia wasn't as well-lit as it had been under Jimmy Ching's management. The clubhouse's interior, pool, and floodlights were dark except for sensors that winked on as I walked past. Every other streetlight was off, too; apparently, Thompkins was watching the bottom line on energy use.

Still, it was likely that the cameras were tracking my every move —and that of Tiki, trotting along the verge with her whiskers twitching and ear swiveling for mice or other edibles.

I walked briskly, scanning for changes to the property since the latest management arrived, and was chagrined to see a couple of new SOLD signs posted on empty lots. "We have to get this shut down," I grumbled to Tiki, who was trailing me in the grass. "We have to!"

Tiki trotted closer and switched her tail in agreement.

I turned into the cul-de-sac where Jimmy Ching's model home stood, now occupied by Thompkins. As I passed the mansion with its drawn curtains, I saw a flash of motion on one side of the building.

Was someone trying to get in?

I slipped behind a fan palm planted near the edge of the property and peered around it.

A figure in black was approaching the back of the house with the furtive movement of someone trying to stay undetected. They were dressed in head-to-toe black, including a ski mask, to try to fool the cameras.

My training and reflexes kicked in and I rushed the figure, hitting the suspect in a tackle and bearing them to the ground. We plowed into the lawn and rolled, separating; as we did so, lights burst on so brightly I was blinded.

I tried to scramble to my feet, but tripped over something—a hissing, spitting bundle of fury that leaped to attach itself to the suspect's leg. The perp emitted a high-pitched shriek, and light gleamed on the barrel of a silencer-equipped gun as they waved it wildly.

"Tiki!" Now all I cared about was saving my crazy attack cat who'd charged to the rescue.

I dove for the suspect's gun hand and wrestled the weapon away, ending up on my knees.

Tiki let go of the intruder's leg and dashed off into the long grass.

The ninja in black scrambled up and made a dash for the road.

"Stop!" I tried to stand, belatedly realizing it wasn't Tiki who tripped me this time, but a darned untied shoelace. I wallowed in a tangle of my own legs like a giraffe stuck in the mud of a watering hole. "Stop!"

But of course the suspect didn't stop, disappearing out of sight behind the fan palm and the turn of the decorative rock wall marking the cul-de-sac's fancy street signage.

"Drop the weapon!" A harsh male voice bellowed, accompanied by the ominous ratchet of a shotgun.

I finally gained my feet; I raised my hands and turned slowly to face the blazing lights. Four New Ohia Security guys were crouched in shooting stances with their guns trained on me.

I wisely dropped the weapon into the grass.

Behind the operatives stood Thompkins, his face red with rage. "Well. Look who killed Jimmy Ching and came back to shoot me."

"I did no such thing." Off in the distance, I heard the roar of a car pulling away as the ninja drove off and escaped. I ground my teeth in frustration. "I took the gun away from someone trying to sneak up on your house."

"A likely story," Thompkins said.

I was swarmed by the security guys, who patted me down, removed my phone, and cuffed me. "Review your surveillance footage and you'll see what happened," I yelled at Thompkins. "This is ridiculous!"

Thompkins's face flushed even redder; the guy definitely had a blood pressure problem. "The cameras are off. We were having a meeting to talk about budget cutting around here."

Of all the days to have the development's surveillance system down!

"Then call Lei Texeira and Pono Kaihale, the detectives working Jimmy Ching's murder. They'll vouch for me. Who was making all the noise out here? It wasn't me attacking myself with my own gun, that's for sure." I used my toe to point to the marks in the grass.

"Someone was sneaking up to break into your house, and we tangled right here."

"You can be sure we're calling the police, all right," Thompkins said. "We'll let them deal with you. Guys, take her to security headquarters for holding." He stomped back into the house.

"I'm pretty sure your story will check out," the security guy who'd put the cuffs on me said, a tad sheepish.

I recognized him as Phil, the young man I'd met the day Pono and I interviewed Ralph. "Did they promote you after Ralph left?"

He nodded. "Turns out I'd been here longest."

"Well, someone dressed like a ninja and toting that gun you just picked up was moving up on your boss's house. In hindsight, I should've let them do whatever they were trying to do. I doubt they knew you were all gathered inside."

"Well, I believe you about what went down," Phil said. "Mr. Thompkins has his undies in a wad, that's all. Embarrassed someone tried to break in. We'll have to let the cops sort it out."

There is something inherently silly about being handcuffed and helped into the front seat of a golf cart for transport. The other three security guys crowded onto the bench seat in back, and the heavily burdened cart drove off at a turtle's pace toward the security headquarters building near the front of the development.

"Do you think it was Ralph?" one of the guys in the back of the cart asked.

"Maybe. The suspect had a wiry build, which could match him," I said, though the perp had seemed smaller than I remembered Ralph to be. "What do you think Ralph's up to, anyway?"

They all stayed quiet, likely remembering they were supposed to treat me as a suspect.

Once we were back at the security headquarters, conveniently located behind the clubhouse, Phil found a small conference room to put me in. "We can either leave the cuffs on, or I'll lock you in," he said. "It's getting late; it could be a while before the police arrive."

"Lock me in," I said. At least I'd be out of the handcuffs and blessedly alone. "Any chance you could bring me a bottle of water? And loan me your phone? I have to make a couple of calls."

To my profound but unexpressed gratitude, Phil unlocked his phone and handed it to me, leaving me in the conference room to get a bottle of water.

A little dizzy but thrilled that I had both a phone and a signal, I called Lei on her cell.

She picked up right away. "I just got off the line with a very angry Roland Thompkins," she said. "I told him that we were coming out, but that he needed to have everyone make a statement with the Hana Police Department and give them the weapon taken off the intruder."

"You vouched for me?" The cockles of my heart warmed. I hoped she would, but there were no guarantees in this world. Working in Washington taught me that.

"Of course I did. You're our eyes and ears in Ohia! And if you said you tackled a suspect and relieved them of a gun with a silencer, I believe you," she said. "Besides, I searched your place and I know you have no such weapon."

"Thanks. Hopefully the Hana PD won't arrest me for trespassing or some such ridiculousness," I said.

"Give me another call if that happens." She rang off.

I quickly looked up Edith's number and called her. My elderly friend sounded a little tipsy and giggled as I said hello. "Kat! We were just talking about you and singing your praises. I have quite a security detail of Red Hatters over here making sure I'm safe."

"That sounds fun. As for me, I am in a bit of a pickle." I described the situation. "I may need legal representation if things get dicey with Thompkins pressing charges or the Hana PD arresting me."

"Sure! Call me back if they don't turn you loose after you give your statement. In fact, let's make sure they let you go. We'll take a road trip down to New Ohia and lend you some support. Josie! Fire up the VW," she yelled, and with that exclamation, ended the call.

"I sure hope one of them is sober enough to drive," I mused.

Phil returned with the bottle of water. I thanked him, handed back his phone, and tried not to resent the click of the door locking behind him as I was left in the makeshift prison.

I was glad for the bottle of water as the minutes waiting in the conference room ticked by. I slid down in the hard plastic chair as adrenaline crash hit my body and bruises I hadn't noticed during the altercation made themselves known.

I was flat on my face, sound asleep and drooling into the carpet, by the time the Hana Police Department arrived. I heard them before I saw them, giving me time to get up and stretch, yawning and tugging my clothing and hair into place.

Raised voices and a kerfuffle out in the hall signaled that the Red Hat brigade had also arrived. Edith's penetrating voice grew louder. "Are you going to advise her of her rights? Because Kat has them and I'm here to make sure they're respected."

"We just want to get a statement," a man said in a weary tone.

The door opened on a dignified-looking, older sergeant paunchily packed into a uniform and accompanied by a much younger officer.

Behind them, in her witch-style red hat, stood Edith. Beside her, Josie dragged her oxygen tank forward. Clara, who was dressed like an extra in a Dune movie, followed with Mattie, leaning heavily on her cane, bringing up the rear.

My heart cockles warmed again, this time with a painful sting to the eye and lump to the throat. "You all came," I croaked.

The four Red Hatters nodded. Edith forced her way between the two officers. "I'll be staying for your interview."

The senior cop rolled his eyes but made no comment as Edith seated herself beside me at the conference table and took off her hat with an air of authority. "Let's get this over with as we'd all like to get home to bed," she said.

The two officers closed the door and took chairs across from us. "I'm Sergeant Franklin and this is my partner, Officer Tunga. We're here to get your statement, in your own words, of what happened outside Mr. Thompkins's house," the senior cop said.

"Sure." I told the story with stops and starts for questions. "And then the security guys and Mr. Thompkins overreacted, cuffed me, and locked me in this room. Unfortunately, the security cameras that would have documented everything were turned off, according to Mr. Thompkins."

"Ms. Smith was manhandled and abused after she did a good deed trying to catch a possible murderer!" Edith exclaimed. "I've half a mind to sue New Ohia Vision for their treatment of her! Kat here saved my life from assassins on Oahu."

"We heard about that," the sergeant said. "Okay. Can you give us any more identifying information about the person sneaking up on the house?"

I shut my eyes, going over all I could remember. "Five foot six or seven, approximately one hundred and forty or fifty pounds, wiry build. Dressed all in black. The suspect's outfit was made of strong, lightweight material. High quality. Was wearing gloves and a mask that covered the whole head. The gun was a Sig Sauer P320 compact with a custom silencer, since that model doesn't usually use a suppressor."

"You know your firearms," Officer Tunga said, surprise lifting his eyebrows.

"We used Sigs in the Secret Service until recently."

The officers seemed to have run out of steam as well as questions after that. Edith stood up. "If that's all, gentlemen? Ms. Smith has a post office to open tomorrow morning. You can reach her there with any follow-up questions. Let's go, Kat."

Sergeant Franklin gave me back my phone. I lifted a hand in farewell to the officers and followed Edith out of the conference room.

The Red Hat ladies embraced me with enthusiasm in the hallway, whooping, hugging, and high-fiving like we'd had a major victory. "Come on, Kat, let's get you home!" Josie said.

Mattie patted my back. "You look a little worse for wear, Kat." She pointed to the grass and dirt stains on my jeans—and on my precious white Nikes, too.

"Yeah, took a bit of a tumble tackling the intruder. I shouldn't have got involved with whatever the intruder was planning," I said. "That burglar would have had quite a surprise when they broke in and found the entire New Ohia Security team having a meeting in Thompkins's living room."

"Sounds like you did them a favor," Mattie said, leaning on her cane as we headed in a group toward the door.

I told the ladies I could get home on my own two legs just fine, thank you—but Josie insisted on giving me a ride in the van. A minute or two later, we pulled up in front of my shack and they let me out.

Tiki had arrived home well before me and yowled a greeting from the beach rock front stoop.

"Hey, girl!" I slammed the sliding door of the van, waved goodbye to the ladies, and hurried over to my cat. "Are you okay? Did that mean person hurt you?"

It was a sign of our increased positive relationship that Tiki let me run my hands over her, checking for injuries. Her body was filling out and her coat wasn't as rough since she'd had a bath and been eating regularly. She turned on her throaty purr.

"You seem okay." I sat beside her, and to my surprise, Tiki hopped into my lap, kneading my pants with her paws.

I waved again as the van containing the Red Hat ladies pulled away with a little *toot-toot* of the horn.

Just as I was about to go inside and call it a night, I remembered what Keone had asked for when we had our last banana talk.

I sighed heavily. "I'm tired and it's been a heck of a long day, Tiki. Do I have the energy for one more phone call?"

Tiki jumped off my lap and headed into the potholed dirt parking lot in reply.

"I see. You're leading me down by the water where I'll have some signal."

I locked the shack and followed the cat across the parking lot to the beach. Once I reached the sand, I toed off my shoes and headed down toward the moonlit water. "Most likely, Ben is going to pull the plug on my opportunity to work with the VP tomorrow," I told Tiki, who was seated on a log cleaning a paw. "And why should I call Keone? I'm just going to be leaving."

Saying the words aloud gave the tears I'd been holding back a chance to escape. I choked on a sob, covered my face with my hands, and sank onto the log beside Tiki.

"I thought I'd never get a chance to get you alone." The voice that came out of the dark was familiar and male—but it wasn't friendly, and it wasn't Mr. K.

32

"Son of a dung beetle." I'd been ambushed on the beach because I made the error of letting my emotions overrule an assessment of my surroundings. I'd have kicked myself if I could.

Tiki drew close to me on the log, her warm bulk against my side, and her tense body and threatening growl broadcasting her intent to protect me. My attack cat's presence heartened me. (How could I ever leave her? But that was the topic that distracted me in the first place.)

I slowly lowered my hands and rose to my feet, turning to face the threat.

A male figure was backlit by moonlight. Standing next to a large bushy beach shrub, it was easy to miss him. "I've been trying to get a chance to speak to you alone, Kat, but it hasn't been easy."

"Ralph?" I finally recognized the voice and put it together with the silhouette before me. "What are you doing here?"

"I'm trying to turn myself in, but it's harder than you know. Ana is completely nuts."

Knock me over with a feather duster, but this I had to hear.

"Come have a seat. Just don't get too close to my cat. She doesn't like strangers. Well, anybody, if you want the truth."

Ralph leaned down and picked up a long, bulky object. He approached and set the thing down on the log. A stray moonbeam caught the rifle's barrel in its gleam. "I'm turning this in as well."

Remembering the terror of that day on the courthouse steps made my anger rise. "Shame on you, shooting at a little old lady!"

"I wasn't shooting at Edith. Or you. I shot at a mynah bird's tail and hit it," he said. "Ana made me do it."

Remembering my training, I bit my tongue on a half-dozen unhelpful responses that would not move the situation forward in a positive direction. Instead, I picked up the rifle and laid it across my knees, immediately feeling better.

I was no longer vulnerable.

Holding a rifle, even an unloaded one, meant I was prepared for deadly force. I'd had an entire class on Use of Firearms in Nonshooting Situations and could take down a perp with an empty weapon of at least a half-dozen types, including a rifle.

Tiki hissed at Ralph, her tail switching irritably. I patted the log on the side furthest from her. "Why don't you have a seat and tell me all about it."

Ralph sat down a safe distance from me and Tiki. "Ana reached out to me in Ohia by phone. She told me that Edith was going to be staying at the museum. She didn't say anything about moving against you ladies at that point. She just talked about how great it would be to see me, and how, if I spied on what you were doing, Thompkins would be pleased." Ralph hunched his shoulders, a silhouette of misery. "She broke up my marriage, you know. I figured, since my wife left me, I might as well see if the two of us could get something going again."

I forced my voice to sound sympathetic. "Oh my. That must've been hard."

"It was! Ana and I met, and she . . ." He hung his head, and I was sure that if the light had been better, I would've seen him blushing. "She made it worth my trip. Then I searched around the museum but couldn't find you. Ana said she knew where you were staying, and we should check to see if the court papers were there and take pictures of them. You know, so I could give Thompkins a heads up." He sighed. "It felt wrong and weird to break into the guesthouse, but it wasn't too bad until we got inside—then Ana went nuts! She tore everything apart, threw all your stuff everywhere, and wrote this ugly message on the mirror for her grandmother. I tried to talk her down, and realized she wasn't right in the head. Then she showed me her gun and gave me the rifle. She seemed pretty unhinged."

"How awful," I said. It had been, for us.

"Yeah. I thought maybe I could minimize things by playing along and distracting her. It didn't work. She told me we should try to stop you and Edith before you got inside the courthouse. She said I should try to scare you with the rifle, then she took off around the side of the building. I fired at the mynah's tail from across the street, but you guys kept going. Then Ana shot at Edith, and that's when I realized she was serious about wanting to kill somebody."

Once again, I bit my tongue on scathing remarks. Ralph was trying to get out of the hole he had dug and justify himself. It wasn't my job to bust him, only to find out what he knew and get him to those who could sort out the situation. "Go on."

"Well, I made a run for it and so did Ana. We got away from the courthouse and hid at a friend's place by the docks. I saw the news and heard the FBI were involved . . . and I snuck away from Ana. I got back to Maui on a friend's fishing boat." He pointed to where a small cabin cruiser rocked at anchor in Ohia Bay. "Can I get your help turning myself in? I know Ana needs to be stopped. I'm . . . honestly afraid of what she might do."

"To whom?"

"To her grandma. To me, for leaving her." Ralph's voice trembled. For the first time, I felt a shred of compassion for this nincompoop, as Aunt Fae would have called him.

"I'd like to trade her location for a reduced charge," he said.

My compassion vanished. Ralph was a coward and an opportunist.

"Let's call Lei and Pono on my cell phone, down here where there's some signal. Then we can go back to my shack and wait for them," I said.

"Okay." Ralph put his head in his hands. I saw how I'd appeared a few minutes ago in his sad, defeated stance.

I got my phone out and speed-dialed Lei. Her voice was gritty with tiredness when she answered. "We're on our way out, Kat. Already partway there."

"I hate to bother you again, but I have someone here who wants to talk to you, and I know you'll want to hear what he has to say."

Lei spoke with Ralph on speaker and agreed to come get him personally rather than call Hana PD, which was one of his conditions for surrender. "I don't trust anybody but you and Detective Kaihale," he said. "And I'll want my deal in writing—what I know about Ana and where she is for reduced charges."

"Okay. We'll wake the DA and ask him to draft something for you to look at on our phones. You should know we'll be returning tonight and taking you into custody in Kahului," she said. "You'll be booked into county jail for holding."

"That's okay. I'll be safe there." Ralph was definitely scared of Ana, and that gave me a bit of a chill.

He handed the phone back to me and I took it off speaker.

"Lei?"

"This is a break in the case at last."

"Agreed." I glanced at Ralph, who was gazing out to sea.

"Beginning to think Pono and I need to buy into one of those condos they're building at New Ohia, there's been so much activity out there."

"It wouldn't be a bad idea if it wasn't a scam."

"Right? See you soon." She ended the call.

I felt bad for my cop friends having such a late night, but heck, I wasn't enjoying a relaxing evening either.

I stood up from the log. "Come on back to my place, Ralph. I'll make you a cup of tea."

"And do you have anything to eat?" Ralph pressed a fist to his midsection. "I left Oahu without any supplies on that boat."

This guy. "Sure."

I glanced at the cruiser he'd come to the island on, rocking gently in the moonlight on the bay. He'd rowed to the beach in a little inflatable I could see in the moonlight beside the pier. I'd bet my pet geckos that Ralph hadn't "borrowed the boat from a friend." He'd stolen it. But that wasn't my problem. Keeping him safely with me until he could be picked up was.

I led the way across the road to the shack, frowning as I noticed that the sensor light on the porch was on.

"Wait here a minute," I directed in a whisper, pressing my new protectee against the wall of the post office. "That light shouldn't be on until we get within twenty feet of the porch."

"Do you think Ana could have followed you?" Ralph went stiff with alarm and hugged the post office for cover as I lifted the rifle into a shooting stance and aimed toward the porch of the shack, scanning through the eyepiece.

"I don't know."

"Wasn't there an alert on us at the airports?" Ralph's whisper had a quaver in it. "That's why I took the boat—and getting here was no picnic on the open sea."

"Maybe she disguised herself and fooled the cameras. Traveled under a fake ID," I murmured. There were ways to do that but they weren't for the average lawbreaker, and Ana was relatively new to a life of crime.

I squeezed the barrel of the rifle, settling the rubber-capped wooden stock comfortably into the notch of my shoulder, my finger curled around the trigger. "Is this gun empty?"

"Yeah. I wouldn't have handed you a loaded weapon."

I didn't need bullets for this heavy club to be deadly. But whoever might be inside my shack wouldn't know the thing wasn't loaded—strategy number one from my class.

I paced forward, sighting through the notches on the barrel at the door of my shack. As I approached, the door opened with its usual spine-tingling creak.

A woman stood framed in the opening, backlit by my familiar dangling bulb. The light illuminated a pistol held down and to the side.

"Took you long enough," she grumbled. "Where the heck have you been?"

❧ 33 ❧

"Mattie!" I lowered the rifle. "What are you doing in my place?"

"I came to check on you, and you left the front door open. Josie had an intuition something was wrong. She gets those, you know." Mattie must have spotted Ralph, because she suddenly raised the gun, dropping into a two-handed shooting stance. "Kat! Get out of the way!"

I shook my head and advanced a step, the rifle lowered and my other hand raised so as not to alarm her further. This lady knew her way around a handgun. "Ralph's in my custody, Mattie. He's turning himself in. Detectives are on their way to pick him up."

Mattie limped out onto the porch. The boxy black Glock was pointed at a terrified Ralph, who'd raised his hands overhead. "That's the guy that shot at you and Edith!"

"Yes." I spoke slowly. "Mattie, put down the gun. He's unarmed and turning himself in. The situation is under control."

"No. I don't believe it. This guy tried to kill you and Edith."

"I did not," Ralph hollered. "Tell her, Kat! Tell her about the mynah bird's tail!"

"I don't care about any mynah bird. This man is dangerous,"

Mattie snarled. I recognized in her staring eyes someone prepared to cross a line to protect those she cared about.

"Would you put the gun down if I tied Ralph up, Mattie?"

"Maybe." Mattie hadn't lowered the weapon an inch.

"Okay. I'll make sure Ralph is no longer a danger to anyone." I backed up, keeping my body between Mattie's line of fire and Ralph, huddled against the post office wall. "I bought some rope at Longs when I was in town. Is it okay if I bring him inside the shack and we tie him to a chair? Then everyone will be safe."

Mattie's eyes were so wide that white showed all the way around the irises. Her whole body trembled like an overstretched guitar string; that couldn't be healthy for someone of her age. "He better not so much as sneeze."

"Ralph. Go along with this, please, or I can't vouch for what she'll do," I hissed at the former security guy as I reached his side.

Ralph had some training, too, because he nodded. He could see Mattie was on the edge. He kept his hands high and allowed me to walk him up onto the porch, past Mattie, and into the shack.

I breathed an inward sigh of relief as I glanced around—Tiki was nowhere to be seen. The last thing I needed right now was to worry about my unpredictable attack cat in this explosive situation.

Ralph sat down on one of my two chairs, his gaze fixed on Mattie, who had followed us inside. Her gun continued to point in his direction. She shut the door of the shack. "Hurry up."

I crossed to the drawer in the closet where I stashed stuff like light bulbs, citronella candles, rubber bands, thumb tacks, tape, batteries—and my Glock and extra ammo. The rope, coiled in a figure eight with a cardboard loop around the middle, lay on top. I reached below it for where my gun was hidden and stared into the drawer in consternation. My Glock and the extra clip were gone. Only a box of bullets remained, nestled beside a pack of AA batteries.

I absorbed the fact that Mattie was holding *my* loaded gun on Ralph.

"What's the holdup?" Ralph waggled his hands. "So to speak. I'm ready and waiting to be tied."

I picked up the rope and held it aloft, turning to meet Mattie's gaze and keeping my expression blank. "Found it."

There was no innocent explanation I could think of for Mattie to have gone through my drawers and taken my gun, but she was the armed one in the current situation. I wouldn't call her out on it and risk provoking her.

I strolled to the kitchen sink and used a pair of scissors to cut the cardboard loop off the rope. I then turned to Ralph and made a production of tying his legs to those of the chair and his arms behind its back. "Are you comfy? Got enough room for circulation?" I asked, testing the give.

"I'm okay," Ralph said. "And as I told you before, I never meant to hurt anyone. My girlfriend Ana is the dangerous one."

"Ana? Edith's granddaughter?" Mattie frowned.

"Yeah. She has it in for her grandma for some reason."

I finished my knots, snipped off the extra rope, straightened up, and turned to face Mattie. "There. He's restrained. Not a threat to anyone, anymore."

"I still don't feel safe," Mattie said. She grabbed the remaining chair, tugged it over near the doorway, and sat down. "Let's all wait for the cops to get here and sort this out."

I crossed my arms on my chest and rolled my eyes. "Come on, Mattie."

"Don't you take that attitude with me, young lady," she snapped. "Now put on some hot water for tea. I need to relax. My leg is really bothering me."

"Where'd you put your cane?" I turned back to the sink and filled the kettle I'd inherited with the shack and put it on to boil.

"Forgot it at Edith's." She rubbed her calf, keeping the gun pointed at us.

She didn't actually need that darned cane, but that was another something I didn't say. "Ralph is hungry. Can I make him a sandwich?"

"I am. Super hungry. Haven't had food in at least a day," Ralph begged. His stomach rumbled loudly for emphasis. "See?"

"Okay. I'm not a monster." Mattie propped the gun on her knee. I could no longer tell if it was pointed at Ralph or at me, and that gave me goosebumps.

A seemingly endless time later, I was sitting in front of a tied-up Ralph, feeding him slices of baloney sandwich like a great big hairy baby bird, when the roar of Stanley's engine filled the shack.

"I'm going to keep you covered until Ralph is safely in custody." Mattie spoke to the back of my head as I fed the last of the sandwich to Ralph, tied to his chair.

I put the plate into the sink and ran some water on it. "Cops don't like other people to have guns out around them. If the detectives see what you're holding, you'll be the one in danger."

I glanced at her sideways. She was thinking this over.

Meanwhile, I heard the murmur of voices and then the thump of footsteps on the porch. A sharp knock at the door. "Kat, you in there?"

"Yes. Ralph is restrained, and Mattie Ramirez, a concerned citizen, is also here." I narrowed my eyes meaningfully at Mattie.

She stood up from her chair and tucked the Glock, gangster style, into the back of her waistband.

I stepped forward and opened the door wide, moving to stand beside Mattie. I pointed to Ralph, bound hand and foot to his chair. "He voluntarily surrendered," I said.

"Great work, Kat," Lei said, looking pleased. Pono nodded.

And then I sidestepped behind Mattie, flipped her over my extended leg, and removed the gun from the back of her pants once she was face down on the floor. I discharged the ammo clip and chambered round and set the cleared weapon on the table. "Mattie broke into my shack and stole my gun. She's been holding it on us since we returned from the beach where Ralph surrendered to me."

Lei had her weapon out and was covering us. "Explain."

Pono shook his head and whacked his ear like his hearing was gone. "What?"

Mattie groaned, sucking air back into her lungs. "Elder abuse," she wheezed. "Assault. I'm pressing charges."

I rolled Mattie onto her back and pointed to her legs. "When I pull up Ms. Ramirez's pants, you'll see marks where my cat grabbed her on the shin and an injury to her knee from when I tackled her. Mattie was the one trying to break into Thompkins's house in New Ohia, carrying a brand-new Sig with a silencer. I believe she killed Jimmy Ching, too."

"Wait, what?" Lei groped for the chair Mattie had recently been sitting in and lowered herself into it, putting her gun away. "Slow down."

Ralph piped up. "This I gotta hear."

"Let me show you." I squatted and pushed the leg of Mattie's black ripstop hiking pants all the way up, over her knee.

Mattie slapped at my hands, squawking in rage. "Don't touch me! I have rights!"

But there was a puffy purple bruise on her knee, and the puncture marks and scratches from a cat's teeth and claws were swelling and red on her calf. "See?"

I glanced at the detectives to see if they were following my deductions.

Lei had a carefully blank expression on her face. Pono rubbed the bristle of his mustache thoughtfully. "Can't hurt to hear your theory, Kat."

"This doesn't prove anything." Mattie sat up and rolled her pant leg back down over the evidence. "I ran into a rose bush and bruised my knee. Sneaking up on Thompkins's house with a silenced weapon? Ridiculous. And I certainly didn't have anything to do with Jimmy Ching's murder."

Ralph wiggled in his bonds. "Would any of you mind untying me?"

Everyone ignored him.

Mattie lay back down and put an arm over her eyes. "I'm tired. I'm old. I've had a long day. I'm not saying another thing without legal representation. Please call my lawyer, Edith Pepperwhite."

"You can't have Edith," I said. "It's a conflict of interest since she's my lawyer already."

"And I'm the one who needs a lawyer most," Ralph said.

Lei flapped a hand. "Nobody's getting a lawyer right now. We're just trying to figure out what's going on here."

"Did you bring my reduced charges agreement?" Ralph persisted.

"About that. We ran it by our captain, and she wasn't willing to sign off until we heard your story," Pono said. "Neither was the district attorney."

"Then I guess I won't be talking until I have a lawyer," Ralph said.

"Dang it, Ralph. Can you at least tell them what happened with Mattie when I brought you up from the beach to the shack?" I said.

"That I can do. But I'd appreciate a beverage, please. That baloney sandwich was dry."

I rolled my eyes but fetched Ralph a glass of water, holding it to his lips as he drank thirstily.

Mattie waved from the floor. "Me too. I'm dehydrated."

"Okay. But I'm not helping you drink it," I grumped.

"Are you alright? You took quite a tumble just now, Ms. Ramirez." Pono fussed over Mattie in gentlemanly "good cop" fashion. He helped her up and then shooed Lei off the chair so the older woman could sit on it. I handed Pono a fresh glass of water to give her, which he presented with a flourish.

Mattie preened at the attention. "At least one person here knows how to behave toward an elder."

I was feeling none too charitable toward a woman who'd basically kicked my butt and escaped me, leaving me humiliated in front of Thompkins and New Ohia's security detail.

Though the solution to recent mysteries came together in a flash for me, it would be hard to prove if Mattie didn't confess. She'd continue to get away with murder while hiding behind her guise of helpless old lady.

I glanced across the room and met Sergeant Lei Texeira's narrowed brown eyes. A telepathic moment seemed to pass between us. She gave a slight nod, and so did Pono from behind Mattie.

"Do you mind if we record this, Ralph, so we don't have to ask you about this particular situation again down at the station?" Lei asked.

"Sure. Whatever gets me out of these ropes faster."

Lei took out her phone and stated the date, time, location, and people present. She recited the Miranda warning and named Ralph, Mattie, and me as having been informed. We all agreed aloud that we'd been apprised of our rights.

Then Lei started in. "Ralph, thanks so much for voluntarily surrendering yourself to Postmaster Katherine Smith and asking for Detective Kaihale and I to take you into custody in the matter of the attack on Ms. Smith and Edith Pepperwhite on the steps of the courthouse on Oahu. We understand you will not discuss those events without representation. But can you explain the series of events that have led to you sitting bound to a chair in Ms. Smith's place of residence?"

Ralph cleared his throat and wiggled, settling more comfortably into his bonds. "I've been waiting for an opportunity to speak to Kat alone and turn myself in. I staked out her place and then met Kat on the beach."

"I bet that was a surprise," Lei said drily.

"She seemed a bit surprised, yeah, but I told her my story and said I wanted to meet you and Pono and turn myself in. So she called you and we discussed it."

"I recall, yes," Lei said and made a twirling gesture for him to speed up his narrative.

Ralph continued. "I surrendered my unloaded rifle to Kat, and we were making our way back to her place to wait for you when Kat noticed the porch's sensor light was on." Ralph described how we'd found Mattie already inside my shack, and how she had a gun and held it on both of us until the detectives arrived, and then attempted to conceal it and pretend nothing was wrong.

"Ms. Ramirez said she wouldn't feel safe until I was restrained, so Kat tied me up to this chair, as you see. But we both knew she was ready to take us down whenever she felt like it. I could tell Ms. Ramirez would have been happy to shoot me. I was the one who wasn't safe."

"Nonsense," Mattie snorted, setting the empty water glass she'd drained on the Formica table. "This is a low-down dog of a man who cheated on his wife with my friend Edith's deranged granddaughter and then tried to kill her."

Smooth as silk, Lei turned to Mattie. "Perhaps you'd like to tell your side of the story, Ms. Ramirez?"

"I'll set this part straight, that's for sure. I came to the shack to make sure Kat was safe, specifically from Ralph and Ana and whoever killed Jimmy Ching. When I got here, I called out her name. No one answered. I tried the door handle, and it was open. I went inside, very concerned. Kat wasn't there, which I thought was odd. I knew she owned a weapon for self-defense so I went looking for it, wondering if she was armed wherever she had gone, or if the perp here," she pointed at Ralph, "might have stolen it. I found Kat's gun, which alarmed me, because it meant the poor girl was without protection wherever she'd gone or been taken. I was going outside to get a signal to call for help when Kat came back from the beach, holding a rifle with the perp in tow. So of course I wanted to get to the bottom of whatever was going on, and I had to make sure both Kat and I were safe.

"To that end, I asked her to tie Ralph up. Once he was restrained, I realized I wasn't sure whose side Kat was on. I thought I'd let you police officers sort it all out when you got here." Mattie blinked big brown eyes. Sitting in the chair in her dirty black outfit, she seemed small and frail. "I'm just a little old lady. What danger could I possibly be to anyone?"

I suppressed a snort. Mattie was as wiry and strong as a woman half her age. I'd seen her speed hiking a trail that would knock most people on their rear ends, even as she pretended to need a cane.

Lei glanced at me meaningfully.

"I'd like to give my version of events," I said in my best Secret Service authority voice. "Let me begin by telling you that I did not leave the shack unlocked." I reached into my pocket and produced a key. "Yes, I went to the beach, but I never leave the shack open anymore. I've been broken into too many times."

Mattie shook her head. "Just because you pulled a key out of your pocket doesn't mean you didn't leave it unlocked."

"You're accusing me of lying, Mattie. Well, two can play that game. Lei, can you ask Mattie to turn out her pockets? Those are cargo pants. They will likely be holding a set of lockpicks."

"Let's address that after you finish your story," Lei said.

I put my hands on my hips, indignation speeding my words. "Events happened as Ralph said, word for word—only I realized when I went to get rope to tie Ralph up that my gun and its ammo clip were missing, and that its make matched the one Mattie was holding on us."

I paused to get a breath. "I believe Mattie came over to talk to me after our recent scuffle in New Ohia, to see what I knew about her activities. I realized it was she who I tried to grab outside of Thompkins's house—I put the size, build, outfit, and mud and claw marks I spotted on her pants together with whoever got away from me."

I met Lei's steady gaze. "I got her gun away from her at Thompkins's house. When I turned out to be missing from the shack, Mattie took that as a golden opportunity to break in and get another one. And one more thing—if she came to my place with no intent of harm, why is her car parked somewhere out of view?"

Mattie folded her arms over her chest. "Do I look like someone who makes a habit of running around at night, tussling over guns?"

"Ms. Ramirez, we need to give you a quick frisk for additional weapons," Lei said briskly. "We should have done that right away after Kat disarmed you. Ralph, Kat—you both need to be searched as well."

"I'm happy to submit to that, since it will substantiate my story," I said.

"And I gave Kat the only weapon I had," Ralph said. "Search away. Just untie me, please."

Only Mattie scowled and said nothing—and then she surged up from her chair and darted out the door into the night.

❧ 34 ❧

"Don't let her get away!" I couldn't get around Ralph fast enough to chase Mattie out the door of the shack. Neither could Pono, catching himself on the back of Mattie's chair in a big stumble.

But Lei was another story. She charged out into the night after the older woman. I heard the thump of their feet receding across the parking lot into the distance. Pono followed Lei, rubbing his leg and cursing under his breath.

Ralph wriggled pathetically. "Would you please untie me? I can help!"

"No way. Just chill."

Though it killed me to stay behind, Mattie Ramirez was the detectives' problem now. They would have to catch her. And when they brought her back to the shack, I had something that I hoped would make her talk.

I glanced around frantically but couldn't remember where I stashed it. I hurried over to the closet and pulled the door open. "There it is!" The super ugly, rhinestone-covered, red ball cap that Mattie'd made for me rested on the top shelf.

This hat was the key to why she killed Jimmy Ching, and why she had gone after his replacement.

It took longer than it should have, but eventually, Lei and Pono returned, walking across the unpaved parking lot holding a hand-cuffed Mattie Ramirez between the two of them. Both detectives were out of breath. Mattie was fresh as an elderly daisy.

"Yay!" I exclaimed. "I was starting to wonder if you'd let her get away."

The porch light went on at the general store and Opal emerged, her white hair pointing in every direction in a fresh case of bed head. "That you, Mattie? What's going on over there, Kat?"

"Everything is under control," Lei hollered to the storekeeper.

Opal was not so easily dissuaded. She slid her feet into her trusty yellow Crocs and made her way across the parking lot, tugging a robe tight around her nightgown. "Is everything okay, Mattie?"

Clearly it wasn't.

"Stay outside, Mrs. Pahinui," Pono instructed sternly as they brought Mattie back inside the shack.

I hurried over and put a hand on Opal's shoulder. "We're in the middle of a breaking investigation. Do you mind staying outside? I'll scoop you in as soon as I can get away."

Opal gave me a long look, and then nodded briskly. "I'm sure you will do right by Mattie, whatever trouble she's in," she said.

I felt a pang of guilt; I was going to try to get her to confess. While that wasn't necessarily in Mattie's best interest, it did serve the greater good. That's what the Red Hat Society was about. I waggled the ball cap. "Red Hat Society, forever!"

With that, I went back inside the crowded shack.

Lei and Pono seated Mattie on her chair, but this time her hands were cuffed behind her back. "Here's what was in her pockets," Lei said, holding up a clear plastic evidence bag that held a set of lock-picks and a small but lethal looking switchblade. "Looks like your version of events holds up, Kat."

Mattie hunched on the chair, petite and vulnerable. She hung her head, her chin resting on her chest. "Mattie, are you okay?" I asked.

"I could use another glass of water," she said.

"So could we," said Lei.

I poured fresh water for everyone and approached Mattie. This time, I held the glass to her lips, and she drank thirstily. Her eyes met mine, and there was defeat in them—but also a proud defiance.

She wanted to talk. I just needed to give her a reason.

"I know this is unusual, but I'd like a chance to ask Mattie a few questions," I said. "I think I understand why she's been doing what she's been doing."

Lei's brows went up, but she reached for her phone and thumbed to the recorder app. She recited the Miranda warning again and set the phone down after once more identifying the date, time, people in the room, and current situation.

"I know why you did it." I held out the sparkling red ball cap toward Mattie. "You did it for Ohia."

Mattie nodded.

"Please speak your answer out loud," Lei said. "And I'm reminding you that you have been apprised of your right to remain silent and to have an attorney present."

"Yes, I have been apprised of my rights, and tonight, I waive them. Kat is right," Mattie said. "I did what I did for my friends. For the town that's my home." Her eyes flashed with pride. "I did it because I could."

That last bit revealed the egotism that came from getting away with murder.

I still needed to get her to say exactly what she'd done, and it had to be eased into. "I'm holding, in my hand, a specially decorated red ball cap that Mattie made when she invited me to join Ohia's Red Hat Society," I said. "Ms. Ramirez has done nothing but try to protect the town. Isn't that right?"

"Everything I've done was to help Ohia," Mattie said. "If that's over, I don't care what happens to me."

Her eyes followed the movement of the sparkling red hat as I held it out and set it on her knees. "You just wanted to protect the town. Tell us how you did that. It began with Kermit Hubbard, didn't it?"

"That man was an evil pervert hiding in our midst."

Lei held up a hand. "Wait a minute. I need you to back up and tell me how you knew this."

"I follow the postings of sex offenders. I didn't kill Kermit Hubbard, but his death was what inspired me to take action. I was concerned about Jimmy Ching. I went to his office pretending I was interested in buying into the senior living building. He told me he was going to the continental U.S. to pitch the development to new buyers and was planning to stay over there from now on. He bragged that there was nothing we could do to stop New Ohia, that not even Edith's court papers would do the job." She gave a dry little cough. "Something had to be done."

I wanted to keep the flow going, so I brought her more water. After a few sips, Mattie continued. "Ching was the one who got the development to this point, and he was leaving to expand it more, and I couldn't let that happen."

She lifted her head, and her brown eyes blazed with conviction. "Some guys just need killing. Jimmy Ching was one of them, and so was Kermit Hubbard. They were both low-down dirty sleazebag blackmailers. One was cheating investors, working for the mob, and laundering money; the other was a sexual predator. They were bad for our town."

"So what exactly did you do to stop Ching?" Lei asked.

"I whacked him. Someone had to do it. Like stomping on a cockroach."

I suppressed a shudder. "Tell me about tonight and what happened at Thompkins's house."

"I thought getting rid of Jimmy would buy us more time than it did—time for Edith's cease and desist to get reviewed. I'd also decided to upgrade my methods. Catching these turkeys unaware was going to be harder now that two of them were down. I bought a gun with a silencer on the black market. I figured once Thompkins was out of the picture, the Changs would get the message and cut their losses in New Ohia."

"Not everyone knows how to use a weapon like that Sig you bought, my gun, and this." I pointed to the switchblade. "How are you so comfortable with weapons?"

"I worked for the CIA back in the day. During the Cold War. A time when men were men, and women were unexpected." Mattie's eyes flashed. "No one ever suspects an elder with a cane, but we have pasts that would make your hair curl. We've seen things, all of us."

"You mean . . . the Red Hat Society ladies? Did any of them know what you were up to?" Lei asked. "Did any of them . . . help you?"

My stomach plummeted. I pictured sweet Josie and her oxygen tank and Hawaiian crafts, Pearl and her wheelchair, graceful Clara with her lovely outfits, and of course my new friend Edith. Each woman was so special. I didn't want any of them going to prison.

What had I unleashed in getting Mattie to talk?

But Mattie shook her head. "No. I knew none of my friends would approve. Edith, especially, wouldn't have wanted me to . . . endanger myself."

I exhaled a breath in relief.

"Is there anything else you'd like to add?" Lei asked gently.

"I think that's quite enough, don't you? You have permission to search my home. You will find evidence there." She straightened up in her chair. "Might as well go out in a blaze of glory."

I could respect where Mattie was coming from without agreeing with it. "Thank you, Mattie," I said. "Is there anything you want me to tell the Red Hat ladies when I see them?"

"Tell them I'm not sorry. I've done worse to protect my country, and I'd do it again." She set her chin. "This is no different."

I exchanged a glance with Lei and Pono. Mattie figured out how to justify her actions, as every criminal did. Even so, I sympathized more than I could show.

"Let's get these two booked into custody," Lei told Pono. "We'll have to go over everything again tomorrow."

"With lawyers present," Ralph spoke up. "Because I'm not saying another thing without representation."

Mattie snorted. "Wimp."

I finally helped Ralph out of his ropes and let him use the bathroom, only for him to have to put on a pair of handcuffs that Pono supplied. It was going to be a mighty uncomfortable drive back to Kahului with all four of them packed into Stanley's extended cab. I was glad I wasn't going to be in on that party. I had plenty of my own "lobsters to shuck" as Aunt Fae would've said.

I watched from my porch as the fully loaded truck left.

Opal appeared in a square of light in the store's doorway, waving for me to come over. "I've got a cup of tea ready for you, and Artie and I are dying to hear everything that's been going on."

"Do you mind if I make a phone call first?" I asked. "I was just going to do that when Ralph interrupted me."

"Sure, but don't take too long." She disappeared.

I headed back down to the beach, rubbing the left side of my chest because my heart ached in anticipation of the call I had to make.

35

I had good signal down by the water, per usual. I walked with bare feet splashing in the foam as I connected with Ben in D.C. "I've made a decision about the VP's special detail," I said.

"Good. Time was running out."

I told him what I'd decided. We discussed details and plans, and I hung up. I didn't let myself wallow or feel anything. I just scrolled to the next number and called it.

"Kat?" Mr. K's voice sounded sleepy. "You know what time it is?"

"Nope. I called about a banana conversation we had a bit ago."

"I need a minute," he said. I could picture him sitting up on the edge of a bed, his big hands scrubbing over a bristle of stubble and pushing though his thick black hair. "What kind of banana situation?"

"The kind where I agreed to call you if something big happened."

He was alert now. "Big? How? Involving cops and a life-threatening situation?"

"Yes and yes."

"Tell me."

I spoke rapidly, filling him in about the evening, beginning with my walk in New Ohia and tackling an unknown perp, and ending with Lei and Pono driving off with two prisoners in custody.

"Thanks for calling to let me know," he said. A beat went by. "Are you okay?"

"Sure. Uninjured. I'm headed over to Opal and Artie's to fill them in. Opal promised me a cup of tea."

"Want some company? After?"

I stared out over the moonlit, restless ocean. The smell of the sea filled my nostrils, and a light breeze played with my hair and rippled a few goosebumps up my arms. Was I up for having Mr. K come over late at night? What did that mean?

"Banana," he said.

"Wait a minute. I was about to say banana."

"Beat you to it." He blew out a breath. "This is awkward. I made the offer to come over, but it's not a booty call. I want to make sure you're okay, and not just physically. It's a platonic offer. Unless . . . you don't want to be platonic, and I'm good with that too. We might not have long together since you're leaving for D.C."

"About that. I'm not ready to leave Ohia. I'm getting into a groove here. I told my boss no and passed on the special detail."

"Ooh."

"Now it's my turn for banana."

"Okay."

"I like you, Keone Kaihale. A lot."

"Oh yeah?" I could hear him smiling. "Well, good news. I like you, too."

"But you're not why I decided to stay in Ohia."

"You sure?"

"Don't joke right now." I kicked the water. A little wave splashed me back, wetting my pants. "I like it here. This town. These people. My cat. My job. I like it all. Not just you. So we're clear."

"I hear you. Message received. Banana over?"

"Banana over."

"There are a lot of murders in Ohia for such a small place," he said dubiously. "You sure you like it there?"

"Dude. I'm standing on a moonlit beach right across the street from where I live. I get to swim in the ocean every day and sometimes I run into sea turtles. I have a cat who has adopted me. I have friends who feel like family—Opal and Artie and Edith and the Red Hat ladies. For the first time in my life, as postmaster, I'm part of a community. I'm hoping we'll figure out the rotten apples soon and clean up Ohia. Not like Mattie tried to clean it up, but in a good way."

"Good speech." He chuckled. "I'd still like to come over, if you're up for more possible banana moments."

"I'd like that. Give me half an hour to talk to Opal and Artie."

"See you soon." He ended the call.

I headed for the general store with a smile on my face.

It had been a tough call with Ben, but I was happy about the decision I'd made. I wasn't ready to leave Ohia. There would be other opportunities with the Secret Service—at least, so I hoped.

It took longer than a half hour to answer all of Opal and Artie's questions, and I was nodding on my feet by the time I headed back to the shack. Even so, my heart speeded up at the sight of a dark green pickup illuminated by the sensor light on the porch. Mr. K was waiting for me.

Keone got out of the truck and met me on the beach rock front step carrying a small duffel. He was wearing a T-shirt so worn it was transparent and a pair of green University of Hawaii sweatpants. He looked delicious. "How about a hug?"

"Yes, please."

We enjoyed that for a long moment. "Thanks for coming over."

"You're welcome." He gave a jaw-cracking yawn. "I won't tell you what time it is, since we both have work in the morning."

"Oh, ugh." I unlocked the shack. "Don't remind me."

Tiki was under the table. She let out a complaint that sounded like a chisel scraping stone. I scurried to do her bidding. "Hey, girl. So glad you weren't here earlier. I'll get your food right now."

Meanwhile Keone undid the strap on the Murphy bed. "I thought we could rest here while you told me everything that happened. I wore my pajamas and brought work clothes in case it turned into a sleepover."

I put my hands on my hips. "Feeling awkward."

"Another banana moment. For me too. This is platonic, remember?" Mr. K twinkled his eyes at me. "Why don't you brush your teeth and think about it."

I went into the bathroom, did my business, and slid into my sleep tee. It was too skimpy for platonic, so I threw my terry cloth robe on over it, wrapping myself up like a mummy and tightening the belt. I was as sexy as a bag of laundry in that outfit.

I yawned as I came out and couldn't stop.

Keone yawned too. "Look what you started."

"They say it's contagious."

We got onto the bed and lay side by side with a couple of inches between us. "So. Tell me everything," said Mr. K.

Tiredness hit me like a brick to the forehead. "I just got done going over it with Opal and Artie. Is it okay if we just go to sleep? I'll catch you up in the morning."

"I thought that's how this might go," he mumbled, sounding half gone already.

I tugged the new comforter I'd bought up over us, then turned over. I reached out and pulled the string, and the overhead bulb went out on one of the longest, strangest days of my life.

❧ 36 ❧

I slept with a man. In the same bed. All night.

Granted, we were fully clothed and actually sleeping with little physical contact, but as I woke up to a ray of sunshine coming through the bullet hole near my pillow and realized I wasn't alone and that the company with me wasn't a cat—I counted it a win.

Keone was still sleeping when I snuck out of the bed and went to the bathroom to hop in the shower, pausing to let Tiki out the front door on my way. I was overdue to wash off the stress from the day before.

I opened the door of the bathroom on a cloud of steam. My hair was in a towel, and I had dressed in the polo shirt and jeans I wore for work. "Do I smell coffee?"

"You do." Keone leaned against the sink, sipping from my DO NOT SPEAK TO ME mug. "How's the water?"

"Still hot. You're welcome to use the facilities."

"Glad to hear it." He handed me a mug from Fran's eclectic collection. This one was emblazoned with the purple Hawaiian Airlines logo. "Hope you take it black."

"You know I do." We smiled at each other a little longer than necessary. "How'd you sleep?"

"Surprisingly well. You?"

"Same."

"Well, I'll just . . ." he made a gesture toward the bathroom.

"Of course." I got out of the way and went to make the bed. The rush of the shower turning on attested to Keone's activities.

I couldn't stop smiling as I shook out the sheets and comforter and fluffed the single pillow we'd ended up sharing with no ill effects. I'd never had this much extended physical contact with another human since before the car accident that ended everything in my known world. "Systematic desensitization," one of the therapists Aunt Fae had taken me to had said. "Kat needs to build up to tolerating touch."

But I didn't want to, and at nine I couldn't be forced to do the therapy, even if the right kinds of interventions hadn't been far away and too expensive. By the time I was old enough to want to get over my touchphobia, I was in a career where admitting any weakness was frowned upon.

"But maybe I'm turning a corner," I murmured. I remembered little about the night except feeling safe and comforted by another human presence.

"Kat?" Edith's distinctive voice came from the door, followed by a sharp knock. "You in there?"

I hurried over and undid the deadbolt. "Edith? What's up?" But it wasn't just Edith on my doorstep: Clara, Josie, and Pearl in her wheelchair were there too. "Good morning, ladies."

"We wanted to catch you before work. Mattie sent me a message that she was being arrested and to come to you to hear about it." Edith peered around the doorjamb. "Do you have company? Someone's in the shower."

"That's Keone Kaihale's vehicle," Josie stated, tugging her oxygen tank into a better position. "Looks like he spent the night."

My face heated as I stepped outside and shut the door. "I'd appreciate it if you didn't share this around the community. It's not what you think."

"I sure hope it's what I think," Pearl chuckled. "You go, girl."

Opal waved from her porch. "Come on over, ladies! I've got some warm banana bread and coffee. Kat can tell you all about it from our comfy chairs."

Edith narrowed her eyes at me. "You're not getting out of a full accounting," she said. "But we can give the lovebirds a little space. Let's go see Opal. There's banana bread calling my name."

The four remaining Red Hatters set off at a slow pace across the potholed parking lot.

I went back inside—only to run into Keone in nothing but a towel. "Oh. Hey. I got rid of the ladies, but they saw your truck and put two and two together that you spent the night. Sorry about that."

"I'm not sorry about it. Okay if I give you a hug?"

"Maybe put your clothes on first? I might be having a panic attack." I lay a hand over my thundering heart. "I'm feeling very odd."

"Maybe you're not afraid. Maybe it's something else." His dimple showed. "Let's give it a try."

The hug turned into a kiss, and who knows where it might have ended if I hadn't heard a holler from Opal's porch. "Get over here, Kat! Time's a-wasting!"

Keone went back into the bathroom to put on his uniform, and I headed out with a fresh cup of coffee to tell the local Red Hat Society that one of their own was a vigilante murderer.

Keone joined me about a third of the way through my interrogation with the Red Hat Society. Wearing his scrumptious white uniform, he sat beside me on a chair Opal reserved for him as I told the ladies last night's events.

Edith interrupted several times asking clarifying questions, but we finally got to the end of my tale. "I asked Mattie what she wanted me to tell you. She said she wanted you all to know she wasn't sorry. She said she'd done worse for her country, and she had no regrets."

The group, seated in a circle on folding chairs Opal produced, were silent, palpably depressed. Only Edith finished her banana bread.

"I'm somehow not surprised she did it," Josie said at last. "Mattie always had an edge."

"Did any of you know what she was up to?" I was almost afraid to ask, but I'd regret it if I let the opportunity pass by to know for sure if any of the rest of them were involved.

All of them shook their heads and murmured negations, including Opal and Artie. "I knew Mattie didn't need the cane," Josie said at last. "But I figured she liked to have it as a prop. Sometimes it's nice when people underestimate you."

"Mostly it's awful, though," Pearl said. "Because I'm in a wheel-chair, people assume my brain is dead too. But I can see how if I was up to something shady it might come in handy."

"Mattie said she did if for the town. To make things better," I said.

"She was the most dedicated of us to the Red Hat principles," Clara said.

"I can't stand the thought of our friend in jail!" Pearl exclaimed and sniffed audibly. Clara fished in a pocket and handed her a packet of tissues.

They each took one and dabbed their eyes and blew their noses. "She had the courage to do what she believed was right," Clara said.

"But it was wrong, and we all know it." Edith shook her head sadly. "Oh, Mattie. If only you'd waited and had a little faith." She straightened up in her chair and set her empty paper plate on the box of Kona coffee currently being used as a table. "I have news. A friend in the judge's office on Oahu leaked to me that our cease and desist order is being granted."

"What!"

"Seriously!"

"Oh my goodness!" The group burst into simultaneous exclamations, and I led a patter of clapping.

"Wonderful news! Exactly what we needed to hear today," Opal said.

Edith pointed to me. "I'd never have pulled off that filing without Kat's help."

"Just doing my former job," I said. "On that note, I'd like to tell you all I declined an opportunity to be reassigned with the Secret Service. I want to stay in Ohia a while longer."

"Yay!" Opal exclaimed. "How much longer?"

I found myself gazing into Keone's warm brown eyes and made myself look away. "Not sure. At least as long as it takes to make sure New Ohia is thoroughly investigated and, hopefully, shut down."

"And my granddaughter Ana is captured," Edith said.

"Exactly," I said. "Ralph was negotiating a deal, exchanging info about Ana for reduced charges. I thought you should know that, Edith. But he didn't seem to know her current whereabouts."

"And unfortunately, on that note, it's time for us both to get to work," Keone said.

The party broke up on a wave of excited chatter and discussion, and another round of banana bread was served.

Mr. K and I walked back to his truck.

"Thanks for the company last night, Keone. You may not realize it, but spending the night with someone is a really big deal for me."

"And you think it isn't for me?" He smiled. "Think again, Trouble."

I cleared my throat. "You okay with helping me find Ana?"

"Definitely," Keone said. "Looks like we've got another case, Postmaster Sleuth."

"I was hoping you'd say that," I said, and reached out to give Mr. K a hug.

Hawaii Time book 3

Want to continue the story? Grab your copy of HAWAII TIME, book 3, and continue reading!

HAWAII TIME

The "witching hour" at the post office in Ohia, on Maui, was the period from three to four p.m. All the folks on the waiting list for their own mailboxes remembered that we closed soon and showed up all at once to pick up their General Delivery mail.

"Kat, I've been on that waiting list for six years," a youngish woman with a sleeve tattoo and purple hair told me. Her hibiscus print aloha shirt sported a brass name tag over the left boob that reminded me her name was Leona and she worked at the Hotel Hana. "When is someone going to die so I can get my own box?"

I chuckled—but the truth was, people had been dropping like anvils in our tiny village due to a rash of murders, so it wasn't that funny. "I'll see what I can do, Leona. What was your last name again?"

"Baxter."

"Gotcha." I pulled her mail from a folder in a stack of temporary sorting files. She also had a package from an online retailer.

"Seriously. Can you check on the status of my postal box?" This lady wasn't giving up.

I chewed my bottom lip. "I'll have to get in touch with my boss in Kahului. Can you step aside so I can wait on the rest of the customers?"

"Don't you have a clipboard somewhere?" Leona didn't budge. "I bet Pua knows exactly where I am in the order of things."

Ugh. Pua Chang. The former postal employee was out on bail, and still a thorn in my side.

"I'm sorry. As you may have noticed, I've been in this job less than a month and I have no help out here. If you could be patient ..."

"Patient! That's what I've been for six years, Kat!" Leona's voice rose. "And now we've got a newbie postmaster who doesn't know her butt from her elbow. Have you lost my application?"

Sometimes it came in handy to be a six-foot-one former Secret Service agent temporarily assigned as postmaster. I straightened to my full height and gazed down at Leona Baxter, speaking in my authority voice. "Is this what's known as 'going postal' Ms. Baxter? You're having a conniption fit about a structural and institutional shortage, and that isn't going to speed up a solution."

"But we like this line fo' speed up," said the customer behind Ms. Baxter, a rotund, deeply tanned man with a bald pate wearing a rust-colored Primo Beer shirt. "No make *pilikia*, Leona. We all gotta take our turn, and you stay makin' da rest of us wait plenny kine." The customers behind him murmured in support of this. Quite a line formed to his rear.

"Humph," Ms. Baxter said, and stomped out with her package and mail. I had only seen that particular expression in writing before, but that's what she said—"Humph!" Over her shoulder she hollered, "I'm calling the main post office in Kahului to complain!"

"You do that," I shot back. "Ask for my supervisor, Mr. Hanoi.

I'm sure he'll do what he can to make extra mailboxes appear out of thin air."

I forced a smile as she disappeared out the glass door and my elderly defender stepped up to the counter. "Here for your mail, Mr. Costa?"

"Yep. Geev' um, Kat," Mr. Costa said.

"What's geev'um?" I fetched his General Delivery mail. "I'm still new to the Hawaiian creole dialect."

He laughed. "Local kine pidgin, you mean. Geev'um means get after it, go for it. You gonna win. Li'dat."

"Okay. And just out of curiosity, Mr. Costa—how long have you been waiting for a box?"

He scratched the white whiskers on his chin. "Mo'bettah you ask how long I've been in Ohia. Cuz I wen' forget." He chuckled, took his mail, and left as I went on to the next customer.

I was getting better at my job, but the truth was I'd been thrown out here in this cozy small town on the "backside" of Maui with very little training. In addition, I'd been up to my eyeballs in crime solving while dealing with the former clerk's pristine reputation even though she'd engaged in criminal activities on behalf of her notorious mob family.

My life had been one long bout of whack-a-mole since I arrived in Ohia. The finer points of how the post office was actually running had been the last thing I'd been thinking about.

Closing time rolled around at last. I said goodbye to the last customer of the day, flipping up the old-fashioned counter and following Mrs. Lagustino and her three grandchildren in the Radio Flyer wagon to the glass doors. As I held the door open for them, my ring of keys in hand to lock up, a tall, slim, outrageously beautiful woman with close-cropped black hair and skin the color of melted bronze walked up to the door. "Kat. It's been a while."

"Sophie!" I dropped the keys on my foot in astonishment. "What brings you all the way out here?"

"Helping you with a big problem you've got." Sophie Smithson was a computer wizardess and the CEO of a top security firm with offices in Honolulu, Beijing, and Thailand. She was also the daughter of Ambassador Frank Smithson, one of my favorite former protectees. "I thought I'd better talk with you in person."

"Heck yeah. Get in here, girl." I swung the door wider. "This I've got to hear, even if it's about a big problem."

"It is big, and it involves your friend Edith Pepperwhite."

My stomach tightened and I realized how empty it was. Had I eaten that day? Couldn't remember. "Can we get some food? I need a little ballast for this conversation."

"Indeed," Sophie said. "And we need a quiet place to sit down."

"Then let me show you my shack. You'll be surprised when you see it." Of that, I had no doubt. My shack still surprised me every day—and not in a good way. I had several "pets" who called it home: a large and unpredictably violent cat named Tiki; a giant, shower-dwelling cane spider named Miss Prissy; and Tweedledum and Tweedledee, the pair of geckos who liked to hang out over the stove and drop their little turds on its surface. "In fact, I know you'll be very surprised."

Sophie's eyebrows went up. She looked like Nefertiti the Egyptian queen with a question on her mind. "This I have to see."

Continue reading by downloading your copy of HAWAII TIME HERE!

ACKNOWLEDGMENTS

Aloha dear readers! 😄

Lots of authors don't bother with these little missives at the end of a book, but I can't resist the chance to talk directly to YOU.

Maybe this is the first TN book you've read, maybe it's the....geez, I lost count! Either way, MAHALO for coming along on another adventure with Kat and her clue crew on Maui. These stories are some of the most fun I've had writing in years, and with the challenges we've all faced in the lately, anything that makes you smile is a win, right? **We need more smiles!**

For those who love to check a map (you know who you are!) Ohia is an **imaginary** town located on the eastern coast of Maui, somewhere between the villages of Hana and Kaupo. Inspired by reading about Louise Penny's beloved Three Pines and Jana DeLeon's Sinful, I wanted to create a place peopled by colorful characters that encapsulated both the small town charms and big issues of Hawaii.

Ohia is where I'd enjoy living. I don't have to fact check every street name; only keep track of my own inventions. I get to imagine there, and that's one of the most enjoyable things about being an author. Kat's shack reminds me of the rustic places I lived in growing up on Kaua'i in a simpler era, as I wrote about in my memoir, FRECKLED.

Recently I introduced a BUY FROM ME option on my website. This is because online retailers are taking a bigger and bigger bite of royalties. I'm the main breadwinner in my household with a retired husband—and every little bit helps!

If you haven't tried that option, check out the link to Hawaii Time. You can get it sent to you via Bookfunnel a week early on preorder (or immediately after 6/23) and save 15% with coupon code 15tobyneal at checkout...*and you'll have my eternal gratitude for helping me stay afloat in challenging bookselling times!*

If that's not your cuppa and you prefer to stay with your favorite book retailer, no worries! All the options are right there, waiting for you to click on your choice.

No book would be complete without thanking my book development team: Laura Adamowich, who brought this manuscript from very rough to polished, and "Eagle Eye" Angie Lail, who added a final shine. Thanks also to my ARC readers who help me by finding any last minute typos and errors. A book truly takes a village!

Until next time, I'll be writing!

Aloha,

Toby Neal

P.S. Don't forget to add a review! They mean so much, I read them all, and they help others find the books!

My favorite grumpy cat, Tiki!

ABOUT THE AUTHOR

Kirkus Reviews calls Neal's writing, *"persistently riveting. Masterly."*

Award-winning, USA Today bestselling social worker turned author Toby Neal grew up on the island of Kaua`i in Hawaii. Neal is a mental health therapist, a career that has informed the depth and complexity of the characters in her stories. Fans call her stories, *"Immersive, addicting, and the next best thing to being there."* Neal also pens romance and romantic thrillers as Toby Jane and writes memoir/nonfiction under TW Neal. Visit tobyneal.net for more ways to stay in touch!

or

Join her Facebook readers group, *Friends Who Like Toby Neal Books*, for special giveaways and perks.